LUNA

By
Richard Matturro

Livingston Press
at
The University of West Alabama

ISBN 1-931982-73-2, library binding
ISBN 1-931982-74-0, trade paper
13 digit ISBN 978 1-931982-73-3
13 digit ISBN 978-1-931982-74-0

Library of Congress Control Number 2005938337

Printed on acid-free paper.

Printed in the United States of America,
Publishers Graphics
Hardcover binding by: Heckman Bindery

Typesetting and page layout: David E. Smith, Gina Montarsi
Proofreading: Tomeika Walker, Ariane Godfrey,
Margaret Walburn, Danielle Hornsby, Gloria Maduka,
Jennifer Brown, Angela Brown
Cover art concept: Mary Trev Thomas
Cover layout: Joe Taylor, Gina Montarsi

This is a work of fiction.
You know the rest: any resemblance
to persons living or dead is coincidental.

Livingston Press is part of The University of West Alabama,
and thereby has non-profit status.
Donations are tax-deductible:
brothers and sisters, we need 'em.

first edition
6 5 4 3 3 2 1

For Mary Trev Thomas

Contents

LUNA

ðũò åẽðáò ; ç̂ îï̂ò ðáé̂ò ó´ áðáëëÜîåé êáêũí ;

Aeschylus *Prometheus Bound 773*

I

River Lord

Zach was early. He was always early for things. It was a vice he was rather ashamed of, since he associated it with middle class values and provincialism. Important people, sophisticated people didn't have to arrive on time. Try as he might, though, he couldn't quite shake the habit. Zach was too afraid of missing something.

He pulled his car into the small parking lot and shut off the engine, then twisted the rear-view mirror slightly so he could see his face in it. Unnecessarily he ran his fingers through his black hair and flashed a smile at the image staring back at him. He tried to gauge whether that smile projected just the right mix of warmth and worldliness. Then he felt silly practicing facial expressions and twisted the mirror back in disgust.

The other cars in the lot were all empty save one. The driver's side door open wide, a balding, middle-aged man in a pale blue jogging suit was bending over and tying the laces of his running shoes. It was the after-work hour, the time when business people flooded out of the nearby office buildings. Some of them used the bike path along the river to run off the accumulated stress of the day. Zach too had issued from one of those buildings, but he had not come to the river for exercise. He had come for an assignation.

Assignation! What a ridiculous word, he thought, a loaded word, like tryst or rendezvous. Why must an appointment between a man and a woman warrant a special word? Why not just "meeting"? He was meeting a woman—that's all. There was nothing sinister about it.

Except, of course, that Zach was married.

He stepped out of the car and set the security alarm, which chirped a response. Then he strolled to the broad grassy strip that separated the parking lot from the river. It was a lovely spring day. Albany has been known to get snow in May, but not this year. The air was mild and warm—so warm in fact that Zach felt overheated in his suit. He wondered if she would think him stuffy because of the way he was dressed. There had been no time to go home and change. His polished black shoes looked absurdly out of place sinking into the grass. He'd probably have to clean them when he got home tonight.

"Beautiful weather, huh?" said a gravelly voice behind him.

Zach glanced over his shoulder. The balding man in the jogging suit was lumbering toward the bike path. Zach smiled goodnaturedly. "Yes, very. Is it Friday yet?"

"Am I sixty-five yet?" The man began his run, waving his hand in the air without looking back. He clopped along stolidly, his age and excess weight showing in every footfall. Zach watched him until the pale blue of the jogging suit disappeared around a bend.

Sixty-five, retirement: it was too far away even to contemplate. Zach was forty, intelligent, reasonably good-looking, successful. In a government town filled with government employees, he had climbed quickly to the upper reaches of the bureaucracy. He was a deputy commissioner, no small feat for a person his age.

Zach walked down toward the water and stopped at the retaining wall. He looked at his watch. It was a surprising place for her to choose, really, by the river. He thought women who placed personal ads usually wanted their first meeting with a man to be in a very public place—a bar, a restaurant, a coffee shop. That way, if the guy looked like a sociopath, the woman could safely extricate herself.

He slipped off his jacket and draped it over his arm, then loosened his tie. Zach didn't really approve of infidelity; nor did he enjoy the prospect of lying to his wife. He had a stubborn habit of honesty—similar to his habit of punctuality, and with as few moral overtones. But Zach had become acutely restless in his marriage. Beth's demanding work schedule often kept them apart, and when they were together, there was a dreadful sameness about their routine. Most significant of all, eight years after their wedding they were still childless.

Zach had contemplated an affair many times before this, yet even now his worst transgression might have remained a promiscuous fancy, had he not seen the ad. He was scanning the women's personals one day when he came upon one that read,

Child of myth seeks god of desire.
Abandon your past; relinquish
your future; pursue only me.

The ad fascinated him. He'd read hundreds, perhaps thousands of them over the years, mainly for his own amusement. Some were quite witty and clever, but it was the utter strangeness of this one that snared his imagination. He knew nothing about the writer, of course, except that she was more original than most, but he convinced himself that she was looking for the same kind of adventure he was, and so he wrote to her.

In his letter Zach was truthful about his marital status, and by means of this frankness he hoped to make clear right up front what he was interested in so that neither of them harbored any false illusions. Then he described himself. He told her his age, his height, his weight, his hair and eye color. In describing his looks he was properly self-deprecatory. Modestly too he intimated that he had a good job, though he did not go into detail. He signed his real name, Zach Tonner, and included his home address. This was safe, for he and Beth *never* opened each other's mail. Zach hoped that by such openness and candor he might gain the woman's confidence so that she would respond in kind.

And she did indeed respond, but her letter, neatly handwritten, told him nothing about herself. It merely proposed that they meet down here on Wednesday at 6:00 p.m., and the letter was signed "Luna."

Whoever she was, Luna seldom passed from Zach's thoughts after he got her letter. He'd speculated about what she looked like. Would she be a drop-dead beauty, the kind that gazes out seductively from the cover of *Cosmopolitan*? Unlikely, really. He was fairly certain that *Cosmo* models didn't advertise in the personals, not in Albany anyway. Would she be too tall? Zach was of average height and rather sensitive about his stature. He feared that tall women despise shorter men, and under no circumstances did he want to be despised.

These thoughts were still passing through his mind as he heard a car pull into the parking lot behind him. He turned and saw a small black compact, pockmarked with rust. Zach wondered if this modest chariot was what a "child of myth" drives, but his feeling of superiority was not providing the composure it usually did. Involuntarily, his heart began to race. He stared at the car for an intolerable minute or two until the driver's door swung open, and he saw a boy get out from behind the wheel, a teenager dressed in jeans and a T-shirt. As he turned back to the river, Zach sighed and told himself it wasn't a sigh of relief. He did not want to admit that part of him hoped this Luna would not show.

Embarrassed by the absurd thumping in his chest, Zach thrust his hands deep in his pockets and tried to look relaxed. He was angry to be in this position, to feel tense and unsure of himself. He liked knowing where he stood. He liked familiar situations that had predictable outcomes. He felt ridiculous standing around in a strange place waiting for a strange person with a phony name to show up. Luna! Even if her name was genuine, Zach didn't much like it. He did not approve of unusual or trendy names. He scorned parents who called their little girls "Ashley" or "Brooke" or "Morgan." If he ever had a daughter, he was damn well going to name her something simple like "Mary." Better an interesting person with an ordinary name than a dull person with an exotic one.

Idly, Zach glanced at the parking lot again and saw that the boy was walking in his direction. He wondered if he'd have to go through the same pleasantries about the weather again. No, he thought, teenagers don't usually make small talk with adults if they can help it. He was probably just coming to stroll by the river.

Zach seemed to be wrong, however. The boy definitely was approaching him. Irritably, Zach turned away, hoping his body language would ward off the intruder. Zach had more important things to do than make inane chitchat with a dumb teenager. Out of the corner of his eye, though, Zach continued to watch him approach, just in case he was a mugger.

When still a few paces off, the newcomer halted. Then a voice inquired, "Are you Zach?"

Zach spun around and stared stupidly at the other figure. From this range, his mistake was obvious. It was not a boy. It was a young woman in her mid-twenties, but Zach's error in perceiving her gender from a distance was understandable. Only an inch or two shorter than Zach, she had close-cropped, dark brown hair, worn the way a boy might wear it, carelessly parted on one side and combed straight. She carried no purse, wore no makeup or jewelry. And Zach could tell by the uninterrupted fall of her T-shirt that she had no bust whatsoever. Her sex was apparent only in the very unmasculine contours of her face. Her eyes were a deep brown like her hair, and these looked out from beneath equally dark eyebrows. She had full lips, but they were not formed into a smile. Rather, she gazed at him with an odd look of solemnity.

"I—I'm sorry," Zach stammered. "Are you Luna?"

"Of course I'm Luna. How else would I know your name?" She spoke in low-pitched, even tones.

"Yes, that's right." Zach smiled a silly, sheepish smile, but the woman continued to eye him gravely.

"Have you been waiting long?" she asked.

"No, not too long."

"I'm not late, you know."

"No, no," Zach assured her, glancing unnecessarily at his watch, "you're not."

On some level Zach perceived that she might actually be pretty, if her hair were not so short and if her figure were a bit more feminine. Perhaps it was his initial impression that she was a boy, though, that made him find something freakish about her, as if some of the spurious maleness still clung to her. Particularly unsettling was her lack of breasts. The thought of making love to her, which was one of the first thoughts that passed through his mind, was mildly repellent. Zach wanted to flee, but a lifelong fear of hurting people's feelings caused him to stay—if only until he found a graceful way to make his exit. Resigning himself to a half-hour in the woman's company, he determined to fill it with small talk. After many years in the professional world, he had acquired the useful skill of making innocuous chatter with almost anyone.

Zach forced a smiled. "Would you like to sit down?"

They sat across from each other at a picnic table. Zach noted the fine, almost invisible hairs that grew upon her upper lip and curved down over the corners of her mouth. Her coloring led him to conclude that she was of southern European ancestry. "Did you get a lot of responses to your ad?" he asked.

"I got twenty-four."

"Really? Twenty-four. That's quite a lot. How many of them have you met so far?"

"None until now."

"You mean I'm your first? Well, I'm flattered," he said, though he did not feel flattered at all. "That was a very interesting ad you wrote, very creative. What exactly were you looking for?"

"I wanted a swain."

"A swain? What's a swain?"

Luna did not seem to be listening. Instead, she was scrutinizing his features, which made Zach feel self-conscious.

"What is it?" he asked.

"I didn't expect you to be this handsome."

"Well, thank you," Zach said, slightly embarrassed. "I am a bit older than you, of course. I turn forty-one on Saturday."

"Age doesn't matter to me."

"Really?"

"No. Neither does appearance," she added, "or race. You could have been black or Chinese or anything."

"Well, that's very democratic of you. What is it that made you choose my letter first out of the twenty-four?"

"You were the only man who said he had brown eyes. All the rest either said they had blue eyes or they didn't say at all. Are men ashamed of having brown eyes?"

"I ... I don't know."

"Your eyes aren't as brown as mine are," Luna continued, "but they're still a nice brown. Brown eyes are much more interesting than blue, don't you think?"

An image of Beth, Zach's very blue-eyed blond wife, flitted through his mind. At this very moment Beth was probably arriving home—where Zach wished *he* was right now. Zach said, "I never thought much about it."

"You also used good grammar. So many of them used bad grammar. 'I *seen* your ad in the paper.' "

Zach smiled wryly. "Good grammar's kind of ingrained, I'm afraid, from being an English teacher."

"You're a teacher?"

"Formerly. Now I'm a full-fledged bureaucrat." He adopted a mock rueful tone. "Like a lot of people in this town, I work for the State of New York. The Education Department, to be specific."

"Why did you change?"

"To tell you the truth, I thought I might have more effect on the cause of teaching by joining the enemy, administration."

"And do you?"

He shrugged his shoulders. "Not very much. I spend most of my days putting out brushfires and trying to convince people that the computer is not going to save American education."

"I don't like computers."

"I sympathize, but don't let my wife hear you. She loves them. Beth designs computer systems for a living."

"Does she?"

He nodded. "All over the country. Last week she was in Maryland, the week before in Georgia, and next week she'll be in California."

"She travels a lot?"

"She travels a *lot*." Zach uttered this last fact grimly, as if it were one of the eternal human woes like death and taxes.

"Why don't you go with her?"

"I did once. She took me to a weekend conference in Boston. At the opening cocktail party all of the computer geeks got together and talked shop, while I was left standing at the refreshment table eating little hot dogs. That was the last time she invited me."

"So you sleep alone often."

"Often enough."

"Is that why you want an affair?"

Zach laughed nervously. An affair had indeed been Zach's motivation for contacting Luna, but the notion had evaporated from his mind the moment he laid eyes on her. There was no tactful way he could tell her this. He said merely, "You get right to the point, don't you?"

"Life's too short."

Anxious to change the subject lest the prospect of their affair be pursued further, Zach looked for something else to talk about. He noticed the unusual motif adorning the front of Luna's T-shirt. Upon a black background were a series of curved and interweaving parallel yellow lines. Earlier, Zach had avoided looking directly at the shirt lest she think he was staring at her breasts—or lack thereof. Now he made an obvious show of trying to decipher it. "That's an interesting pattern," he said. "What is it supposed to be?"

Luna glanced down. "Oh, the shirt. I sent away for it." She stood up so he could view the rest.

The parallel lines, though stylized, were now seen to be tracks, something like railroad tracks, but held aloft in a series of exaggerated humps by crisscrossed scaffolding. Printed across the bottom of the shirt was the legend, "Kennywood *Thunderbolt*."

"Oh, I see it now," Zach said. "It's a roller coaster."

Luna nodded and sat down again.

"Where is Kennywood?" he asked.

"Pittsburgh."

"Are you from Pittsburgh?"

"No, I've never been to Pittsburgh, but I'd love to go someday."

Zach laughed.

"What's funny?"

"I've heard people say they'd love to go to Paris, or to Rome, or to London, but that's the first time I've ever heard anyone say they'd love to go to Pittsburgh."

Luna continued to watch him somberly, showing no recognition that he had made a joke. She clarified, "I mean for the roller coaster. The *Thunderbolt* is one of the best wooden coasters in the world."

"Is that so? I didn't know that. The best *wooden* coaster, you said?"

"As opposed to steel. Most of the new ones are steel, but the wooden ones are better."

"I see. So you're a roller coaster aficionado. I haven't ridden one since I was a kid."

"Are you afraid?"

"Actually I'm rather afraid of getting ill. As I've gotten older, I've developed an embarrassing tendency toward motion sickness."

Luna seemed to weigh this in her mind for a moment before saying, "That's all right." Something in the way she uttered it made Zach feel as if he'd just been forgiven for having a minor character flaw.

"Well, we've established that you're not from Pittsburgh," Zach continued. "So where *do* you hail from?"

"I live here in Albany."

"But where were you born?"

She looked over at the water. "I was born in the glen in springtime when the riverbank was knee-deep in wildflowers."

"That's very poetic."

"At my birth they said I was destined to wander."

"Who said that? Was that your horoscope?"

"It was meant as a curse."

"A curse? Why would you be cursed?"

Luna shrugged her shoulders. "Wandering has never seemed like much of a punishment. It's always sounded sort of nice. Of course that's probably because I've never been anywhere."

Zach stared at her, puzzled, but he determined not to probe further. She was, after all, a young person, and young people often try to make themselves appear more interesting than they really are by saying outrageous things. Zach was too old to be taken in by it. "But you live here in town now. Where?"

"Lark Street."

Of course, Zach thought, nodding to himself. Lark Street was Albany's Soho, or the closest thing to Soho the city could boast, a seedy downtown strip of bars, brownstones, and tattoo parlors where the unconventional and the dysfunctional converge. Where else would a hermaphrodite who was destined to wander call home?

"Well, as you could tell from my Delmar address," Zach said, adopting the mock ruefulness again, "I live in the 'burbs.' I have a little square of green, on which sits a raised ranch, a two-car garage, a maple tree in front, and a deck behind. To complete the picture, I have a gas grill on the deck which I've used a total of four times."

"Do you have children?"

Zach looked at her. It was a normal enough question, but for some reason he had not anticipated it. "No," he said, a slight confusion in his voice.

"Do you want children?"

"Oh, yes," he answered enthusiastically. "Doesn't everyone?"

"No, everyone doesn't," Luna snapped. "But if you want them, why don't you have any?"

He shrugged his shoulders. "We're waiting."

"What are you waiting for?"

The bluntness of the young woman's question and her impertinence in asking it might have justified an indignant response, but Zach had a dislike of unpleasantness, which made him inclined to ignore most offenses. There was something else too that prevented him from being annoyed. This particular topic was a sore one between Zach and his wife. Luna's question, for all its want of tact, was far from impertinent. On the contrary, it was a most pertinent question indeed, and one Zach had asked himself many times. What in hell *were* they waiting for?

Zach averted his eyes. "Oh, you know, it's a big step. We want to make sure we're prepared for it. Beth's at a critical time in her job right now, and she doesn't feel she can leave."

"I see," Luna responded dryly. "You're waiting until a child fits into your wife's schedule. How old is she?"

"Beth? She's thirty-six."

"Well, I wouldn't wait too much longer if I were you. Don't you know that for every year after thirty-five that a woman puts off having her first baby, she increases the likelihood that her child will be retarded?"

"I ... believe I read that somewhere."

"And I suppose after you have children, you'll put them in day care."

"Well, yes, probably. Beth would want to go back to work."

"Of course!" she said angrily. "So for eight hours a day your children will be raised by morons. Why do women have children if they're going to pawn them off on someone else?"

The irony of the situation was not lost upon Zach. He had contacted this strange person with the intention of having an affair with her behind his wife's back. Yet in their first few minutes together she was admonishing him for not conducting his family life properly. He wondered at her surprising passion. A thought occurred to him. "Do *you* have children, Luna? Is that why you—"

Luna's eyes opened wide, her expression of angry incredulity cutting off his words. Abruptly she stood up. "Look at my hips," she demanded.

Startled by the request, Zach obeyed and found himself staring at her crotch, which hovered at eye level before him.

"Do I *look* like I've had children?"

Her hips were quite slim, which was her point, no doubt, though Zach knew well enough that skinnier women than Luna had borne children. Staring at her this way, however, Zach noticed for the first time the subtle curves barely visible beneath her jeans. Thin as Luna was, her torso was unmistakably feminine.

Zach looked up at her face again. "I'm sorry. I meant no offence. I just thought you might be a mother yourself."

Luna scowled and sat down. "I *never* want to be a mother."

Amazed at her vehemence, Zach dared not pursue the matter further. Somehow his plan for light conversation had been thwarted. He determined to bring things back to the comfortably vapid. After a suitable pause he asked, "What do you do, Luna?"

"What do I do? I do—as you see."

"I mean for a living. How do you pay the rent on Lark Street?"

She appeared irritated at the question, or perhaps she was still vexed by his innocent suggestion that she might be a parent. In any case, she turned away from Zach. For a while he thought she would not answer at all, but after a few moments she said simply, "I sell shoes."

"Really? Where?"

"Florsheim's at Crossgates."

Zach said, "That must be interesting."

There was mild bafflement in her eyes, and Zach realized how stupidly patronizing his comment was. To make up for it, he tried to think of something intelligent he could say about shoe retailing, but even *his* powers of shallow discourse had their limit.

He changed the subject. "So you live on Lark Street. I haven't been up that way for a while. There used to be a funky little restaurant at the end of the street. Is it still there?"

"Yes."

"We could have met there. You could have saved yourself a trip all the way down here."

"I like to come down here."

"Well, yes, it is a nice spot." Zach glanced vaguely in the direction of the water. "Sometimes you forget the river is here, even though it's so close."

"I never forget it's here," Luna said. After a moment she added, "My father is lord of the river."

Zach looked at her. "Excuse me?"

"My father is lord of the river."

"Your father is lord of the Hudson River?" Zach wondered if this was merely Luna's eccentric way of saying that her father, like Zach, worked in the vast state bureaucracy and was in some way responsible for maintenance of the waterways. "Who is your father?"

"Inachus."

"Inachus? Is that his first name or his last name?"

Luna did not answer. Instead, she got up from the picnic table and strolled to the retaining wall, Zach following. He surmised that she was just pulling his leg. Deciding to play along, he quipped, "Well, if your father is truly lord of the river, he's done a very poor job of taking care of it. Why did he let it get so polluted?"

Luna stared into the water. "He doesn't give a damn about pollution. It's no skin off his ass."

Zach laughed nervously, wanting to believe that she was still teasing him, but the serious look on her face belied a jest, and there seemed to have been a touch of real bitterness in her voice. He puzzled for a moment, but decided the enigma was best left unsolved. He'd now spent a sufficient amount of time with her, thus fulfilling any social obligation he might have had. Zach looked at his watch, and Luna noticed the movement as she was meant to.

"Do you have to be somewhere?" she asked.

"Home," he said apologetically. "Beth's *not* traveling this week, for once, and she'll be expecting me."

"I see. Well, I won't keep you then."

The awkward moment had arrived. Zach could never be so cruel as to say bluntly, "I'm sorry, but I don't want to see you again." Like most men he preferred the innocuous "I'll call you," but Zach was in a quandary. Since he didn't have Luna's phone number, he could hardly pretend any intention to call her. He could, of course, ask her for her phone number, but to do so with the express purpose of *not* calling her seemed particularly duplicitous. He was trying to think of a way out of this dilemma when Luna abruptly solved it for him.

She took a step closer and, leaning up, kissed him lightly on the cheek. It was a strange, unromantic, almost familial kiss, the sort you might give your mother or cousin, a kiss two women friends might exchange after an absence.

Luna said, "I like you, Zach. Your eyes are sad, but they're kind. I want you to know that I don't expect you to take me out and spend money on me. I can pay my own way. I have a lot of money."

"That's nice of you, Luna, but it's really not necess—"

"What I'm telling you is that you won't be able to pay me for anything I give you. Is that clear?"

"Yes."

She turned toward the parking lot, hesitated, glanced at Zach again. "Saturday is your birthday?"

He nodded.

"I'll spill wine for you on Saturday," she said. Then without another word she strode away.

Zach had intended to accompany her to the parking lot as the only polite thing to do, but he was so startled that he seemed rooted to the earth where he stood. He watched her retreat, watched her until she drove off, disappearing from view. Only then did he raise his hand to his cheek and touch the spot where her lips had brushed him, ever so lightly.

II

Project Manager

"WORK LATE?" BETH asked over her shoulder.

"No," Zach said, taking off his jacket and draping it on a kitchen chair. "I was meeting an exotic woman who offered to be my sex slave."

Beth glanced at him briefly, then resumed slicing the celery. "Does she know that you leave your dirty socks on the window-sill?"

Zach smiled at his wife. From the back he watched her elbow bob up and down as she chopped. For some reason he found her enormously endearing right now: safe, sane, smart-assed Beth. He even rather liked how substantial she was. Four inches shorter than Zach, Beth was not fat, but neither was she thin. She kept her weight within a moderate range that long ago she had determined was healthy. When he was feeling particularly discontented, Zach wished her hips and her thighs were not quite so healthy as they were, but at this moment the full womanliness of them pleased him. So did her fine blonde hair, which reached unglamorously to her shoulders.

Beth was of Scandinavian descent, had the high cheekbones and the broad face of a Brunhild. No one would call her beautiful;

nor had Zach married her for her beauty, though he admired her clear, light skin and the intelligence in her eyes. What had drawn him to her was her sharp-edged mind and a kind of crisp, no-nonsense attitude toward life which mirrored his own. Zach had decided they were meant for each other. Winning her love had not been easy, for women such as Beth do not blindly follow their hearts. Zach had accepted the challenge, assuring himself that once achieved, her love would prove stronger than the love of one who gave her affection more willingly.

From behind, Zach slipped his hands around Beth's waist and kissed her on the neck. She did not stop what she was doing.

"Well, if you told me you worked late," she said, "I was prepared to faint. I had the smelling salts all ready."

"Sorry to disappoint you. Where is it? I've never seen smelling salts. I always wondered what it looked like."

"You're the only deputy commissioner in New York State history to leave at five o'clock on the dot every day of the year."

"I like to set an example for my staff. Is smelling salts singular or plural, I wonder?" Zach gave her a squeeze, then pulled down the dictionary from its place among Beth's cookbooks. "You never hear anyone say 'smelling salt,' right? It sounds like it's plural when you say, 'Quick! Madame Fotcheldorf's passed out! Get some smelling salts!' But other times it sounds singular: 'The smelling salts is in the medicine chest.' "

"Madame Fotcheldorf?"

"You know, the famous Viennese contralto." He opened the dictionary and flipped through the S's scanning for the term, but his eye lit on another word. He held the page closer.

"What's the verdict?" Beth asked. "Singular or plural?"

"Do you know what the word 'swain' means? It's a rustic or peasant, specifically a shepherd. And it can also mean a male admirer or suitor."

"Fascinating," she commented.

Zach stared at the entry a moment, then shook his head to himself and closed the book. Now he drew a bottle of red wine from the cabinet and opened it. Hearing the pop of the cork, Beth turned and looked at him. "You're having wine? It's only Wednesday."

"I noticed." He took a stemmed glass down from the shelf and put his fingers on another. "Does that mean you don't want any?"

Beth's pause was only momentary. "Don't be silly."

Zach filled both glasses, handed her one, and then clinked it with his own.

"What are we drinking to?" she asked, smiling at him.

He looked around. "Home."

"Home? You're always making fun of this place."

"To home," he said, raising his glass.

"To home," she repeated, and they both took a sip.

Leaning against the countertop, Zach gazed idly out the window over the sink. A squirrel scampered across the lawn in the late afternoon sunshine. "We have such a nice backyard, and we rarely set foot in it, except when I cut the grass."

"Which you regularly complain about doing."

"Maybe we ought to put up a privacy fence."

"What are you planning to do back there? Sunbathe in the nude?"

"Good idea. But we never use the yard because the neighbors can see right in."

"The last time we talked about it, you said we never use the yard because we never have time."

"That's true too, but if we had a little more privacy, maybe we would make time to use it."

With the back of her hand, Beth pushed a strand of her hair from her forehead. "A fence won't do much good anyway. The neighbors could still see in from their second floor windows—unless, of course, you were planning to build a fence twenty feet high."

"Against the code, unfortunately." Zach turned from the window and smiled slyly. "I guess we'll have to limit our nude sunbathing to St. Thomas."

"St. Thomas? We've never been to St. Thomas."

"I know, but maybe we should go. Maybe we can take a cruise."

"You get seasick whenever you're on a boat."

"I'll take Dramamine."

Beth looked at him. "You'd be willing to spend a week spaced out on a cruise ship just so you could ogle some naked young women."

"Maybe I'd ogle you."

"Sorry, but I'd be in a bathing suit."

"You say you hate bathing suits."

"I hate *buying* them because they never fit right. But I have no intention of trying to compete with nubile young things who have nothing better to do with their time than work on their tans and improve their muscle tone."

Zach took another gulp of wine, then rolled up his sleeves. "Can I help?"

"You can cut up two more onions." With emphasis she added, "I don't care *who* has to smell my breath tomorrow."

"Do I dare ask how your day went?"

"Only if you really want to know."

Zach wished life didn't require quite so many lies to smooth social intercourse. He said, "Of course I want to know."

While Zach sliced the onions, and then while he sliced the carrots, and then while he pulled apart the lettuce, arranged it in a bowl, and set the table for dinner, she told him about her day. In this continuing saga Zach already knew the whole cast of characters, the denizens of Beth's office. He knew their names, their qualities. He knew the heroes, few in number, their valor limited and careful. He knew the villains, whose knavery was so palpable and shameless that no sane person would employ them. And he knew the ineffectual group that formed the middle, a kind of Greek chorus whose simpleminded commentary accompanied the high action swirling around them. This regular company, occasionally supplemented by other actors when Beth traveled, peopled the ongoing drama of her work life.

Beth felt a need to rehearse this chronicle. She had a tendency toward moodiness and would stew all evening if Zach did not let her tell her story. Yet she did not require anything more from Zach than that he be in the room to listen. She certainly did not want his advice. When on occasion she had presented him with a problem at work and he had volunteered a solution, she accused him of meddling, or trying to shut her up prematurely. So Zach learned to make only the most innocuous sounds of commiseration and otherwise to keep his mouth zipped.

After twenty minutes the narrative finally came to an end, or at least a cessation, and only then did Beth ask Zach how his own day had been. Zach said simply, "It was quiet." This was not only his most common response to the question, but it was also the truth, as far as he could tell. Moreover, this was probably the highest praise Zach could bestow upon a day at work. Most days were a lot like all other days, and Zach felt no inclination to allow his work life to stretch beyond its proper nine-to-five boundaries.

One glass of wine consumed and several sips into the second, Zach began to feel a warm sense of well-being. He watched Beth as she stirred a pot on the stove. "We should do this more often."

"Do what more often?"

"Have wine in the middle of the week. It makes you feel a little more genteel at dinnertime, doesn't it?"

"I suppose so, but I'd better not have *too* much gentility tonight. I've got to look over some stuff from work."

Zach furrowed his brow.

"I know you don't like it when I take work home," she said, "so I usually don't do it, but I've got to have this—"

"Did I say anything?" Zach protested.

"Okay. Sorry. It'll only take an hour or so anyway."

"It's all right." He paused. "Did you find out when you have to leave next week?"

"Well, I wanted to talk to you about that. They'd like for me to be out there Monday morning."

"Monday morning? In California? That means you'd have to

leave on Sunday."

"I know. I thought I'd be able to leave later, but everyone there is going to be ready to begin Monday morning, and I'm project manager this time. If I get an early start, I may be able to finish by Friday and be back for the weekend."

"Any time you've said that, it's never happened."

"I wish you wouldn't do this whenever I have to go somewhere. You know it's my job."

Zach frowned. It was a perpetual struggle between them. Zach resented how often Beth was away; then he kicked himself for resenting it. He was supposed to be an enlightened man, after all, supportive of his wife's career. Resignedly he asked, "When is your plane?"

"Ten a.m. Sunday."

"Saturday's my birthday. Remember?"

"Of course I remember. It won't interfere with Saturday."

"We had planned to go out to dinner. I was hoping we'd have a nice evening."

"We can still do that."

"It's not the same, not if you have to rush off to catch a plane the next morning."

"I'm the one who has to rush. I don't see why you should care. You can sleep late the next morning if you want to." She turned back to the stove.

"You think birthdays are silly, don't you?"

Beth sighed. "Do we have to talk about this?"

"Last October I got the impression you celebrated yours mainly to please me."

"Listen, Zach, I know birthdays mean a lot to you, so I'm willing to celebrate yours any way you want."

"But why don't you like celebrating yours?"

"It's *my* birthday, for God's sake. If I don't feel like making a fuss about it, that's my business. Why should I have to feel guilty for disappointing *you*? If anybody should be disappointed, it's me."

"But you're *not* disappointed."

"No, I'm not."

"Why?"

"Because I'm not a kid anymore."

"In other words I'm still a kid."

Beth shook her head. "It's not like this is a special one, Zach. When you turned forty last year, we had an enormous bash. This year it's just forty-one. What's the big deal?"

"No big deal, I guess. Forget about it."

She turned to him, exasperated. "Listen, we'll celebrate your birthday Saturday night, all right? We'll carouse until dawn if you'd like, and I'll stumble to the airport half-asleep. Will that satisfy you? Nothing is going to deter us from celebrating your damn birthday!"

"Thanks," he said flatly. "That really makes me look forward to it."

"Zach, what the hell do you want me to do?"

He stared down into his glass. "Spill wine for me."

* * *

WHEN ZACH ARRIVED at work the next morning, he found someone already seated at his desk hidden behind a copy of the *Times Union*. Zach said, "Good morning, Bob."

"Did you see this?"

Zach flopped his briefcase on the desk. "What's up?"

"It's what's down!"

"Okay, what's down?"

"My damn stock is down." He let the top half of the newspaper fold over now. Bob was about five years older than Zach and had a scattering of gray hair and an expanding midsection to prove it. The small mustache he wore did little to improve his looks. Bob was dressed in a rumpled gray suit, the tie askew. A colleague in the Education Department who had once been Zach's peer, Bob now ran a smaller division in the same building.

"What have you got stock in?" Zach asked, taking off his jacket.

"PVA's."

"PVA's?"

"Point-of-sale video advertising."

"What the hell is that?"

"It's great stuff. They're little, individual TV screens mounted over each supermarket checkout. They play constant commercials to entertain you while you're waiting in line."

"Why would you invest your money in something so obnoxious?"

"That's the whole point, Zach. This is America. The more obnoxious the concept, the more likely it is to succeed."

Zach walked around to where Bob was sitting. "Do you mind?"

"Oh, sure." Bob moved to a less comfortable seat on the other side of the desk. "Hey, I've got a joke for you."

"It's too early in the morning."

"No, this is a real good one, and it's almost clean. These two dogs meet in a vet's office. Have you heard it?"

"Yes. Why do you read your paper up here anyway? Why don't you read it in your own office?"

"You have a better view."

Zach turned around in his chair and looked out the window. It *was* an impressive sight, and this view was indeed one of the perks of his position. The Education Department sat at one end of a quarter-mile-long mall, a broad slab of poured concrete, gleaming white in the sunshine and lined on both sides with tall, equally white government office buildings like his own. The design was modernist to a fault and, like most modern architecture, soulless as well, despite its stark beauty. The whole complex was constructed in the 1960s when few questioned spending public money on temples of bureaucracy.

At the far end of the mall, though, opposite Zach's building, was the old state capitol. This structure, built in the 1800s, was a monument to a different era. A gray square pile of rough-hewn granite blocks topped with pointed towers, it once dominated the little city the way a French castle dominated a medieval town. Its height had long since been surpassed by the blank white monoliths nearby, but it stubbornly hung on as the real seat of power in the state.

"Why don't you read the paper at home," Zach asked, "before you come in to work?"

"Judy won't let me. She doesn't like me to read anything at breakfast, not even the back of the cereal box. She says it's one of the few times we get together as a family, and we should *interact*." He uttered this last word with sarcastic emphasis. "Does Beth let you read over breakfast?"

Zach leaned back in his chair, still gazing out the window. "We both read."

"Really? That's great."

"She reads the newspaper and I read a book."

"Every morning?"

"Every morning."

"That's great. But see, that's because you don't have kids, so you can do whatever you want. You're lucky."

Zach twisted around in his seat. "How old are yours now, Bob?"

"Nine and six."

He shook his head in disbelief. "I remember when they were born."

"I know. Time flies when you're having fun, right? It doesn't seem that long ago that my 'disposable income' referred to the money I spent on diapers."

"So they're both in school now."

"Michael's in first grade and Amy's in fourth. Both know how to read. They read to *me* now instead of me reading to them."

"They read to you?"

He nodded. "I get a real kick out of it. Last night Amy read me this story about the seven-league boots. You know that story?"

"No."

"You put on these magic boots and you can travel long distances with each step. It's corny, of course, and I have to help her with some of the words, but listening to her read still gives me kind of a thrill."

Zach was silent.

"And let me tell you," Bob continued, "one of the fringe benefits of their being in school now is that it's caused a major improvement in Judy's disposition."

"Has it?"

"*Major*," he repeated, "in all kinds of ways—if you take my meaning."

"Will Judy be going back to work?"

Bob lifted his shoulders. "Who knows? When she left her job to have Amy, she said she wanted to go back as soon as she could, but now that she's got a taste of being home and not having to worry about jerky bosses and office politics and all that crap, I'm not so sure. Really, though, I don't care if she goes back or not. It's nice having her home when I get there."

"I wouldn't mind if Beth were home a little more."

"What am I hearing? The patter of little feet in your future? Are you two thinking of taking the plunge?"

Zach averted his eyes. "No, not yet."

"It would be a big switch for you, a lot of changes. Once you have kids, say good-bye to your free time."

"We don't have much free time anyway."

"And your privacy goes right out the window."

"We don't seem to need privacy anymore."

Bob narrowed his eyes. "Hey Zach, is everything all right?"

"Yeah."

"You sure?"

Zach brushed some non-existent lint off his trousers. "So what about the two dogs?"

"What two dogs?"

"The ones that meet in the vet's office."

"Oh, the joke! Okay, these two dogs meet in a vet's office. One's a German shepherd and the other's a Labrador. So the shepherd says. . . ." Bob hesitated. "I thought you said you heard it."

"I lied."

Bob shrugged. "Well, anyway, the shepherd says, 'What are you in for?'"

At that moment Zach's secretary appeared at the door. "Excuse me," she said. "The commissioner's on the phone and wants to know if you can come over a little early. He's got a meeting at ten-thirty."

Zach looked at his watch. "I'm on my way."

"It's about the cuts, isn't it?" Bob asked.

"If I tell you, I'll have to kill you."

"Well, be sure to let him know how indispensable I am. Okay, Buddy?"

"Maybe it's *me* he'll decide to get rid of." Zach slipped on his suit jacket.

"You? Fat chance! If he got rid of you, where would he get all the neat statistics he feeds the governor?"

At the door Zach paused, remembering something. "Hey Bob, who's in charge of the Hudson River?"

"The last time I looked, it was God."

"No, I mean what agency?"

"I don't know. Why?"

"Just curious. Do you know any state employee named Inachus?"

"No. Is he Pakistani?

Zach shook his head. "Remember to shut off the lights when you leave."

* * *

THE COMMISSIONER WAS staring into his computer terminal as Zach entered his office.

"Good morning, Hugo."

"Morning, Zach."

Zach stepped behind the desk and peered over his boss's shoulder. "Where are you?"

"Athens. It's a forum on Attic art."

"Would you rather I—"

"No, no. It's all right. Some idiot is going on about his pet theory of red-figured pottery. Sit down." He signed off, then turned to his subordinate.

Hugo was a commanding presence. In New York State, commissioners do not work their way up through the ranks of civil service as lesser bureaucrats do. They are appointed directly by the governor, so they must be not only prominent people in their fields, but political animals as well. In other words they must look the part they are chosen to play, and Hugo did. He was tall, with a handsome, hatchet face and a fringe of white hair that ringed his otherwise bald head. His voice was a deep baritone that immediately drew respect. The only thing unattractive about his demeanor was a set of bifocals that enlarged his already liquid blue eyes. Something about their watery gaze always made Zach mildly uncomfortable.

The commissioner smiled. "I don't know how you resist the Internet. In some ways, Zach, you are a bloody reactionary."

"I prefer to think of myself as an unreconstructed traditionalist."

"Well, *you* were the English teacher. I bow to your superior vocabulary. I taught mathematics, as I'm sure I've told you—back around the time of the Spanish-American War."

Zach looked at him. "Do you ever miss it, Hugo?"

"Times like these I do. I won't say teaching was a snap, but at least I didn't feel like I was always in the middle of a damn typhoon." Hugo's eyes crinkled as he leaned back in his chair. "I used to love numbers. Oh, to return to the simple beauties of the logarithm!"

"Is there beauty in a logarithm?"

"There is indeed, but it doesn't reveal itself readily. You fellows who taught English think you had it hard unlocking the splendors of Shakespeare for high school kids. Let me tell you, the bard is simple by comparison. What's the wonderful speech from *Macbeth*?

Will all great Neptune's ocean wash this blood
Clean from my hand? No; this my hand will rather
The multitudinous seas incarnadine,
Making the green one red.

"Students don't have to understand every word of that to see the beauty in it. Hell, Shakespeare probably *knew* people wouldn't understand it the first time around, and that's why he provided his own translation in the last line. But the beauty of John Napier's creation isn't quite so easy to grasp."

"John Napier?"

"You see what I mean? You've never even heard of him. John Napier, a contemporary of Shakespeare, was the inventor of the logarithm. He was a Scottish mathematician, a bit of a crank: an ardent Protestant, as only a Scot can be. In his spare time he designed war machines, which, no doubt, he would like to have used against Catholics if he got the chance. Anyway, two years before he died, he published the first logarithmic table, the forerunner of the one that's printed now in every high school math book in the world."

"I'm impressed."

Hugo smiled. "Don't lie. You're thoroughly underwhelmed, but you prove my point." Leaning over, Hugo drew something from a bottom drawer and placed it on the desk between them. It was a small set of polished wooden rods attached to each other, but free to slide back and forth. Engraved on them was a series of numbers.

Zach picked up the device. "What is it?"

" 'Napier's bones' it was called ... a slang term that stuck. That's a reproduction. It was an early computing tool Napier invented, a precursor to the slide rule. Are you old enough to remember the slide rule?"

"No, but I've heard legends." Zach slid the smooth rods and watched the numbers line up. "It's very ... elegant."

"Yes, it is, and it works too. I've used it."

Zach replaced it carefully on the desk.

"My only point," Hugo continued, "is that beauty comes in many guises. We've just got to have the nerve endings to appreciate it. If a scientist can perceive loveliness of form and function in a double helix, why shouldn't a mathematician find an exquisite table of numbers as beautiful as the Parthenon?"

"No reason. I stand corrected."

"Corrected never. Merely better informed, I hope." Hugo allowed his smile to take on a rueful cast. "But beauty, I'm afraid, is not our theme today." He looked at Zach significantly. "I spoke with the governor. It's going to happen."

Zach watched him silently.

"Even some of our friends have started calling us 'the empire.' "

"And 'the empire' can't strike back anymore?"

"Not effectively. Not this time. I used all the arguments you gave me, but his back is against the wall. With Clinton in the White House balancing the federal budget, he can't be seen to do any less—especially since he's got national aspirations himself. And cuts are the only way to do it. He told me I can make the usual statement to the media opposing the measures, but if I put up anything more than a token resistance—well, you get the picture."

"So what do we do?"

"All we can do is limit the damage."

"And how much damage do they require?"

"The loudest proposal is twenty-five percent."

"Eliminate *twenty-five percent* of the department?!"

Hugo waved his hand dismissively. "I said the *loudest.* That figure is merely for the galleries. The governor thinks the final figure will be ten percent."

"Ten percent will still be a massive hit."

"I know. To make it more palatable politically, he wants the cuts to be made across the board. If we eliminate ten percent of the clerks, in other words, then we eliminate ten percent of their supervisors, and so on up the line."

"How far up?"

Hugo sighed. "All the way up. The governor asked me how many deputy commissioners I had. He actually didn't know, Lord love him. When I told him twenty-one, he did the simple arithmetic and said I'd have to cut two of them."

"Close down two whole divisions?"

"Combining them is the preferable choice, and that's where you come in. You've been involved in this battle from the beginning. Now it's time to negotiate the peace. I'd like for you to come up with a plan that will accommodate the ten percent loss."

"It's going to be a thankless job to suggest which two of my counterparts should leave."

"I know it, but it won't come from you. It will come from me."

"Is there anyone who's planning to retire soon?"

Hugo shook his head vigorously. "That can't have anything to do with it. We've got to have a more logical reason for closing divisions than the age of the person in charge. We're going to have to live with these changes, remember."

"I understand."

"Besides, we can offer them a pretty sweet deal. The governor has tentatively approved a very generous severance package." He pushed a thin folder across the desk. "The outline of it is in there. See if you don't agree."

Wordlessly Zach took the folder.

"This won't come as a surprise to anybody, Zach. Anyone with half a brain has anticipated it for years."

Zach nodded, stood up to leave. "What's our timetable?"

"Theoretically, the legislature could come to an agreement tomorrow, but they won't. Instead, they'll spend the better part of a month haggling over the goddamn numbers." He was quiet for a moment, then lifted the small wooden device from his desk and stared at it. "Did I really say 'goddamn numbers'?" He sighed, shook his head wearily. "And to think I used to love numbers."

III

Arch of Triumph

ON SATURDAY EVENING Beth took Zach to dinner at Les Pyrenees, a small, country-style French bistro located some miles from town. Zach had a genuine love for French cuisine, which was not unconnected to his belief that he had Gallic blood running through his veins. Zach's surname, Tonner, was French for "thunder," and one family account had it that an aristocratic ancestor first came to America to escape the French Revolution. Whether or not Zach believed in the blueness of his blood, he tried to make the most of his ethnic heritage.

Zach had studied French in school, but found that he was hopeless at foreign language. What words he learned, though, he pronounced beautifully. He grew to love French wines and had an enviable collection of dusty bottles in his basement. He read in translation French literature and studied French history and architecture. A framed poster of the two dissimilar steeples of Chartres hung in his office; another of Notre Dame's rose window hung in his study at home. When Zach and Beth had toured France, he made an almost religious pilgrimage to places he had read about. For his pains, he was duly snubbed by Parisian shopkeepers like any other American.

Les Pyrenees was set just off a rural highway. Originally a private home, it had but a single dining room with a low, heavily timbered ceiling and rosy-red plaster walls. On this particular evening they shared the restaurant with only one other party, a couple about their own age with a girl of five or six. Perhaps fearing that the child would disturb them, the waiter seated Zach and Beth at the opposite corner of the room. Into two slender flutes he poured a split of champagne.

"What's your grandfather cooking tonight?" Zach inquired.

The young man glanced over his shoulder at the kitchen, then looked at Zach significantly and made a small bouncing motion with his hand.

"*Pierre Lapin*?"

"It was hopping around the yard an hour ago."

Zach winced. "I only eat bunnies if they're made out of chocolate. I guess we'd better pick something from the menu. Give us a few more minutes."

"Take your time." The young man made his way over to his charges at the other side of the room.

"It's hypocritical, really," Beth commented.

"What is?"

"That you're willing to eat cattle without a second thought, but you won't eat a rabbit because it's cute and fuzzy."

"You're right. It *is* hypocritical. I'll call him back and tell him you want it."

"I didn't say I'm not a hypocrite."

Zach smiled and raised his glass. "To Pierre, who gave his life for the greater glory of *la patrie!*"

"Don't be silly," she chided. "The toast has to be to you tonight."

"All right then. To me, whose life, unfortunately, wouldn't add to the greater glory of anything."

Beth furrowed her brow. "Gloomy thoughts, aren't they, for your birthday?"

"No, no. I didn't mean anything by it." He buried his nose in the menu. "What are you going to order?"

She ordered sole, and Zach ordered steak *au poivre*. Over Beth's protests that she didn't care what color wine she drank, he nevertheless ordered two bottles, a Pouilly-Fuissé to go with her fish and a good Bordeaux to go with his beef. Perhaps to please Zach on his special day, Beth refrained from talking about work over dinner, and both of them avoided the topic of her imminent business trip. When the waiter cleared the dishes, Zach told him they would hold off on dessert while they enjoyed more of their wine. Beth's bottle was less than half-consumed, but Zach's was nearly empty. Beth watched him refill his glass.

"Are you planning to drive home tonight?" she asked.

"If I say yes, will you wrestle me to the ground for my keys?"

"I have my own keys."

"Damn. We haven't wrestled in years."

Beth reached for her purse.

"It's a little premature, though," Zach said. "I'm not ready to go yet."

Instead of her keys, Beth produced a small, neatly wrapped package tied with a ribbon and a red bow. "Happy birthday, Zach."

Zach grinned and grasped the package, showing considerable patience in slipping off the ribbon before tearing the paper. The box had the name of a local jewelry store embossed on the lid. Inside, nestled upon a small mattress of cotton, was a gold tie tack with a miniature *Arc de Triomphe* upon it.

"It's ... lovely," Zach said, turning it over in his hands.

"Well, I know men don't wear them too much anymore, but when I saw it, I thought you might like to have it."

"Thank you." Zach leaned over the table and kissed her. "I almost wish I was wearing a tie tonight so I could use it." He put the tack in the box and replaced the lid. "Maybe now I'll have to go out and buy a new one to go with it."

"That wouldn't be a bad idea. I think you have the same ties you owned when I met you."

"Well, they don't go out of style. They just get a little wider or narrower, but once you have a good selection of every width, you never need to get any new ones."

"Some people would disagree with you."

"Yes, I know: tie manufacturers. I wonder when the custom of wearing neckties began, and how it changed from being a matter of choice to a tyranny."

"I'd prefer that particular brand of tyranny to the one that governs women's fashions. You don't have to wear stockings to work every day."

"Neither do you. You could wear pants."

"I can't wear pants to work."

"Why not? Lots of women do."

"Whenever I wear pants to work, Ed Bumpus looks at my ass all day."

Zach laughed. "So the tyrant isn't really women's fashions. The tyrant is your office mate." He took a sip of his wine. "You could also stop wearing makeup."

"I wear hardly any as it is, just eye liner and a little lipstick."

"Is that for Ed Bumpus too?"

"It's so my face doesn't look completely washed out."

"I think you're pretty enough without it."

"I think we've had this conversation before." Beth paused. "In any case, wearing a tie is a small price to pay for the advantages it gives you."

"What advantages are those?"

"The advantage of having a prominent, highly-paid position. The advantage of having a private office with a window instead of a shared cubicle like I have."

"I have those things because I wear a tie?"

"Yes, and because you have a Y-chromosome."

Zach let the comment pass. He mused, "I've often wondered what would happen if I showed up at work without a necktie, or wearing sneakers."

"Don't try it. That tie which you consider such a tyranny protects you from a lot of things you wouldn't like very much at all."

Something in her tone, the know-it-all certainty of it, riled Zach. With more vehemence than he intended, he complained, "I hate ties. I hate everything about them." No sooner had the words passed his lips than he realized his blunder.

Beth said flatly, "That's nice to know. You must really like your birthday present."

"I'm sorry. You know I didn't mean it that way. I love the tie tack."

"You don't have to lie."

"I'm not lying."

They fell silent. Zach looked across the room at the other small party. The waiter had rolled the dessert cart up to their table, and the little girl pointed to one of the pastries, then giggled, holding her hand over her mouth.

"Their daughter is quite well behaved," Zach commented. "I was worried she might start squawking in the middle of dinner, but she's been very quiet."

Beth glanced over now too as the waiter place a huge tart in front of the child.

Zach chuckled. "I wonder if she'll be able to eat that whole thing. Do you suppose it's her birthday too?" He turned back to Beth. "You know what Bob told me this week? His children read to him at night."

"Oh?"

"I know what you're thinking: that's because Bob can't read. But it's quite a scene to contemplate, isn't it? Bob sitting on the sofa while his daughter reads fairy tales to him. He's such a buffoon with all his crude jokes, but he seemed really tickled telling me about it."

"So?"

"So nothing. I was just making an observation."

Beth put down her glass. "I think I'm beginning to understand now."

"Understand what?"

"The gloomy thoughts, the complaint about ties, and now wistful talk about children."

"What do you mean?"

"I'm watching a male mid-life crisis unfold right before my eyes."

Zach turned away. "Please, Dr. Brothers, no self-help book psychoanalysis tonight."

"That *is* why you brought up children, isn't it?"

"Don't be ridiculous. I only brought it up because Bob happened to mention them."

"And you envy him."

"No, I don't envy him."

"What is it then?"

"Nothing."

"I don't believe you."

"Believe what you want," Zach snapped. After a moment he added, "But I don't see why we always avoid the subject."

"Listen, Zach, if you want to talk with me about children again, fine, but let's do it the right way. Let's wait until sometime when we haven't both been drinking."

Zach looked over at the other party again. Holding the fork with her small fist, the girl skimmed some of the whipped cream off the top of her tart, then delicately tipped the fork into her mouth. "No," Zach said.

"No what?"

"No, let's not wait. Let's talk about it now."

Beth sighed. "What do you want to say?"

"Do you ever want to have a family?"

"I told you I did."

"Not recently."

"How often do you need for me to say it to you? Weekly? If so, I'll put a reminder in my calendar."

"I don't think there's room for me in your calendar."

She shook her head, gazing down at the table. "Is this really the way you want to spend your birthday?"

"I just want to know if I can ever expect to be a father."

"Don't I get any say in the matter?"

"Yes, of course you get a say. This is your say. So say something."

"I've told you already why I don't want to start a family yet."

"Well, how long do you want to wait? One year? Two years? Three? Don't you know that for every year after thirty-five that a woman puts off having her first baby, she increases the chance that her child will be retarded?"

Beth eyed him quizzically. "That's what you're worried about? Having a retarded child?"

Zach was silent.

"There's another reason to hold off," Beth continued. "It seems my husband is going through some emotional crisis right now. If you don't mind, I'd like to see the upshot of it before we talk seriously about having children."

"That's just another excuse."

"Don't label my reasons excuses just because you don't agree with them. This is a much bigger step for me than it is for you. I'm the one who'll have to leave work."

"I wish you cared half so much about us as you do about your damn work."

"That's what this is really about, isn't it? If I really loved you, I'd give up my job and give you children instead."

Zach fumed, unable even to look at her. Abruptly he stood. Without calculating the tip, he threw far too much money on the table and headed for the door.

Beth caught up with him in the parking lot just as he was about to get into the car. "I'd better drive, Zach."

He spun around, his face red with anger, but after a moment's hesitation he merely muttered something and walked around to the passenger side.

Beth did not start the engine immediately. Instead, they both sat for some time listening to the night sounds that drifted in on the cool air. Finally, her tone conciliatory, Beth said, "I'm sorry I got my back up. I'm a little sensitive on this issue. Don't think I haven't thought about it." She paused. "Here, you forgot this." She held out the small jewelry box he had left on the table.

Zach opened the box again and looked at the shiny tie tack. "I'll tell you," he said softly. "I'll tell you what I envied. I wanted to hear—"

He couldn't finish. To his alarm Zach realized he was holding back tears. He turned from his wife and looked out the side window so she wouldn't see.

"You wanted to hear what?"

After a long silence he said, "It was stupid, I know. But I wanted to hear the story. *I* wanted some little kid, some daughter of mine, to read *me* the story of the seven-league boots."

* * *

THEY DID NOT talk on the drive home, nor did they exchange more than a few words before retiring that night. The next morning Zach uncharacteristically lingered in bed while Beth quietly packed her bag and departed for the airport. An hour or so later, barefoot and clad in his pajamas, he made his way to the kitchen. On the table he found a note propped up against the coffeepot. Beth had jotted down the name of the motel where she was staying in California and the phone number in case he needed to reach her. The note ended with, *I'll try my best to be back by Friday. Hope you're feeling better this morning. Love, Beth.*

The pot of coffee was still warm. Zach sat wearily at the table and poured himself a mug. The house seemed very still, very empty. As he sipped his coffee, he reread the note in an attempt to raise another human voice in the silence. When he came to the last sentence, he frowned. *Hope you're feeling better this morning.* She made it sound as if he had been sick last night instead of heartsick. That kind of tactfulness was typical of Beth. Her errant husband had acted badly, and so she offered him a face-saving excuse: it was merely his temporary indisposition. Zach put the note down in disgust.

Well, how would he spend this quiet, boring Sunday? He ran his hand over his chin, feeling the stubble. No reason to shave today. From the liquor cabinet he extracted a bottle of Canadian whiskey. A dollop added to his coffee might be a good way to begin. Zach smiled wickedly to himself, knowing how strongly Beth would disapprove. Perhaps he wouldn't bother getting dressed either. He looked down at his feet. Maybe today he wouldn't even put on his shoes. Zach unscrewed the cap and held the bottle over his cup, then stopped suddenly.

Shoes.

"I sell shoes," Luna had said.

Zach thought of the strange young woman he'd met by the river. He thought of her short-cropped hair, her boyish figure, the odd things she'd said. She worked at Florsheim's at Crossgates. The shopping mall would be open this afternoon. Zach glanced up at the kitchen clock. For an absurd moment he considered driving over there to see her.

No, no, he had enough trouble right now without complicating his life further. He lifted the bottle again, but once more hesitated. He looked over at Beth's note and reread the last line: *Hope you're feeling better this morning.* His lips tightened.

Slowly, Zach lowered the bottle and replaced the cap.

IV

Blood Sport

THE MALL WAS already crowded when Zach arrived at two p.m. Clean-shaven now and dressed casually in jeans and a sweater, Zach strolled along the concourse wondering why he was doing this. He didn't want an affair with the strange young woman. Perhaps all he really wanted was to take some silly revenge on his wife. And why? Because Beth wouldn't agree to have children? Because Beth didn't understand him? Because Beth presumed to understand him too well? Or was the reason even shallower than these? Was it just because Beth was away again, and Zach resented being alone on this dull Sunday in May? None of the options covered Zach in glory, and he knew it.

Zach came to a stop some distance from Florsheim's so that he could peer into the store without being noticed from within. In an otherwise flashy mall, the shop reflected the conservative appeal of its merchandise by keeping glitz to a minimum.

Only two persons were visible. One was a broad-chested, big-armed young man in his late twenties. He was dressed in a stylish business suit, and he carried himself with a small air of importance, the store manager, perhaps, a title that used to mean something before retail America was turned over to teenagers. He was tending a gray-haired gentleman seated in the small row of chairs.

It occurred to Zach that Luna might have the day off. He wondered if he should go into the store and ask after her, or if it might be better all the way around simply to go home. Zach stood for a moment, unable to make up his mind. He looked at his watch.

"Do you have to be somewhere?" a voice behind him asked.

He turned around and saw Luna, a cup of coffee in her hand. She was wearing a long green skirt that reached to her ankles. Pinned to her blouse was a plastic badge with the company logo and the name "LUNA P."

Zach smiled. "Hello, Luna."

"I'm glad you came to see me." Her deep brown eyes examined him more closely. "You *did* come to see me, didn't you?"

He was about to lie and say he was just passing through the mall and thought he'd drop in to say hello, but he feared this pretence would disappoint her. "Yes, of course I came to see you. I thought we might have a drink together."

"I don't get another break until four o'clock."

"That's all right. I can come back at four."

"Are you sure you don't mind waiting?"

"No, I can amuse myself."

"All right." She proceeded toward the store, then hesitated and looked around at Zach again, taking in his attire. "I like you better this way."

* * *

ZACH HAD ALL he could do to occupy himself for two hours in the mall. He tried to think of something he needed to purchase, but nothing immediately came to mind. Then he remembered the tie tack and his own proposal that he buy a new tie to wear it with. Pleased that he now had a mission, Zach strode to a large department store at one end of the mall. In the men's wear section, he took what for him was a leisurely amount of time sorting through all the available patterns and colors before making his purchase.

Nevertheless, from the moment he had conceived the idea to the moment he left the store carrying a flat, rectangular box, a mere eight minutes had elapsed. Afterward he regretted having to tote the damn thing around for the rest of the day.

Zach browsed in a bookstore for a while. He wandered into an electronics shop. He examined some cooking gadgets in a kitchen store. Finally in desperation he bought a newsmagazine, carried it to a coffee bar, and spent the remainder of the time becoming much better acquainted with current events than he had intended.

When Zach returned to Florsheim's at four, he found the young man alone and bending over the displays in the front of the shop. Zach stood for a moment, looking in both directions.

"She'll be right back, Big Guy," the young man said over his shoulder.

Zach stared at him. "Excuse me?"

"You're here to meet Luna, aren't you? You're Zach."

Startled to find his anonymity shattered, Zach admitted that he was.

"She just went to the restroom." He jerked his thumb in the direction of the public facilities down the mall. The young man straightened up now. His face was open, confident, and innocent. He held out a beefy hand. "My name's Scott."

Zach took the hand, which squeezed his mercilessly.

"Luna says you're an English teacher."

"Well, it's been some years, really, since—"

"I liked English. You know what my favorite book was?"

"No. What?"

"*Moby-Dick*. I read the whole thing, not the abridged version. It was the longest book I ever read."

"That's great," Zach said without enthusiasm.

"People who haven't read the book but only saw the movie, they think it was Ahab who's tied to the whale at the end, because that's the way it is in the movie. But it wasn't Ahab; it was that other guy—the Arab, right? What was his name? Fadoola?"

"Something like that."

"That's right. Something like that. Anyway, the book was way better than the movie. What's your favorite book?"

"I'm not sure."

"Books have it all over movies. And television is even worse. Some nights I go home, I don't even turn the TV on. I just read all evening. You ever do that?"

"Sometimes." Zach looked down the mall, hoping to be rescued.

Scott followed his gaze. "Women!" he exclaimed good-naturedly. "They always take a long time in the john, right? Now guys, they know just what they have to do and they do it." He thrust his arm out stiffly to indicate the straightforward way males accomplish things. "But women? They always have to sit down and think about it for a while." In a quieter voice he added, "Luna's a nice girl, though."

"Yes, she does seem to be."

"If I wasn't married—I'll tell you the truth—I'd go out with her myself."

Glancing down, Zach saw the broad, bright wedding ring on Scott's left hand. Zach slipped his own left hand in his pocket.

"And she's a good worker too," Scott continued. "Some of these kids we get in here, you should see how they act to the customers: like they're doing the customer a favor by waiting on them. But Luna's always polite to people. And honest? I can leave her alone here anytime, and when I cash out at the end of the day, everything will tally up perfectly—to the nickel. She's real reliable too, always on time, never late. She's a very good worker, a very nice girl."

"How long has she worked here?"

"Six months. We hired her for the Christmas season, then asked her to stay on."

Zach thought of something. "Scott, has Luna's father ever stopped by the store?"

"Her father?" Scott looked puzzled. "No."

At this point, Zach distinguished Luna threading her way along the concourse. He shook Scott's hand again. "Well, it was nice meeting you."

"Same here, Big Guy. Don't do anything I wouldn't do."

* * *

ZACH TOOK LUNA to a restaurant in the mall. He chose a small booth in the bar section where they could be alone, then ordered two glasses of white wine. While they waited for their drinks to arrive, Luna maintained the solemn expression she wore on their previous encounter. Zach wondered what, if anything, ever made her smile—or laugh. Despite the skirt and blouse, her boyish demeanor still predominated. In fact, the more feminine attire seemed to accentuate it, as if she were a boy trying to impersonate a girl and doing it badly.

Two glasses of wine were set down in front of them, and though Luna tried to pay for her own, Zach prevailed upon her to let him treat. He clinked her glass with his, and they both sipped. Zach glanced at the nametag pinned to her chest.

"What does the 'P' stand for, if you don't mind telling me?"

"Planitis."

"Planitis," Zach repeated. "What nationality is that?"

"It's Greek." Luna took another sip of wine. "Did you enjoy your birthday?"

"Yes, very much. We went out to a French restaurant. I like French food."

"Is that a present?" she asked, indicating the flat package Zach had placed on the table.

He glanced down at it. "Oh, this? No, it's just a tie I bought."

"Can I see?"

For some unaccountable reason Zach felt embarrassed to show it to her. He opened the box and revealed a standard silk tie, red with a repeating pattern of small yellow diamonds upon it. Luna examined it. "You bought this for yourself?"

"Yes."

"Do you like it?"

"Well, I *bought* it," he responded, as if this were sufficient answer.

Luna looked noncommittal.

Irritated that his fashion sense had been called into question, Zach quickly replaced the lid on the box and stowed it out of sight. "So," he said after a moment, "have you met any more of your correspondents?"

"No."

"Why not?"

"I have no interest in meeting any others."

"Aren't you a little curious?"

"Curious about what?"

"To see what they're like."

Luna furrowed her brow. "Why would you want me to go out with other men?"

He was taken aback by the question and could think of no response other than a foolish grin, which seemed all the more foolish compared to the grave expression on the young woman sitting opposite him. Finally Zach just shrugged his shoulders. "Well, it's none of my business anyway."

"It isn't?"

Zach changed the subject. "Is Scott your boss?"

Luna nodded.

"He spoke very highly of you. Somehow, though, he got the impression I was an English teacher."

"You are, aren't you?"

"It's nice of you to pretend I have an honest calling, but as I told you, I'm a bureaucrat, a rather overpaid one at that, which is the very worst kind." He paused. "Scott seems a friendly sort. Is he a good boss?"

"Yes. He doesn't like what he's doing, though. He'd rather go into business for himself. A friend of his owns a sporting goods store downtown, and he wants to sell the business. Scott would like to buy it, but he hasn't got enough money. He asked me if I wanted to invest in it."

"Really? How much did he want from you?"

"Ten thousand dollars."

"Ten thousand dollars! What made him think you had that kind of money?"

"I told him. I said I was looking for something to invest in."

Zach narrowed his eyes. "Are you going to do it?"

"I don't know. Scott's very good at managing, and he knows quite a bit about sporting goods, but one should be careful with one's investments."

"I think that's *very* wise." Zach spoke with emphasis, and his tone implied that he was using his utmost restraint to keep from giving advice to someone who sorely needed it.

Luna looked at him. "You don't think I'm very smart, do you?"

"Of course I do."

"You don't. I didn't go to college, but I'm not stupid."

"I'm sure you're not."

She seemed unconvinced. Luna asked, "Do you know who the second President of the United States was?"

"What?"

"Who was the second President?"

"John Adams."

"How about the third?"

"Jefferson, right?"

"And the fourth?"

"Was that the other Adams?"

"No, it was Madison. How about the fifth?"

"*That* was the other Adams."

"No, that was Monroe. The other Adams was sixth."

Zach smiled indulgently. "Do you know all the Presidents, Luna?"

"Yes."

"That's ... impressive." There was a condescending edge to his voice.

Luna narrowed her eyes. "Tell me why you're here."

"I came to visit you."

"Surely not just to mock me."

"Of course not."

"When I saw you here, I assumed it meant you wanted me. Was I wrong?"

Zach hesitated. For the first time he realized that the most probable interpretation of his visit was that he had decided to pursue the affair with her. The most damning alternative was that he was merely toying with her, and Zach did not want to believe that about himself.

"Well?" she demanded. "Do you want me or not?"

"I ... I do."

She fixed her deep brown eyes upon him. "Do you?"

"Yes."

Luna glanced at her watch. "I have to get back." From a small notebook in the pocket of her skirt, she ripped a sheet of paper and jotted something upon it, then pushed it across the table to him. "There's my address," she said. "You can come for dinner."

Zach was startled. "Dinner?"

"I *know* how to cook," she said with some annoyance. "I won't poison you."

"But, do you mean tonight?"

"No, not tonight. Come Friday at seven." She stood up. "I can't have you over tonight. I'm bleeding."

* * *

THAT EVENING ZACH drank the whiskey he had refrained from drinking in the morning. While he sat alone in the kitchen intermittently raising the glass to his lips, he looked at the slip of paper Luna had given him. Written in her neat hand was the name "Luna Planitis" followed by a Lark Street address and a phone number. Zach did not want an affair with Luna, and he didn't know how he'd gotten into this.

Nevertheless, as he continued to sip the whiskey and to fall under its influence, he kept thinking about her and especially about the last thing she had said to him. "I'm bleeding." What kind of woman would refer to her menstrual cycle that way? She'd said it resentfully too, as if such a thing shouldn't be happening to her at all. Did this boyish-looking person consider her gender a mistake, a cosmic taunt? The oddest thing, however, was Zach's reaction.

Somehow he found the image of Luna bleeding, bizarre though it was, strangely attractive. Zach was not religious, but he was put in mind of the curious biblical locution of being washed in the blood. "I'm bleeding," Luna had said, and thereby she had been made clean.

* * *

It was nearly two a.m. before Zach collapsed into bed. The next morning, his head feeling several times larger than usual and a throbbing pain behind his eyes, he sincerely regretted the events of the previous day. Moreover, even though there was no one else privy to them, he was thoroughly embarrassed by the wild thoughts he'd had the night before. With the reasonable light of day shining upon him again, he determined to call up the young woman and end this silliness once and for all. He would tell her the truth. He would explain that though he was indeed experiencing some problems with his wife, it would be wrong to jeopardize his marriage. He would apologize to her, take all the blame upon himself, and wish her luck in finding a "swain" better suited to her. Having once formulated this plan, Zach felt much better, almost as if he had already carried it out.

Yet he postponed calling her. On Monday night he put it off until Tuesday, and on Tuesday he put it off until Wednesday. On Wednesday night Zach accepted Bob's invitation to get a bite to eat after work and watch a ball game on TV. It was nearly eleven when Zach finally got home, and he convinced himself that this was too late to phone Luna. Then on Thursday night Beth called.

Zach was sitting in his study reading when the phone on his desk rang.

"How are you, Zach," she asked. "Have the dirty dishes reached the ceiling yet?"

"Not yet, but I'm working on it. How are you? Are you coming home tomorrow?"

From the brief silence at the other end of the line, Zach knew the answer. "That's why I called," she said. "I really thought we were going to finish by Friday, and we almost did, but then we ran this trial program yesterday, and it crapped out right in the middle. We ran it four more times, but it kept crapping out in the same spot, so today we got two guys on the phone from *my* shop, and they—"

"Beth, I really don't need to hear this."

"I just want you to understand that it's been frustrating for me too."

"I'm sure it has," he said flatly.

She paused. "How have you been feeling?"

"How have I been feeling? I've been feeling fine. I wasn't aware that I'd been ill."

"I mean, since our talk Saturday night."

"I feel fine."

"Well, anyway, if we're able to fix this problem tomorrow—and I'm pretty sure we can—I'll be coming home Saturday. There's a flight that will bring me in at noon, your time."

"My time," he repeated, finding something irksome in the phrase.

"Yes. I'll have to leave Friday night to make the connections. The client's planning a small party for us, which I'll have to skip."

"So I should be properly grateful."

"No, that would be asking too much. After a week like I've had, I'd like to relax for an evening, but don't worry: I won't. Instead I'll spend the whole damn night running around in airports so I can get home in time to hold my husband's hand."

"Beth—"

"Good-bye, Zach," she said, and the line went dead.

V

Swain

AFTER WORK ON Friday Zach went home to change his clothes and also to collect two things he wanted to take along to Luna's. Not very well concealed by a paper bag was a bottle of wine from Zach's cellar. Better concealed in his trousers pocket was a small, unopened packet of condoms.

The address she had given him corresponded to a brownstone with a seedy T-shirt shop in its basement storefront. Zach found Luna's name among a half-dozen others, her apartment a third-floor walkup. He pressed the little square button alongside her name and a few moments later heard her voice crackling through the speaker. Once inside the door, Zach was assaulted by the smell of decay, the peculiar odor of old city apartment buildings. He mounted the stairs in a drab hallway dimly lit by bare, twenty-five-watt bulbs.

When Zach reached the top floor, Luna was waiting for him on the landing. She wore an apron over jeans and a loose-fitting, short-sleeved shirt. Though she maintained her usual solemnity, she appeared pleased to see him and ushered him to her door. As he stepped over the threshold, he inhaled a much more inviting aroma, simmering meat and the unmistakable bouquet of evaporating wine. "What are you making?" he asked.

"*Coq au vin*. It's French. You said you liked French food."

Zach smiled broadly. "I do. And it looks like I brought an appropriate wine." He handed her the paper bag. "It's also French."

Luna slipped the bottle out and examined the label. " 'Chateau Talbot,' " she read aloud, anglicizing the name as she pronounced it. "Is it good?"

"Yes," he said, smiling more to himself now than to her, "fairly good."

She took his jacket and disappeared into the adjoining kitchen to open the wine. Zach looked around. He was standing in her living room, but she had apparently brought in a table for the occasion. It was already set for dinner, complete with candles and even a few wildflowers in a vase. Though the table cut down on the available floor space, the room looked tidy enough. Lark Street was a notorious student ghetto, and Zach had rather expected a typical young person's pad: funky, cluttered, all flash and trash. Instead, the room looked oddly conventional, almost petit bourgeois. A faded pink carpet with a flower pattern covered the floor. Against the wall was an old-fashioned sofa, and before it a fake cherry coffee table. The furniture looked well used, nearly but not quite dilapidated.

The only elements of the decor that looked out of place and did indeed resemble a student apartment were a series of large posters. Yet these were not photos of rock groups or movie stars. As Zach made his way around the room examining them, he saw that each one was an image of a different roller coaster. One pictured the Coney Island *Cyclone*. Another, its view from a sandy shoreline, showed a gleaming white coaster, eight or ten stories tall. It bore the injunction, "Ride the *Giant Dipper* at Santa Cruz Beach Boardwalk!" A third poster showed a maze of interweaving tracks with the Rocky Mountains standing starkly in the background. At the top it read, "*Mister Twister*," and below, "Not to see Elitch's is not to see Denver."

One final poster hanging over the sofa pictured something so impossible that Zach had to lean over to make sure it was an actual photograph. Against the vibrant blue backdrop of a lake two slender humps of red track rose so high into the air that they seemed a cartoon exaggeration of a real roller coaster. The scale of the looming structure could only be gauged by the low buildings at its base and by the size of the train itself, which, caterpillar-like, was just cresting the first hill, high above everything else. Zach sucked in his breath. "Holy Jesus!"

"That's the *Magnum*," Luna said over his shoulder.

Zach turned around. She was holding two glasses of red wine. "It looks ghastly!" he said, motioning toward the coaster photo.

"It's two hundred and five feet tall. It's steel," she added, handing him a glass, "but it's configured like a wooden coaster."

"And wooden coasters are better. See? I remembered. Where is the *Magnum*?"

"Cedar Point. It's in Ohio, not far from Toledo."

"And you've never been to Toledo?"

"No."

"But you'd love to go there someday."

"You're making fun of me again."

Zach laughed. "No, I'm not really. You just have a lovely way of wanting to visit cities no one else wants to go to. But we have our toast." He touched her glass with his own. "May you ride the *Magnum* before you die!"

After they had both sipped, Luna furrowed her brow. "What kind of wine is it?"

"*Saint-Julien*. It's a kind of Bordeaux," Zach clarified. "It'll grow on you. Trust me. It'll taste even better with food."

"Dinner's nearly ready. I'll just be a few minutes."

"Anything I can do to help?"

"Of course not. You're the guest. Would you like to hear some music?"

Luna switched on an ancient phonograph and placed the

needle on a record. As she left the room, Zach heard a female voice issue from the speaker.

There's a saying old
Says that love is blind,
Still we're often told
"Seek and ye shall find."

He recognized the introduction to Gershwin's "Someone to Watch Over Me." From the primitive sound reproduction and the style of the singing, he guessed it was a vintage recording from the 1920s or 30s.

Zach strolled to an open doorway and stepped inside. It was Luna's bedroom, a tiny chamber only slightly larger than the bed itself. The bed was neatly made. There was a single window that looked out on the building next door. The walls, painted a dreary off-white, were bare save for a framed photograph of a horse. Zach took a sip of the wine and returned to the living room.

I'm a little lamb who's lost in the wood.
I know I could always be good
To one who'll watch over me.

At the dinner table two places had been carefully set. Zach gazed down at the china. All the pieces were of the same pattern, each one bearing an idealized, sentimental image of country life: a covered bridge, an old fashioned well, a rural stone wall in front of an apple tree, a red schoolhouse. Zach lifted one of the plates and examined it. "Where did you get the dishes?" he called into the kitchen.

"I bought them," was the reply. "Do you like them?"

Zach hesitated. "Um ... sure. How did you happen to pick this particular set?"

"I like dishes with pictures on them."

Zach put the plate back.

Won't you tell him all my love I will save.
I'll be his slave. Oh, how I crave
Someone to watch over me.

Luna carried in a salad bowl and the remainder of the wine. "What kind of dishes do you have?" she asked.

"We have two sets, actually."

"Are you Jewish?"

He smiled. "No. We just have a good set for company and then an everyday set for ourselves. Beth picked them out."

"What do they look like?"

Zach shrugged his shoulders. "I forget what they're called. The everyday set is just plain white, and the Noritake is white with a black and gold edge."

"Noritake?"

"It's a Japanese company. They make china."

"Oh. Mine comes from England." She said this with a touch of pride in her voice.

Luna disappeared once more into the kitchen. When she returned, she had removed her apron and was carrying the *coq au vin.* She placed the platter in the center of the table and proceeded to serve Zach, then herself.

"It looks wonderful," Zach proclaimed. In fact, he thought the sauce was a little thin. Nevertheless, when he tasted the chicken, he concluded that it wasn't bad. He said, "Delicious!"

She had been watching him for his reaction. Now she began to eat.

Their conversation during dinner was sparse, and all of it initiated by Zach. Luna appeared never to have mastered the art of integrating discourse with dining—or perhaps she had just never practiced it. And though she was obviously making an effort to be dainty while she ate, she was not overly successful. She consumed her food rather too quickly, and she had a tendency to drop things from her fork before they reached her mouth. She also had an appetite that was not dainty at all. As the wine began to have its mellowing effect upon him, though, Zach found something charming in Luna's quirks. When she offered him a second helping, he accepted.

The dessert was a chocolate mousse, also of Luna's own making. Any reservations Zach had about its quality were overcome by his appreciation that she had worked very hard to create this dinner for him. Zach pronounced the dessert excellent, and he devoured it all.

The first bottle of wine emptied, Luna retrieved a second one from the kitchen, an undistinguished red from California. "I'm afraid it's not as good as yours," she apologized as she poured it into their glasses. "I don't know much about wine."

Zach waved away her fears. "Don't worry about it. After the first bottle, they all taste good. The only thing I have to be concerned about is driving home afterward."

"You don't have to drive home. You can stay over."

At any time in the past, such an invitation from a woman would have brought on an immediate physical reaction from Zach, but now he merely smiled and lowered his eyes shyly. In an odd way he was really enjoying Luna's company, but he still could not picture himself going to bed with her.

Zach sipped the new wine, which, true to his prediction, did not taste bad at all. He asked, "Who taught you how to cook? Your mother?"

"I taught myself."

"Well, you did a very good job of it. My mother tried to teach me, but I had no interest in learning. It's probably just as well, because she wasn't really a very good cook."

"Is Beth?"

It was the first time Luna had uttered his wife's name, and for some reason Zach felt uncomfortable hearing it from her lips. "She's a good cook," he answered simply. "But tell me about your family, Luna. Do you have any brothers or sisters?"

"No."

"So you're an only child. You've never had to deal with sibling rivalry then. Lucky for you. And your parents: what are they like?"

"We could sit on the couch."

Zach glanced over at it. "All right."

They moved to the sofa, Zach sitting first and Luna sitting close enough by his side that he was induced, almost without thinking, to put his arm around her. It was the first time he had touched her since the brief kiss she'd given him down at the river. He could feel her ribs under the smooth garment, and as he casually ran his hand up and down her side, he could tell that she wore no bra. He looked at her profile.

"You have no holes in your ears," he observed.

"Holes?"

"For earrings. You must be the only woman of your generation—that's leaving aside the men—who hasn't had her ears pierced."

"I think it's *barbaric*."

"I can't say as I disagree with you. And you don't have long painted nails either, or purple hair."

She made no response except to turn toward him, their faces inches apart now.

Zach laughed nervously. "Of course, you might have a tattoo on your chest."

Luna's deep brown eyes stared into his. Quietly she said, "I don't." Then she lifted her hands to her shirt and began to unbutton it.

Zach had the strongest urge to stop her, to grasp her wrists and make some absurd speech about this being too soon and they should get to know each other a little better first, but he could not. In paralyzed fascination he watched as she unfastened the remaining buttons and pulled the shirt open, then slipped it off.

Luna had no tattoo. And as Zach had surmised all along, she had no breasts to speak of either. Light brown nipples, only a little larger than Zach's own, merely indicated where the breasts should be. More startling to Zach was that Luna did not shave her body hair. Clumps, dark as that which grew on her head, peeked out from under her arms. The greatest surprise, however, was what happened to Zach as he looked at her. Unexpectedly the ground had shifted, and Zach was no longer wondering if he wanted Luna. As he gazed at her, he found that he coveted the strange person seated beside him. Yet there was in his desire a curious dread. Involuntarily, he pulled Luna to him.

* * *

ZACH TOOK PRIDE in his lovemaking, and if he'd had time to think about it, he probably would have wanted to impress upon Luna how a truly sensitive man treated a woman. Indeed, out of habit—at first on the couch and later when they had undressed and lay together in bed—he practiced those erotic techniques that he knew women enjoyed. After a while, though, he became drunk, but not with alcohol. Luna's body exuded the sharp, acrid smell of sweat, as if she had not washed today and perhaps not the day before either. Instead of finding her odor offensive, Zach became intoxicated with it. Embarrassed at first to reveal how strongly the fragrance attracted him, he eventually became too tipsy with it to care. He buried his nose in the dark clumps under her arms, inhaling the outlandish bouquet. This barrier crossed, he hunted out all her other animal scents, following each one to its own private lair.

And he touched Luna, felt compelled to touch her everywhere, to experience her fully, without restriction. He pressed his chest upon hers, rib to rib, nipple to nipple. Her legs were unshaven, and Zach ran his hands upward on her calves, excited by the mild resistance of her hairs. He did the same on her forearms. Then, when he returned to the fine down that grew upon her upper lip, they began a new kind of embrace.

Their mouths less than an inch apart, Luna sought his breath, beckoned it out to play with her own, inhaled his as he inhaled hers. Like the scent of her body, Luna's breath was curiously enticing. Zach couldn't say if it was bad or good, only that it was foreign and that he craved it, wanted to draw it inside himself. Eventually they coupled in the conventional way, but it was in this other congress, in the small gap between their parted lips, a fearful no-man's land, that the real intimacy took place. Their breaths, more naked than their bodies, met there, mingled, and danced a strange cotillion together.

The old mattress barely recorded their brief shudders at the end. Nevertheless as Zach lay awake afterward, he knew something significant had happened. In the dim light he gazed at the young woman dozing in his arms, her head resting on his chest. He stroked her hair lightly and listened to her even breathing. Partly thrilled, partly horrified, Zach knew that he had experienced passion for the first time.

He'd never understood the word before. Romeo felt passion for Juliet. Antony felt passion for Cleopatra. Paris felt passion for Helen. Does that mean passion is love?

Yes.

But it can't *just* be love. In church they talk about the passion of Christ, and they mean the suffering he endured at the crucifixion. Does that mean passion is pain?

Yes.

But it can't just be pain either. Suffering, even great suffering, doesn't require so profound a word. Nor does love. Passion is the way people describe a single-minded zealousness in pursuit of a cause, an idea, a person. Yet that still doesn't get to the heart of it. Passion means something else too, something that brings it right back to love again, and right back to pain.

Zach understood now. In a little room in a little city on the banks of a river ruled by the Lord Inachus, Zach had finally figured it out. He looked at Luna sleeping upon him, hair on her legs, hair under her arms, reeking of sweat and of sex. From her parted lips, drool slid down her chin and moistened his chest. Zach understood now. At the very center of passion is madness.

VI

Teacup Puppy

Zach was in the midst of a dream when Luna woke him. He dreamt that he was teaching again, and he was late for his first class of the semester. His battered old book bag hanging open with his lesson plans hastily thrust inside, he was rushing down the hall to his class. All he could think of was how bad a first impression this was going to make on his students. How was he going to maintain discipline after this? Zach couldn't believe he had allowed himself to get into such a mess. It wasn't like him to be late for things, and even less like him to act contrary to his own best interests. Just at the moment when he reached the door to his classroom and was about to pull it open, a voice from outside his dream asked, "Do you believe in God?"

Zach woke with a start. Through the window the light of morning lit the small room, and for a moment Zach forgot where he was. Then he saw Luna, still naked and sitting up in the center of the bed solemnly watching him.

"Did you say something?" he asked, squinting at her.

"Do you believe in God?"

Zach's relief at coming out of the disturbing dream was replaced by a vague apprehension as he recalled the events of the previous evening. Rubbing his eyes, he felt a wave of guilt wash over him. He'd gone from fantasizing about adultery to committing it. Now he was a man who cheated on his wife. It made him feel small and common, and that hurt his pride. Zach looked at Luna again. "What time is it?"

"I don't know. Early. We have lots of time."

Sleepily, he sat up now too and blinked at her.

"So, do you?" she asked again.

"Do I what?"

"Do you believe in God?"

"That's an odd question to ask a person just waking up. Do you ask everyone that?"

"Everyone?"

"Everyone you sleep with."

Even before the wrath that rose in her face could register on Zach's consciousness, he felt the stinging pain on his cheek where she hit him. So hard was the slap that he nearly fell back down onto the bed. "Do you think I'm a *whore*?" she shouted.

He stared at her, shocked. "No, of course not."

"You think I sleep around!"

Smarting from the blow, Zach felt his own anger rise. He had not been struck by anyone since high school, and he'd never been struck by a woman. "For Christ's sake, Luna, you advertised in the personals! You slept with a married man! What am I supposed to think? That you're a goddamned virgin?"

"*I am*," she said. After a pause, and in a much smaller voice, she amended, "I was."

Still rubbing his cheek, Zach straightened up again and examined her grave features. "Do you mean it? I was your first?"

Instead of answering, she pushed aside the covers, revealing a small bloodstain on the sheet, dark brown now from having dried overnight.

Zach sighed. He could now add this guilt to that which he was already feeling. "I'm sorry, Luna. I had no idea. Why didn't you tell me?"

"What difference would it have made?"

The difference was that Zach probably would not have gone to bed with her at all had he known. He had an embarrassing sentimental streak, not to mention a latent sexism. He considered a woman's virginity a gift she bestowed upon a man, and he felt thoroughly unworthy of that gift.

They both fell silent now, Zach looking glum and avoiding eye contact. After a long interval he said, "I don't."

"You don't what?"

"Believe in God."

"Why not?"

"Who can account for what they believe? I just don't."

"Do you believe in an afterlife?"

"No. As far as I'm concerned, this is the only life you get."

"You don't think anything lives on after you?"

"Nothing but your genes, I guess, if you have children." He looked up at her. "Do *you* believe in God?"

"I believe in many gods."

Zach smiled. "I guess I shouldn't be surprised. You even advertised for one, and I had the audacity to answer." He pulled his knees up and wrapped his arms around them. "Folks who believe in God are probably better off."

"Why?"

"Haven't you ever read about it? When people are taken hostage by terrorists, it invariably turns out that the ones who fare best are those who have faith in God, while atheists like me despair and die. True believers come through medical operations better, and life-threatening illnesses, and disasters and tragedies of all kinds. The statistics are there to prove it. It's rather depressing really."

"Why is it depressing?"

"As a rational person I hate to admit the obvious conclusion: there's survival value in believing a lie."

Luna was silent.

"I've been asked to play God recently. At work I'm going to change the destiny of two people. I have to pick two of my counterparts to leave their jobs at the Education Department."

"Why do you have to do it?"

"Ironically enough, because I've been so active over the years in trying to *save* people's jobs. By default I've become the expert on departmental structure, deployment of staff, allocation of funds." He shook his head, dismayed at the string of phrases he'd just used. "Talk about depressing: I used to be an expert in Shakespeare and Chaucer and Milton. Now I'm an expert in bureaucratic jargon. Quite a metamorphosis, isn't it? Changing from the butterfly into the caterpillar instead of the other way around."

"You could change back."

"No, I couldn't. You don't know what an insidious trap some jobs are. People call it golden handcuffs, as if it's the money that shackles you. Well, the money is good, but ultimately it's not the money. It's the contract."

"What contract?"

"The contract you make with yourself, and with your spouse, and with the world at large. Leaving your job would be crazy, and you've promised them all that you won't do crazy things." Zach glanced at her. "But I'm probably boring you with work talk, and I'm definitely boring myself. Tell me more about you, Luna."

"What about me?"

"Tell me what you do with yourself—when you're not selling shoes, that is. Do you do normal things like read books, or go to movies, or do laundry?"

"Of course I do laundry. Did my clothes look dirty?"

Zach laughed. "No, they didn't look dirty." He glanced around the room and focused on the single item hanging on the wall, a photo of a horse standing in a field. "Tell me about the picture."

"That's Nutty. He was my horse when I was growing up. He's dead now."

"So you know how to ride. I always wished I knew how."

"I could teach you."

" 'Had we but world enough, and time.' " Zach looked at the grainy photograph. "A horse would have been out of the question in a Connecticut suburb, where I grew up. I would love to have had a smaller pet, though, a dog or a cat. Most of my friends had pets. My parents weren't willing to get me one, though. They were afraid I wouldn't take care of it, or that it would mess up the house."

Zach leaned back. "I used to read lots of comic books when I was a kid, and in those days there was an advertisement that appeared regularly on the back cover. It showed a tiny dog sitting in a teacup. According to the ad, all you had to do to receive the live puppy was to fill out the form at the bottom of the page and mail it in with a dollar. It had to be a rip-off. No dog, even the smallest Chihuahua, could fit in a teacup, and no company could stay in business very long selling mail-order canines for a buck apiece. But children love puppies, and children are gullible, so thousands of little kids must have sent in their crumpled-up dollar bills, and I was one of them. I was six or seven at the time, and after I sent in my dollar, I would go and sit on our porch every day waiting for the mail, hoping the puppy would arrive. Weeks went by, maybe months, and no puppy appeared. Finally I told my parents about it. My father laughed, and my mother scolded me for wasting my money."

He shook his head. "The worst part was feeling so stupid afterward. How pathetic I must have looked sitting on the porch steps with my chin resting on my palms waiting for the damn puppy that would never come. I'm still embarrassed by it."

"Why?"

"I was so naive."

"Are you happier now that you're cynical?"

Zach looked at her. He was about to protest, but suddenly had the strongest urge to feel her skin. He reached toward her, hesitated. "May I touch you?"

"Of course you can touch me. We're lovers now."

Zach caressed her bare shoulder. There was an absolute genuineness about her and a simplicity that Zach found endearing. He remembered the unexpected desire, the mad passion she had aroused in him. That passion was now being succeeded by an equally unexpected affection. He ran his hand over her scalp, feeling the shape of her head. "Tell me why you wear your hair like this?"

"Do you prefer long hair?"

"I thought I did. Now I don't know anymore."

"I could make you breakfast."

Considering the large dinner he had consumed the night before, Zach was not particularly hungry, but the thought of having breakfast with her sounded so appealing that he accepted her offer. Luna leapt from the bed, and Zach watched as she slipped her clothes back on and disappeared from the room. When he was alone, he rubbed his cheek where she had struck him. It was still a little sore, but he couldn't summon up any hostility toward her. On the contrary, he felt an odd tenderness. He gazed down at the bloodstain. Obeying a sudden impulse, he touched it lightly, then grazed his lips with his fingers.

Over breakfast Zach once again tried to engage Luna in conversation, but with as little success as he'd had the previous evening. Eventually he accepted this idiosyncrasy of hers. He waited until the dishes had been cleared and the final round of coffee had been poured. Then he said, "I've enjoyed this, Luna. Thank you."

"You're welcome."

"I don't just mean breakfast. I mean ... everything."

"I knew what you meant."

"And to think I almost didn't show up. I considered calling you a dozen times and begging off."

"What made you come?"

Zach smiled. "Something my dad used to say: sometimes it's better to jump out the window first, *then* decide whether you want to fall."

She looked at him.

"I'd like to see you again," Zach said, "if that's possible."

"You can see me all day today. I have no plans."

"I wish I could, but Beth is coming home at noon. I have to get back before she does, or I'll have some difficult explaining to do. Another time, though—soon."

"I have next Saturday off."

"That's Memorial Day weekend. Even Beth gets that off." Zach frowned. He now faced the dilemma of all men who cheat on their wives. Was this to be the first of many times when he would disappoint his lover in favor of his wife? Zach felt like a heel. Worse, he felt common again. He said, "Let me see if I can work something out. Maybe we could get together next Saturday for a little while."

No sooner were the words out of his mouth than Zach realized that this compromise was even worse. He was tossing the young woman a bone, demeaning both himself and her in the process. He'd condemned this behavior in other men. Now to his shame he saw it in himself.

Zach leaned across the table. "Listen, Luna, I don't want you to tie yourself down waiting for me. If something else comes up and you want to make other plans, go right ahead. But I'll call you as soon as I know. All right?"

"All right."

As they continued to sip their coffee, Zach looked for signs of resentment in Luna's face, but he saw only that she was pondering something. After a few moments she asked, "What will happen to the two people?"

"What two people?"

"The two in your department who are being fired."

"They're not being fired," Zach corrected her. "They won't be out on the street holding 'Will work for food' signs, if that's what you're thinking. People at my level don't get fired, unless they're caught with their hand in the till. They'll both leave with very golden handshakes."

"You mean they *want* to leave?"

"It's entirely possible. There are lots of folks in the department who would take any opportunity to jump ship if the inducement were sweet enough, and I think the package we're offering is very sweet indeed. They'll probably take it."

"But what if they don't?"

He hesitated. "Well, they won't really have a choice."

"It sounds like being fired." Luna was silent for a moment. Then in her usual even tones she said, "Don't do anything bad."

"What?"

"Keep in mind that I'm your lover now, Zach. Be merry. You don't have to do bad things anymore."

* * *

WHAT ON EARTH does she mean when she talks like that? As Zach drove away from Lark Street, the words echoed in his brain. "Don't do anything bad." "I'm your lover now." "Be merry." Imagine! She told *him* to be merry, a woman who never smiles. Yet Zach could not help his growing fondness for her. He was touched by the care she had taken in making him feel welcomed. Then there was the strange lovemaking last night, touching her, smelling her, mingling his breath with hers.

He thought of the blood on the sheet. Zach had never been with a virgin before. Beth was not a virgin when they married. In fact she'd told him once how she lost her virginity. Having reached her senior year in college and deciding it was high time, she'd simply asked a male friend in her dorm to sleep with her. When it was over, she thanked him, and they went right back to being friends again. The incident was perfectly in character for Beth.

He remembered *their* first time, his and Beth's. During the foreplay she'd actually said to him, "Would you care for some fellatio?" and she'd said it matter-of-factly as if she were asking him if he'd care for some bean dip. Zach had been mildly shocked, never having heard a woman utter "fellatio" before. Yet he had admired Beth's crisp, straightforward approach. It seemed intelligent, adult, even sexy at the time, and he came to share it. Over the years of their marriage she had often told him how pleased she was that neither of them was a tiresome romantic. What would she think of her sophisticated husband now if she knew that last night he had been driven half mad by the smell of a young woman's feet?

Zach realized that he was experiencing two contrary feelings.

On the one hand he felt guilty about cheating on Beth. On the other hand he felt a very unsettling elation. Much as he would not like to acknowledge it, Zach's new status rather fed his pride. Possessed now of both a wife and a mistress, he felt curiously dignified, a member of an ancient brotherhood, like the kings and potentates of old. His tarnished morality took on a queer charm. If truth be told, he felt more guilt about this elation than he did about his infidelity.

These thoughts were still passing through his mind when Zach reached Delmar and turned onto his street. As he came within sight of his house, however, all his deliberations abruptly halted. Parked in the driveway was Beth's car.

"Oh my God," he gasped aloud. Zach looked at his watch. Her plane came in early, nearly a half-hour before it was due. Now he'd have to come up with a lie much quicker than he had imagined. Where had he gone this morning? Out for a drive? Out to visit someone? Out to buy something? His mind raced. A newspaper! He'd popped over to the convenience store for *The New York Times*, but all the copies were sold out. It was not a terribly creative excuse, but it was the only one he could come up with at short notice.

Zach parked next to his wife's car and was practicing the story as he strolled up the walk. The door from the driveway opened onto the kitchen, and when Zach entered it, he was surprised to find Beth seated at the kitchen table. He broke into a big smile. "Beth, you're home early!" He leaned over and kissed her on the cheek. She did not kiss him back.

"Where were you?" she asked, her voice calm and strangely flat.

"I just thought I'd take a ride this morning to pick up a—"

"I mean last night."

He hesitated. "Last night? Oh, did you call last night? I must not have heard the phone. I fell asleep in front of the TV for a while, and then I went to bed early. I didn't even check the messages yet this morning."

Beth looked away from him. Distantly she said, "I was wondering how much longer to wait before calling the police. It's a good thing I didn't call. That would have been even more humiliating."

"What do you mean?"

She took a deep breath. "You didn't fall asleep in front of the TV last night, Zach. I know, because I was here. We finished early on Friday. You made such a deal on the phone that I caught a flight yesterday. I got home around eleven last night." She added, "I've been awake for the last twelve hours waiting for you."

"Oh."

"So I'm going to ask you again: Where were you?"

Zach bit his lip. He realized the futility of lying to her. Sighing, he pulled out a chair and slumped into it, then stared down at the table for several minutes. Finally, resignedly, he said, "I was with someone."

"A woman?"

"More or less."

"Is that supposed to be funny?" For the first time Beth's voice revealed an edge of anger. "Shall I assume you slept with her, or do you have some other story to tell me?"

"I don't have any other story."

Beth lowered her eyes and winced. That's when Zach realized how painful this was for her. He felt ashamed of himself. "Beth—"

She raised her hand to silence him. Without looking up she said, "I want to know one thing before we say anything else about it. Did you use a condom?"

"Jesus, Beth!"

"Did you use one?" she repeated more insistently.

"Is that really all you—"

Beth turned on him, fury in her eyes. "Goddamn you, Zach! *Did you use a fucking condom?*"

Unconsciously he backed away from her. "Yes."

She exhaled and broke eye contact. In a barely audible voice she murmured, "All right. All right." The words were not directed at Zach. They were uttered mainly to calm herself, almost like a mantra. "All right. All right. All right," she repeated. "People have gotten through this before. They don't die." For a few minutes Beth did nothing but breathe deeply. Then, having achieved some level of composure, she looked at him again. "How long has it been going on?"

"It hasn't *been* going on. This was the first time."

"Were there others before her?"

"No, there weren't any others."

"So who is she? Do I know her?"

"I doubt it."

"If she's a friend of mine, I don't think I'll ever be able to forgive you."

"I'm sure you don't know her. You don't travel in the same circles."

"What circle does she travel in?"

Zach shook his head and lifted his shoulders. "Her own, I suppose. I can't imagine her in anyone else's."

"You're infatuated with her."

"I'm too old to be infatuated with anybody." The words, once spoken, made him feel such a stab of despair that he added, "Unfortunately."

"Does she know that you're married?"

"She knows."

"So much for sisterhood. Is she younger than I am?"

"Yes."

"Of course. And prettier too?"

Zach looked at her. "Do you really want to know all these things?"

"Yes."

"Why?"

"I want to know about the competition."

"She's no competition for you. You're my wife."

"How comforting. Lucky, lucky me. Does she have thin thighs?"

"Come on, Beth."

"I want to know. Does she?"

"Yes."

She averted her gaze, and again Zach could see the pain in her features.

"Beth, I'm sorry."

"Are you?"

"I'm sorry I hurt you. I wasn't going to tell you, at least not like this."

"And not this soon either, I'd wager. You probably wanted to fuck Miss Thin Thighs several more times first." She paused. "Do you love her?"

"Don't be ridiculous."

"I didn't realize I was being ridiculous. It seems like a logical question to ask. You could answer no if the answer is no. You could say what most men say: 'She doesn't mean anything to me.' "

Zach was silent.

"I see," she said quietly. "So you *do* love her."

"No, I don't love her. I don't even know what love is."

"That's quite evident."

"She means *something* though. She's a human being, for God's sake."

Beth glared at him. "And what am I? A bloody orangutan?"

"You know that's not what I meant."

"If I believe you that this was the first time, there must be something special about her. What is it? Is she more intelligent than I am?"

"No."

"Is she more—what?—voluptuous? Are her tits bigger than mine?"

"Hardly."

"Then what is it?"

"I don't know."

"So how did you meet Miss Thin Thighs?"

"Please don't keep calling her that. She has a name."

"Pardon me, but I don't know her name."

"Her name is—." Zach almost said it. Then, remembering his

own initial reaction to Luna's name, he feared that Beth might have the same reaction. He did not want to see her sneer. "Her name isn't important."

Beth was silent for a moment. "So what do we do now, Zach?"

"What do you mean?"

"Where do we go from here? Do you want a divorce?"

"Of course not. Do you?"

"I don't know. That depends."

"On what?"

"Lots of things. I want to find out why you did this."

"I don't know the answer to that. It just happened."

"No, Zach. I'd accept that answer from a hydrocephalic, but not from you. I know you, Zach. You don't do things without thinking. So what is it? Has the marriage gotten humdrum for you? Are you bored?"

"No," he protested.

"Not even a little?"

Zach spread his hands. "All marriages tone down after a while. That's to be expected."

"So you *are* bored."

"Well, aren't you a little? At least occasionally?"

"Zach, you may find this hard to believe, but I'm not. I have many things in my life that keep me from being bored. I have a challenging job. I have friends. I have interests that I pursue. You, on the other hand, are bored with your job, bored with your social life, bored with this house and this town, bored with most things, in fact. It's little wonder our marriage can't compensate for all the excitement you lack. That's too great a burden to put on any relationship."

Zach turned away from her. "Do you have to reduce this to a sermon from a damn self-help book?"

"We're going to have to do something, Zach. Will you go to counseling with me?"

"So I can hear the same sermon from some blowzy divorcee with a master's degree in psychology? No thanks."

"You really hate women, don't you?" Beth shook her head. "Well, if you won't go to counseling with me, I'll go alone. You may not want to admit you need help dealing with this, but I do."

Beth got up now and went to the sink. Zach watched as she filled a tumbler with water and methodically drank it all down. He muttered, "Nothing deters you from taking care of yourself, does it?"

"What do you mean?"

"The earth could open and swallow me whole, but you'd still keep up your fluid intake to avoid getting a yeast infection."

The fury rose into her pale blue eyes again, and she lifted the glass in the air. Zach thought for a moment that she would throw it at him, or dash it to the floor. Instead she slammed the glass back down onto the countertop, but not hard enough to break it. "Go to hell!" she shouted as she stalked from the room.

Zach stared down at the table and let the quiet descend upon him. He wanted to feel remorse for hurting Beth, and he did feel it, but at this moment he had an embarrassing urge to laugh. In fact, he had all he could do to keep from giggling. It was not that hurting Beth gave him joy. Zach was no sadist, for all his faults. Yet he was experiencing an undeniable pleasure, and perhaps relief too, in her distress. If Beth was truly hurt by his infidelity, didn't that mean she cared for him? It was a pathetic line of reasoning, of course, and Zach knew it, but he felt almost giddy from having finally gotten his wife's attention.

VII

Testing

Beth avoided Zach for the rest of the day, and in the evening she carried the cot from the basement and set it up in her room. Zach tried to speak with her, but she refused. When he went to bed that night, he felt lonelier with his wife across the hall than when she had been across the country. All day Sunday she likewise shunned his company, and on Monday morning Beth rose early and sped off to town before he got up.

At work that day Zach felt thoroughly miserable and would have preferred to hole up in his office and see no one. He was especially not in the mood to conduct a delicate interview, but that's exactly what he had scheduled.

The commissioner had instructed Zach to disregard the ages of the deputies when choosing who should leave. The first thing Zach had done was to ignore that directive. In the personnel records he'd looked up all twenty of his counterparts, and he found that only two were past sixty, both gentlemen who had been with the department for many years. Zach predicated his reorganization plan on the departure of these two individuals.

Zach did not see himself as doing anything particularly noble or ignoble in this. He'd worked in state service long enough to know that reorganization plans come and go. All other things being equal, if it was necessary to cut people, it would be best if they were near retirement anyway. With this simple strategy in mind, Zach had resolved to call upon the two men casually to sound each of them out about an early departure, and his first meeting was with Winston Munser, head of the Testing Bureau.

Testing was housed in a large, open work area with dozens of desks lined up in neat rows, but as Zach strolled through the office that morning, very little work was actually being accomplished. Only a few of the desks were occupied, and these by employees who did not seem engaged in anything more productive than reading the newspaper. Knots of others stood around chatting. At the far end of the unit Munser's secretary was giggling on the phone when Zach strode up to her desk. "I have an appointment with Win," he said.

The secretary put her hand over the receiver. "You can go right in."

Winston Munser had thin gray hair, which he combed straight back, and his pasty complexion was interrupted by vague red splotches on his skin. Munser did not rise when Zach entered; nor did he smile at his colleague. He merely peered over the top of his reading glasses, his expression bordering on the supercilious.

"How are you, Win?" Zach inquired.

"Sit down," Munser responded.

Zach sat. He could tell from Munser's face that there was no point in making preliminary small talk. "Hugo's asked me to come around this week."

"So how big is it going to be?"

Only the legislature in its infinite wisdom knows that, but Hugo thinks it'll be about ten percent."

Munser's lips tightened. "Does he plan to make cuts in Testing?"

"I honestly don't know, Win."

"We can't process the exams as it is. How are we supposed to do it with fewer staff?" He turned away disgustedly. "I *taught* business. No one would stand for this in the private sector."

"Actually, what I came for today was to get your opinion of the severance package."

Munser eyed him. "What severance package?"

"The commissioner's proposed a salary and benefits package for those who choose to leave."

"A buyout?"

"Yes, and if enough people volunteer for it, we can minimize the layoffs."

"How much is it?"

"A month's pay for every year of service up to fifteen, along with continuation of health benefits for three years. Pensions kick in at the normal time."

Munser looked skeptical. "Has the governor signed off on it?"

Zach nodded. "Somewhere in the bowels of the capitol the bean counters determined that there will be a net savings." He paused. "Obviously it's best for those who can use it as an early retirement."

"Which means," Munser added bitterly, "the most experienced people will leave." He lifted the papers from his desk and began to straighten them unnecessarily. "Who's supposed to take this buyout?"

"It's offered across the board, from rank and file right up to the top."

"Up to the top?"

"Well, I don't expect that Hugo himself is going to take advantage of it, but it's offered at the deputy level—our level," he added significantly.

Though Munser's expression did not change, there was something going on behind his eyes. "One month's pay for every year of service?"

"Up to fifteen."

"And health benefits for three years."

"That's right."

Munser sat in thought for a moment. "Hugo just wants my opinion of it?"

"Yes."

He shrugged his shoulders and gave a noncommittal grunt. "All I can say is, if the state cripples its own departments, no one should be surprised if the best people leave." He turned his attention back to his work. Without looking up he asked, "Have you got what you came for?"

Zach nodded. "Yes, Win. I have."

* * *

THE SILENCE BETWEEN Beth and Zach lasted until Zach came home from work Wednesday. Beth told him she wanted to talk, and so once again they sat across from each other at the kitchen table.

"We have to come to some understanding," Beth began calmly.

"I agree," Zach said.

"We can't go on living under the same roof like strangers. This has been hell for me, and I can't get anything done at work."

Zach was silent.

"It's not the end of the world just because you had an affair. We're both adults. We can get past it if we want to. I've made an appointment for counseling this week, and you're welcome to come with me. But the bottom line is: I won't tolerate your seeing another woman while you're living in this house. So you have to ask yourself, Zach, if she means enough to you to throw the marriage away."

"She doesn't."

"Does that mean you're willing to give her up?"

Zach hesitated. "Yes."

"Are you sure?"

He sighed, nodded his head. "Yes, I'm sure. I'll tell her. I'll tell her it's over."

* * *

LATER THAT NIGHT Zach phoned Luna.

"Hello, Zach," she said when she recognized his voice. "I'm glad you called."

"Well, I need to see you. If you're still free Saturday, can we have lunch together?"

"I made plans."

"Oh." Zach could not hide his disappointment. He wondered if she had a date with someone else, perhaps one of the other men who responded to her ad, but he knew he had no right to ask. He said, "Is there another time I can see you?"

"You can see me Saturday. Come with me."

"Where are you going?"

"Lake George."

"Alone?"

"Not any more. Pick me up at noon."

"Wait," Zach said, fearing she was about to hang up. "Why are you going to Lake George?"

Her bafflement was apparent to Zach even over the phone. "To ride the *Comet*, of course."

VIII

Comet

A POOR MAN'S Miami Beach: that's how Zach liked to refer to Lake George, a resort area in the foothills of the Adirondack Mountains, a honky-tonk lakeside community of beachwear shops, wax museums, video arcades, and miniature golf courses. It is also the home of a large amusement park called the Great Escape.

Saturday turned out to be an impeccable spring day with a cloudless blue sky. At the appointed time Zach pulled up in front of Luna's apartment and found her waiting at the curb. She was dressed in a T-shirt and shorts. On her shirt, "The Great Escape, Home of the *Comet*" was superimposed on an image of a roller coaster, but Zach's attention was drawn to her exposed legs. He remembered their night together, but pushed the thought from his mind.

Luna slid into his car and kissed Zach on the cheek as if it were the most natural thing in the world. Having spent the week feeling guilty about what he had done to Beth, Zach now began to feel guilty about what he was going to do to Luna. He didn't want to spoil the day for her, so he decided to postpone telling her until later, perhaps on the drive home.

"I'm glad you could come," Luna said when they were underway. "Now we can ride the *Comet* together."

"Wait a minute. I said I would go with you to Lake George. I didn't say anything about riding a roller coaster. I told you, I get motion sickness."

"Motion sickness comes from repetitive movement. Nothing repeats on a roller coaster. You won't get sick."

"How can you be so sure?"

"Don't be scared."

"I'm not scared!" Zach protested, though of course he was. "Why did you need to go up there today anyway?"

"This is opening day. I want to see how the *Comet* got through the winter."

"You talk about it like it's a house plant."

"Wooden coasters are alive. They breathe. Weather affects them. Temperature and humidity affect them. They feel different over time."

During the sixty-mile drive up to Lake George, Luna told Zach the *Comet*'s history. The coaster had originally come from Canada, where it once stood at Crystal Beach on Lake Erie. When Crystal Beach closed, it was dismantled and stored in a warehouse until the Great Escape bought it at auction and carted it piece by piece across the state to where it now stands. Luna seemed to have an encyclopedic memory for facts about the coaster. It had originally been built in 1927, but had given its riders such a thrashing that it was redesigned twenty years later. Its track was 4,197 feet long. Its first hill was ninety-five feet high, with a drop forty-nine degrees off the horizontal. The *Comet* was the fifth wooden roller coaster in New York State, and only the second one built in the past sixty years. There were presently about a hundred wooden roller coasters in the country, Luna told him. Among them the *Comet* was one of the best.

Zach listened with bemused fascination, as if permitted an inside view of a bizarre cult. He had never seen Luna so animated before. He asked her more questions, not because he was interested in roller coasters, but because he loved hearing her talk about them.

Luna told him that the original creator of the ride was one Harry Traver, an amateur engineer and maniacal coaster designer, who was credited with some of the most ferocious roller coasters in the country, including the *Lightning* at Revere Beach and the *Cyclone* at Palisades. So intense was Traver's 1927 ride at Crystal Beach that a first-aid depot was located in the station, along with a nurse to attend traumatized passengers. In 1947 Herb Schmeck and John Allen moderated the coaster and renamed it the *Comet.* In Luna's opinion Traver, Schmeck, and Allen were in an elite company of master roller coaster designers, a small pantheon to which she admitted only one other man of similar stature, Frederick Church. It was Church, she told Zach in reverential tones, who designed the greatest roller coaster ever built, the *Airplane Coaster* at Playland in Rye, New York.

These rides dated from the golden age of roller coasters, and now all them were gone—all, that is, except the *Comet.* Luna reserved her highest praise for the owner of the Great Escape, Charles Rood, who saved it from destruction. Though he had bought the coaster for $210,000, he spent over three million dollars meticulously reconstructing it—much more, Luna stressed, than it would have cost him to build a completely new ride.

"Why did he do it?" Zach asked.

"He loved the *Comet.*"

Zach smiled indulgently. He knew of Charles Rood from the newspapers, where his picture often appeared in the business pages. Though not so rich or so famous as Walt Disney, Rood nevertheless had Disney's knack for turning family entertainment into healthy revenue. Shrewd businessman that he was, Rood may have had many reasons why he wanted to rebuild the *Comet,* but Zach was sure that sentimentality was not one of them.

When they arrived at the amusement park, Zach parked amidst the sea of other cars and followed Luna to the entrance. He scowled at the twenty-dollar-plus admission price since he had no intention of riding any of the rides, but before he could reach for his wallet, Luna hurried him past the entry gates to a special courtesy booth.

"Would you tell Charley I'm here?" she said to the teenage attendant.

The girl obviously recognized Luna and immediately placed a phone call. "Sir, Luna is here." She paused, then laughed. "Yes, Sir. I'll tell her, Sir." The girl hung up. "He says to go ahead in. He'll catch up with you later. He's got a pesky salesman in his office that he can't get rid of."

Zach had watched this exchange in amazement. Once they had entered the park he asked, "Who's Charley?"

"Charley Rood."

"Charley Rood?! You know Charles Rood personally, the owner of the park?"

"Of course I know him."

"Charles Rood is a millionaire, a multi-millionaire!"

"Is he?"

"Of course he is!" Zach exclaimed, coming to a stop and looking all around him. They were in a mock English village with winding streets and quaint Tudor buildings. "He *owns* all this, for God's sake. How else do you think he could spend a fortune building a roller coaster?" Zach stared at her. "How do you know him?"

"Let's go." Luna grabbed his arm.

The Great Escape sprawled over 140 acres. Luna led Zach on a circuitous path that passed a children's storybook land, a town out of the old west, a jungle region, a water playground. Eventually they climbed a small rise at the very rear of the park, and a massive structure loomed into view. They stopped and stared.

The roller coaster stood on a plateau before a wooded slope, its huge expanse of crisscrossed scaffolds gleaming white in the sunshine. Soaring nearly a hundred feet in the air was the great parabola of its first summit, topped with fluttering banners like the turret of a medieval castle.

Zach swallowed hard. Though he had seen roller coasters all his life, he looked at one quite differently when he was faced with the prospect of actually riding it. He turned to Luna with the intention of declining, blaming his motion sickness again rather than the embarrassing truth that he was afraid, but when he looked at her, he saw something that shocked him even more than the immense coaster. Luna was smiling.

Ever since he had met the strange young woman, he had been struck by the undeviating seriousness of her countenance. Now he was stunned by the alteration. Upon her lips—and in her dark brown eyes too—was the most winsome, unaffected look of pure joy. He didn't think he had ever been so charmed by someone's smile, so rare a thing it was in her.

"Isn't it beautiful?" she said as she gazed at the coaster.

Zach wanted to say yes, but what he found beautiful was not the mammoth white structure she looked upon. What he found extraordinarily lovely was the completely transformed visage before him.

"Come on," Luna said, taking his hand.

She led him down the path to the entrance. Zach still would have preferred to beg off, but he was so captivated by her expression that he dared not do anything that might erase it.

The queue was fairly short, for this was not yet the height of the season, and it took but a few minutes shuffling in line before they reached the station platform. When the train came to a halt and the previous passengers had vacated their seats, Zach reluctantly followed Luna into one of the waiting cars and sat next to her. He pulled down the safety bar, which locked into place on his lap; yet he felt anything but safe. From a loudspeaker above, a voice intoned a list of warnings and prohibitions ending with, "Enjoy your ride on the *Comet*." After checking the lap bars, an attendant held a thumb aloft, the all-clear signal, and in the control booth a young man released the brake.

The train slid slowly out of the station into the sunlight. Following a gentle downward incline, it curved behind the platform toward the lift hill. Zach could see the chain up ahead, black with grease and running between the tracks steadily toward the summit. Though he had not been on a roller coaster since he was a boy, he recognized immediately the unmistakable din of the chain. Its low-pitched rattle aroused an instinctive dread, like the whir of a dentist's drill. The train glided to the bottom where, with a lurch, it was snagged by the chain. Then, accompanied by the familiar ratcheting clatter, the cars were hauled upward.

Zach gripped the safety bar. He could not believe he had allowed himself to do this. As the train mounted the steep incline, the tall, slender structure swayed and vibrated with its burden. Longingly Zach looked at the narrow catwalk alongside the track and wished he were on it, wished he were anywhere, in fact, than where he was. Though an avowed atheist, he prayed that God would look mercifully upon his many sins and not choose this moment for a reckoning. As the train climbed higher, the scaffolding to either side disappeared, leaving only the vacant air and the ground far below. Zach ceased looking to his right or his left, but kept his eyes fixed forward, fixed upon the summit, which—impossibly—seemed to recede skyward the higher up he went.

When they had nearly reached the apex of the hill, Zach felt Luna's hand gently touch his white, bulging knuckles. He forced a weak smile. Luna said quietly, "Have no fear, Zach. I'm with you. Nothing bad can happen to you." And then they went over the top.

It is the sensation of imminent death that provides the thrill of a roller coaster. Zach saw the tracks drop away at an appalling forty-nine degrees off the horizontal. Every nerve of his body screamed panic. It was not that Zach feared he would die in the plunge; it was that he *knew* he would die. Ten thousand years' accumulated experience of his species told him that. Zach clung to the bar, and as the train plummeted, an incomprehensible, guttural sound escaped his lips.

And he did not die. In what seemed but nanoseconds, the train had traveled from its zenith to its nadir and was already climbing uphill again, its forward momentum hastening it toward another, shorter summit. There were screams all around Zach, but they were squeals of delight. The train hurtled down the second hill, then banked on a curve, shoving Zach against the side of the car. The currency of terror had now been exchanged for that of speed. The train tore over the tracks, flew through the turns, bunny-hopped over hillocks, causing Zach to rise involuntarily from his seat. Though he had never ridden a horse, absurdly he felt like he rode one now. He held onto the iron rein of the iron steed, and somewhere in its mad career Zach lost his fright.

The entire circuit took but a brief two minutes, and then, after one last, long dash at the station, the train was seized from below by a pair of unseen brakes and brought to an abrupt halt. There was cheering from several quarters, but in Zach's car a strange quiet reigned. Luna watched him, waiting for his reaction. Hesitantly she asked, "Did you like it?"

Zach gazed up at the scaffolding over his head. He looked at the cars behind filled with happy, raucous passengers. He glanced ahead toward the station where they would soon disembark. Finally he turned to Luna. Zach said, "I don't suppose we could ... ride again."

Luna screeched. The woman Zach thought would never smile now tilted her head back and shrieked to the cloudless heavens. Despite the cramped seat they shared and the lap bars that held them fast, she threw her arms around Zach and hugged him. Into his ear she whispered, "I love you."

* * *

THEY RODE THE *Comet* three more times together, and at the end of the fourth excursion, there was a white-haired gentleman in a green, checkered sports jacket waiting for them on the platform. About sixty-five or perhaps older, he had a sharp, pointed nose and the fuller frame that comes at the end of the middle years. Zach recognized Charles Rood from his photographs.

When the cars came to a stop, Rood extended his hand and helped Luna out. "How is it running today?" he asked.

"Faster," Luna told him. "Faster than last year."

"Maybe I should install brakes before the fan turn."

"Don't say that, Charley, not even as a joke."

Rood laughed good-naturedly.

"Charley, this is Zach."

Rood shook Zach's hand. "How do you do, Zach."

"It's very nice to meet you." Zach unconsciously slipped into the formal tone he reserved for very important or very wealthy people.

"Zach's a teacher," Luna volunteered.

"Really? What do you teach, Zach?"

"Well, actually I'm—." Zach hesitated, glanced at Luna. "I teach English."

"I admire teachers. I had wanted to be a teacher myself, but I wasn't smart enough."

"I'm sure that's not true," Zach said politely, though he suspected false modesty and condescension on the older man's part.

As they strolled down the exit ramp and away from the ride, Luna expanded on the roller coaster's performance, using phrases like "negative g's" and "air time." Zach got the impression, though, that these issues were of much more concern to Luna than to Rood, who merely nodded and smiled. When they stopped, Rood took note of Luna's T-shirt. "We've got a new one this year," he said, then peered at a small gift shop nearby. "They've got them over there, I think. Go pick one out. Tell them I said you can have it."

"Let me pay for it this time, Charley."

"Don't be silly. If they want my okay, I'll be right over here," he added, indicating a bench.

She hesitated.

"Go ahead," Rood prodded. "I consider it an investment. You're a walking advertisement."

Luna acquiesced. As she left them, Zach frowned, annoyed to see the rich man press gifts upon her like a sugar daddy. Rood repaired to the bench and patted the seat next to him. "Take a load off, Zach."

Anxious to keep up a conversation until Luna got back, Zach commented, "This must have been quite an undertaking—moving a roller coaster."

Rood smiled at him, glanced down at Zach's left hand where he wore his wedding ring. "It took forty-nine tractor trailers to haul it across the state. All the parts were numbered. The world's largest erector set, I liked to call it. You want to know what the hardest part was though?"

"What?"

"Getting the damn town to grant a permit. I had to attend public hearings, complete environmental impact statements, pay the salaries of a whole battery of lawyers. It took only nine months to build the coaster, but nearly four years to get permission to do it. And you know what the principal complaint was? The neighbors were concerned about the noise. Can you beat that? Why the hell would anyone who's worried about noise live next door to an amusement park in the first place? For the record, I don't think the *Comet's* noisier than any other ride. Hell, the eighteen-wheelers barreling along Route 9 out there make more of a damn racket than any ride I've got in the park, and they do it twelve months a year. But we had to compromise. I wanted to put the coaster right out there in the front of the park where people could see it from the road. It would have been better than a billboard. Instead, to be a good neighbor, I put it way back here in the woods."

He paused and looked toward the gift shop. "I hope they have her size."

Zach found his resentment toward Rood growing. "If you don't mind my asking, how do you know Luna?"

"She appeared out of the blue one day shortly after it was announced that I was going to rebuild the *Comet*. Without an appointment or so much as a phone call she showed up at my office and asked me what trains I was going to use. The old trains had to be replaced, and at that time there were only two manufacturers, the Morgan Company and the Philadelphia Toboggan Company. Morgans were molded fiberglass jobs. PTC's were the old-fashioned boxy-type. Either one came with a six-figure price tag. Well, Luna was there to tell me that only the PTC trains would do."

He snorted. "Can you just picture it? I'm in my office sitting behind my big desk—speechless—while this slip of a girl is telling me how to spend thousands of dollars of my own money. I thought she was a nut, frankly, and the only reason I didn't show her the door was that I was too flabbergasted. After I listened to her for a while, though, I was impressed by how knowledgeable she was about roller coasters; so earnest too, so concerned that I make the *right* decision, the right one for me, she said, and the right one for the coaster. When she was done, I thanked her and told her I'd give it serious consideration."

"And did you?"

Rood pointed to the coaster where the cars were just now ascending the lift hill. "PTC trains. That was only the first of many visits. Once construction began, she used to drive up two or three times a week to watch the progress. She was on the site so often that I had the foreman issue her a hard hat. And she'd plague me with questions while she was here. Was I going to follow this or that specification? Eventually we let her see the blueprints so she could check the details herself. I remember watching her walk the length of the construction site examining the pilings and matching them with the ones on the drawing."

He smiled. "I suppose I'm making it sound like she was a pest, but she really wasn't. The whole crew got to like her. She'd sometimes stop at a diner on the way here and bring them coffee and a whole crate of doughnuts. She would drive up on some of the coldest days of the winter too. One night when she got in her car to go home, the damn thing wouldn't start. Have you seen her car?"

"Yes."

"Well, then you know the thing is a piece of junk, so it was no surprise she had trouble with it, but just try to get a mechanic up here after dark in January. This place may be a bustling little burg in the summer, but in winter the natives roll up the streets at night and retire early. I must have made half a dozen phone calls before I could coerce someone to leave his cozy television set and come and fix her car." Rood shook his head. "Yes, she was here all the time that year. I joked with my wife that some morning I'd roll over and find Luna there in my bedroom asking if I was going to use Douglas fir for the tracks." He laughed. "My wife didn't exactly see the humor of that."

Zach didn't quite see the humor of imagining Luna in Rood's bedroom either. He scowled slightly and turned away.

"I suppose she is a bit of a nut," Rood continued. "I've met coaster nuts before, of course. It's a whole sub-culture. They come in all shapes and sizes, all types and all ages. Oddly enough, many of them are lonely young women."

Zach looked at him. "Why is that?"

Rood lifted his shoulders. "It would take a wiser man than me to tell you." He had been intermittently keeping an eye on the gift shop. Now one of the teenage sales clerks stuck her head out and looked in his direction. Rood waved at his employee and gave her an exaggerated nod. "But where would the world be without a few nuts? They said I was nutty when I announced I wanted to bring the *Comet* to Lake George."

"Why *did* you do it?"

Leaning back on the bench, Rood gazed at the gleaming white structure. "Ghosts."

"Ghosts?"

"It's something Luna said to me once, and it's true. They haunt old amusement parks. Had you ever been to Crystal Beach, Zach?"

"No."

"Well, I grew up near it. I come from western New York, so I used to go to Crystal Beach every year as a boy, and I used to ride the *Comet*. I loved it, loved the whole park, and I was very sad when it closed. When amusement parks shut down, they evict too many ghosts, ghosts of entertainers who got their start crooning in the ballroom, ghosts of lovers who met on the midway fifty years ago, ghosts of young sailors who spent their last night ashore riding the bumping cars before shipping off to Europe, ghosts of kids who had their first paying job in the adult world running the carousel. A lot of memories die when an amusement park dies." He paused. "Did you know that I once sold this park?"

"I remember reading about it in the newspaper."

"It wasn't as lucrative as I thought it should be. I decided to invest in something that had a better return." He shook his head. "It was the worst decision I ever made."

"Why?"

"I built this park, for God's sake, and I didn't like seeing anyone else fool with it or maybe close it! Well, it's rare in life that you get a second chance, but a few years later the park was up for sale again. Without hesitation, I bought it back. Then I went in the hole to buy the *Comet*, and I started my battle with the damn town so I could build it. After it was approved, I hired a crackerjack construction firm that promised they could put the thing up in less than a year. We had what turned out to be the most severe winter in two decades, but by God they delivered. Now I'm planning to build even more rides, which might make me rich or might put me in the poor house, but I can tell you, Zach, that I've never been happier. I learned a lesson from the experience. It was late in life, but I learned it."

"What was the lesson?"

Rood looked Zach in the eye. "The only important investment a man ever makes," he said, tapping his chest, "is the one he makes right here."

IX

Ruins

"Did you tell her?"

Zach was seated in the lamplight of his study pretending to read a book. He glanced up at Beth, who was standing in the doorway. He lowered his eyes again. "No."

"You didn't tell her."

"I intended to, but—"

"But you went to bed with her instead."

"No, I didn't!" he shot back angrily.

Beth pursed her lips. "So what *did* you do?"

"Nothing."

"All day you did nothing?"

"We went to an amusement park."

"An amusement park," Beth repeated flatly. "Splendid."

"Listen, Beth, I'm sorry. I will tell her. I just couldn't tell her today. She was so—"

But Beth was no longer listening. She disappeared into their bedroom, and presently Zach heard her rummaging through the closet. Bureau drawers were opened and slammed shut. There was the clinking of little bottles being snatched up together, the rustle of papers, then finally the latching of a suitcase. Beth appeared at his doorway again, her suitcase in one hand, her attaché in the other.

"I'll be staying at Jean's for a while," Beth announced without emotion.

"Beth, don't do this."

"I'll stop by in a few days to get some more of my stuff."

"Beth—"

She turned on her heel and strode away. Over her shoulder she said, "Call me when you grow up."

* * *

It was not a terribly original taunt, and surely no worse than many others the two had exchanged over the eight years of their marriage. Maybe it was even justified under the circumstances, but for some reason it festered in Zach. So that's what she really thought of him, childish and immature. Instead of feeling lonely, Zach felt angry, angry at her for leaving him, angry at her for not bothering to listen to his reasons, angry at her for taking refuge with her obnoxious friend Jean, who would now function as a kind of gatekeeper between them if he phoned her. But he was damned if he'd phone her!

He could just imagine the things Beth would say about him. She would accuse him of having a mid-life crisis, of being infatuated with a younger woman, of fearing the onset of middle age, or death, or God-knows-what, and wanting one more fling. Soothingly Jean would tell her not to blame herself, that she was not responsible for her husband's behavior, only her own. Beth's primary duty, after all, was to take care of herself. Beth would like hearing that advice. She would feel "validated."

Zach drank himself to sleep that night, and when he awoke late on Sunday morning, it took him a while to recall the events of the previous evening. As soon as he remembered his wife's flight from the house, though, and the injunction she'd hurled at him, he became angry all over again. He spent the day puttering around, obstinately determined to stay busy and not think about her.

But the following morning Zach began to feel the loneliness set in. Deciding that the best distraction might be to get out of the house, he called up Bob.

"What are you up to, Buddy?" Bob asked.

"Nothing much. You have any plans for today?"

"Hell, Zach, it's Memorial Day. We're doing what all patriotic Americans do. We're filling the neighborhood with the tantalizing aroma of charcoal lighter. You and Beth want to join us?"

"Beth's ... away."

"So come by yourself. Judy bought enough to feed the Russian army—if there still is a Russian army."

"Sure you don't mind?"

"Are you kidding? It'll give me somebody to talk to. Her whole fam-damnly is coming over."

A couple of hours later Zach pulled into the driveway next to Bob's home, which, though in a different suburban neighborhood, was otherwise indistinguishable from Zach's. As he walked around to the back of the house, Zach smelled steaks on the grill, and he heard a booming male voice.

"So the contractor, he says to me, 'This yard's too small for a pool that size.' So I give him the tape measure and tell him to go out to the edge of the property. But he says, 'That won't leave you with hardly any space on the side.' 'Fine with me,' I tell him. 'Less grass to mow.' " The speaker broke into an explosive laugh. Dressed in shorts and a Hawaiian shirt stretched to its limit around his middle, he was seated on the deck with a can of beer in one hand and a pretzel in the other.

Bob, who was standing over the grill, noticed Zach rounding the corner of the house and waved to him.

Zach mounted the stairs to the deck and was greeted by Bob's wife, Judy, who then introduced him to her sister and her sister's husband, Ron, who had been holding forth. Ron put down his beer long enough to give Zach a wet handshake. Judy also introduced her mother, Elda, a lady of grim demeanor and extremely large proportions seated precariously on a lawn chair. Finally Judy coaxed the children to interrupt their noisy board game long enough to say hello to Zach.

"Get yourself a brew," Bob told his friend.

"Yeah," Ron chimed in. "'Beer—it's not just for breakfast anymore.'"

Zach bent over the ice chest and looked in vain for something other than Budweiser. He drew out a can and popped it open.

"So, what do you do, Zach?" Ron asked him.

"I work with Bob."

"Oh, so you're on the sugar tit too."

"Ron!" hissed his wife, her finger going to her lips and her head tilting toward the children.

Laughing again, Ron waved his hand dismissively. "You state workers got a racket; that's all I can say. More power to you. Watch out, though. I hear the governor's gonna do some housecleaning."

"Zach doesn't have to worry about housecleaning," Bob assured him. "He's the commissioner's broom."

Though he did his best to make casual conversation during the meal, Zach felt awkward. He couldn't remember the last time he had been at a social gathering without Beth. He wondered if this is what it felt like to be divorced.

Divorced. The word startled him a little and caused him to shudder, even though he had only spoken it in his mind.

After dinner, Ron left the deck briefly for the bathroom, and Bob took the opportunity to slip away from the house with Zach.

"Tell me the truth, Zach," he said as they walked up the residential street. "Do I or do I not have the quintessential in-laws? I swear they're right out of central casting. A blowhard brother-in-law, bratty kids, and a sourpuss mother-in-law wide as a billboard. 'The few. The proud. Elda.' Ain't marriage grand?"

Zach was silent for a moment. Then he said simply, "Beth left me."

Bob stopped in his tracks. *"What?!"* Hurriedly he caught up with Zach again. "What happened?"

"She found out I was seeing someone else."

"Were you? Are you?"

Zach nodded.

"No shit!" Bob looked genuinely shocked. "I thought you were straight as an arrow. Who is she?"

"Just someone I met."

They reached the end of the suburban block, and Bob looked over his shoulder. "Come on," he said, turning the corner, "let's go this way in case the 'king of boors' decides to follow us."

Halfway down the tree-lined street he led Zach through a pair of iron gates. Inside, the path wound its way through an artificial reserve dotted with willows, stone seats, and pseudo-classical columns, many of them artistically incomplete. Zach recognized the all-too-familiar landscaping. "A cemetery?"

"I come here for walks," Bob told him. "I like it because it's quiet."

" 'The grave's a fine and private place, but none I think do there embrace.' "

"Huh?"

"Andrew Marvell."

Bob shook his head. "Sorry. Never read it. I taught history."

They followed the curved path until they were well out of sight of the main gate. "What are you going to do?" Bob asked.

"I don't know yet."

"Do you think Beth will come back?"

"Only if I give the other woman up."

"Are you going to you give her up?"

"I don't know."

"Is she a real looker?"

Zach snorted. "I don't think most people would describe her that way. She's a kid, really, a skinny, scrawny kid."

Bob lowered his voice. "She's not underage, is she, Buddy?"

Zach shook his head, glanced at the monuments on either side. Most of the headstones were of modern design, carved with crisp, sharp lettering and perfect, machine-tooled etchings of Jesus, or angels, or lilies, or praying hands. As they followed the winding path deeper into the cemetery, however, they passed into the older portion where the trees were gnarled and the stones crooked. The lettering on the markers was crude, shallow, and worn with age. Zach paused in front of an unusual stone, a pockmarked cube of marble upon which sat a small cherub hunched over in grief, probably a child's grave.

Bob came to a stop by Zach's side. "What's she like, this other woman?"

"She sells shoes. She loves roller coasters. She likes dishes with pretty pictures on them. She's got a photograph of her deceased horse on her bedroom wall. She thinks her father owns the Hudson River."

"What?!"

"She's naive, not well-educated, a sloppy eater, doesn't wash very often, and she's probably the most politically incorrect person I've ever met."

"So what is it you like about her?"

"Everything."

Bob sat down on a bench across from the grave marker, and Zach joined him. Over their heads the gentle spring breeze rustled the willow. "Listen, Zach," Bob said quietly, "it'll pass. Trust me, Buddy, it'll pass."

"Will it?"

"You and Beth have a good thing going. We've known you guys a long time. Take my word for it. It'll pass." Bob hesitated. "I never told you this. I never told anybody in fact, but I had a bad time a few years ago myself."

Zach looked at him, interested.

"Judy and I were fighting a lot, usually over the kids. And about that same time they hired this new woman in Certification."

"Did you have an affair?"

"Close. Damn close. And for a while I really wanted to go through with it. This girl was really nice. I took her to lunch a few times, and I think she would have been willing. Sometimes you can tell."

"So what happened?"

"I came home after one of those lunches. We were sitting at the dinner table, and the kids were raising hell as usual, and Judy was telling them to be quiet. There was nothing particularly special about it, just a typical evening meal, but I looked around the table and said to myself, this is my family—*my family*. Do I really want to risk losing all this just for a roll or two in the hay? I decided I didn't."

Zach turned away and gazed again at the unusual monument across the path.

"Do you understand what I'm trying to say, Zach?"

"I understand." He stared at the tiny, grieving cherub. "But I don't have a family."

X

Curriculum

That night when he came home, Zach almost called Luna. He pulled out the slip of paper she had given him with her name, address, and telephone number neatly inscribed. He carried it to the phone, stared at it for a while, even doodled a heart on it, but in the end he tossed the paper onto his dresser unused. The following night Zach considered calling Beth instead. Mentally he composed the apology he would make to her, the terms of self-abasement he would use. He only changed his mind when he discovered that she'd been in the house that day. She'd stopped on her lunch hour apparently. Another suitcase was missing from the closet, and more of her clothes had been removed. Zach's anger rose again, and he lost the inclination to call.

Pencilled on his calendar at work the next day was a meeting with Gus Kostas, the other deputy commissioner he had selected for early retirement. Kostas's office was not on the grand concourse. Instead, his window had a good view of some rather shabby downtown neighborhoods. Kostas was standing at his window when Zach arrived that afternoon. Zach paused at the threshold and coughed slightly to announce his presence.

Kostas turned around and smiled at his colleague. "Zach, you caught me playing hooky."

Dressed in a rumpled brown suit, Kostas was a man of medium height with unkempt gray hair and black bushy eyebrows. His sixty-three years had cut deep crevices in his cheeks and on his forehead.

"Don't feel bad, Gus. You should see how much time I spend daydreaming."

There seemed to be years of accumulated clutter in the office: cardboard boxes filled with papers, books stuck every which way on the shelves, a desk littered with loose-leaf notebooks and correspondence. A few old diplomas and certificates hung on the wall, along with a large chart of the state school districts with boundary lines drawn and redrawn upon it. Hanging directly over the desk was a framed photograph of Franklin Roosevelt.

Instead of leaving the window, Kostas motioned for Zach to join him, and he pointed down at the street where a small knot of teenage boys were flipping cards at the curb. "I've been watching my constituency. Today's a school day," Kostas added, "so they're playing hooky too. Hardly a day goes by that I don't see kids down there, school or not." He paused. "When I was growing up in the Bronx, my pals and I would sometimes skip school too. We'd spend the day playing stickball in a vacant lot. Have you ever played stickball, Zach?"

"No."

"It was a poor boy's pastime. All you needed was a broom handle and an old tennis ball. It was a cutthroat game with its own rules: one strike and you're out."

"What are *they* playing?"

"A betting game. We used to play that too. Cigarettes hanging from our lips, we felt awfully cool flipping those cards and gambling for nickels." Kostas offered Zach a seat and returned to his desk.

Zach said, "I didn't realize you grew up in New York."

"I wasn't so very different from the fellows out there. Some of my friends ended up in jail, and some of them died." Kostas looked down at the desk. "One friend of mine—Arnie Chaparos—was killed in a knife fight. They fought over a dice game. He was sixteen, and died right there in the parking lot. I've thought about Arnie many times over the years, wondering what would have become of him if he'd taken a different path and been allowed to grow up."

"What caused *you* to take a different path?"

Kostas seemed surprised at the question, but pleased. "Reading the *Odyssey*."

"The *Odyssey*?"

"It was assigned in high school English class. I wasn't much of a reader then, but for some reason I started that book, maybe because I was Greek, and the book was about a Greek. Before long I couldn't put it down. I loved all the marvels in it, the gods, the monsters."

"Yes, but the *Odyssey* isn't exactly a how-to book for becoming a peace-loving adult. It's filled with violence and greed and deceit. Odysseus is little more than a pirate."

Kostas smiled. "Which goes to show that literature doesn't have to be socially redeeming to be ... well, socially redeeming. A few years later I was teaching Latin and Greek in a New Rochelle Catholic school."

Zach thought of something. "I met someone of Greek descent recently. The last name was 'Planitis.' Do you know anyone by that name?"

Kostas shook his head. "No, I've never heard a Greek name based on that root before."

"What is the root?"

"It sounds like the same one we get the word 'planet' from. It means 'wanderer.' "

"Wanderer!" His brow furrowed. "What about the name Inachus?"

"Oh, that's from mythology. Inachus was a river deity."

"The lord of the river," Zach muttered to himself.

"He was father of the unfortunate Io, a young woman beloved

of Zeus. She was forced to roam the earth an exile. It's there in your Bulfinch. Why do you ask?"

"I just realized that someone's been having a bit of fun pulling my leg." Zach paused. "Well, I should probably stop wasting your time and get down to the reason for my visit. The commissioner asked me to come around."

He related to Kostas the same information he had given Munser. Once more Zach took special care to watch Kostas's reaction as he detailed the severance package.

When Zach was through, Kostas said, "Well, if it has to be done, it has to be done. In some ways I'll envy the people who opt to leave."

Thinking that perhaps he had not made himself clear, Zach reiterated that the buyout was open to everyone at every level, including deputy commissioners.

"There are days, let me tell you," Kostas sighed ruefully, "when there's nothing I'd like better than to pack it in. If I tell my wife about this, she'll encourage me to take it. Elaine's always wanted to travel."

"Where would you go?"

"Her heart is set on Hawaii, God knows why. Myself, I'd like to see Greece once before I die. Ancestral homeland and all that rubbish. I'd like to see the Parthenon, the ruins at Knossos, visit the sacred isles and cross over the Hellespont to Troy."

"It sounds long overdue."

Kostas sat for a moment in thought, then shook off the reverie. "But it will have to wait. I've worked too long on the classics project."

"What classics project?"

"It's something I've spent the last seven years developing. As you well know, students graduate from high school today without having read a word of Shakespeare, Homer, Dante. I may be a dinosaur, but I think that our experiment in 'educational relevance' can safely be judged a failure. The classics project is a basic course in the world's great literature that will be part of every student's education in New York State, and I'm within a year or two of having it instituted. If I retire now, the project will die as sure as I'm sitting here. So Greece—and Hawaii—will just have to wait."

Zach forced a smile. "Do you really think teaching the classics will make a difference?"

Kostas rose from his seat and went to the window again. "To be perfectly honest, I don't know. Reading the *Odyssey* may not have saved Arnie Chaparos's life, but in some odd way it saved mine. I'm betting on something, Zach, like those hip young fellows down there are betting. I think that knowing the peculiar monsters we've struggled with over the generations gives us perspective. If we understand ourselves a little better, maybe we won't need to end our lives bleeding to death in a parking lot."

* * *

Zach sat alone in his study late that evening. Up until today he had all but decided that Kostas and Munser were the right ones to cut. His meetings with them had been mere formalities. Discovering now that Kostas had no intention of retiring early, Zach was left with only two options: ignore Kostas's wishes, or choose a younger deputy.

Reluctant as Zach was to cut anyone, surely the most humane thing was to retire the oldest first. Kostas had earned a rest. Easing him out now would be the best way the Department could thank him for all his years of service. Zach was not completely happy with this alternative, but he had looked at all sides of the issue and made the best decision possible. Was it not a sign of maturity to make difficult choices? Now he should put the matter behind him.

Even as Zach congratulated himself for his resolution, he heard a voice in his head say, "Don't do anything bad. Keep in mind that I'm your lover now. You don't have to do bad things anymore."

Bad things? What bad things? This was not a moral issue. This was an everyday bureaucratic matter, a small quandary about job shuffling, with no ethical overtones. Besides, was he a child that he should be lectured in right and wrong? Hardly! He was old enough to know that damn few questions of morality are answerable in the pure, lovely opposites of black and white. Perhaps in the rarified atmosphere of Luna's simple world there are no shades of gray, but here on this earthly plane, gray is the tincture of everything.

She had a lot of nerve admonishing him on morality anyway! How honest had she been? It was just too much of a coincidence that "Planitis" should mean "wanderer," and her supposed father, Inachus, should be a character out of a mythology book. She had lied to him about everything. Zach wanted to be angry with her, and by God he *was* angry with her.

Unmoved by his bluster, the voice in his head repeated, "I'm your lover now. You don't have to do bad things anymore."

XI

Wanderer

On Saturday morning Zach called Beth. Her friend Jean answered the phone, and Zach could hear the disapproving brusqueness in Jean's voice as she notified Beth that he was on the line. When Beth picked up, Zach asked her simply if she would come home. To his surprise she agreed without argument, and around noon her car pulled into the driveway. Zach, who had been watching for her at the kitchen window, came out to meet her.

"How have you been?" he asked.

"Okay." Her voice was neutral. "How have you been?"

"A little lonely. It's good to see you."

"Well, we've got a lot to talk about," was Beth's non sequitur. To it she added, "Besides, I own this house as much as you do. I felt ridiculous sleeping on a couch like a damned student again."

Zach helped carry her luggage inside, and while she unpacked, he sat on the bed watching her and feeling no small joy to have her back in the house again. He volunteered, "I cleaned the bathroom."

"Congratulations."

"It was a tossup between that and buying you flowers."

"You made the right choice." Beth hung up an armload of suits in the closet.

Zach lowered his voice, more serious now. "Beth, about last weekend: I realize how it must have seemed to you. I promised to tell her, and then I didn't. That was wrong of me."

"Yes, it was."

Zach frowned, wishing that just once she would cut him a little slack, especially when he was offering an apology. "Well, all I wanted to say was that you had a right to be angry. For what it's worth, I haven't seen her since. What I have done, though, is think a lot about you and me. I've probably sold our marriage short, but I don't want to give up on it. We have a lot going for us."

Beth put down the skirt she had just lifted from the suitcase. She drew a chair from the wall and sat down facing him. "What, for instance?" she asked.

"What do we have going for us? All kinds of things. We have a lot in common. We're both well educated. We're a good match intellectually."

"What else?"

"We come from similar backgrounds, and we have similar philosophies. We agree about politics and religion and social issues. We differ on some things, of course, but that's to be expected."

"All right, so we're smart, middle class, and liberal. Does that mean we have a good marriage?"

"Not in and of itself, but it's a basis for one. It means we're mentally compatible."

"And physically?"

Zach uttered a silent curse. How did Beth have the uncanny ability to zero in on his most secret anxieties, even ones he was barely aware himself? He said, "Our physical relationship is fine."

"Fine," she repeated flatly. "I'm surprised you didn't choke saying it. The irony is, Zach, that I do consider it fine even if you don't."

Beth was telling the truth, and Zach knew it. During all the years of their married life she'd had no complaints about sex, so long as the frequency did not exceed once or twice a week. In her eminently practical way Beth considered sex to be good for you, a healthy activity like jogging or eating fiber.

"Listen, Beth, I know I've shown some dissatisfaction over the years, but if we just dwell on the past, how are we supposed to move beyond that?"

"Do you *want* to move beyond it?"

"Yes."

"Does that mean you'll go to counseling with me?"

Zach hesitated.

"That's what I thought," she said wearily, getting up again.

"Just because I won't go to a damn therapist, it doesn't mean I don't want to save our marriage. There are other ways of solving human dilemmas, you know. People managed for thousands of years before psychologists began converting their family rooms into clinics."

"I already know what you think of counseling. If you don't want to go, fine, but don't disparage something that I find beneficial."

"I'm sorry. I didn't mean to disparage it. I know it's helpful for a lot of people."

"Simple, impressionable people, right?"

"No, of course not."

"If you're not willing to go with me to counseling, what are you willing to do?"

"Well, I'll start by doing what I should have done last weekend. I'll talk to ... the person I was seeing and tell her it's over."

Beth carried a small stack of blouses to her dresser and placed them neatly in the drawer. "That won't be necessary."

"What do you mean?"

"I spoke to her myself."

Zach's eyes opened wide. "*You what?!*"

"I spoke to your friend 'Luna.' "

"How did you know—"

"You weren't very discreet," Beth continued, without turning around. "You left her name and address right on top of your bureau. I thought the little heart next to her name was sweet, by the way. I phoned her, told her who I was, and asked if we could meet for coffee."

"And she agreed?"

"Why shouldn't she agree?"

Zach shook his head in consternation. "I can't believe you'd do that. You had no right."

"I had every right." Beth pushed the drawer shut, turned around and faced him. "I *am* an interested party, you know, and I have a responsibility to myself."

"But *why* did you see her?"

"Because I wanted to find out if there was any point in continuing the marriage. I'd already heard your version of the story. I wanted to meet this 'Luna' character and see where she stood."

"And where did she stand?"

"She agreed to end the affair."

"*She did?* How did you get her to agree to that?"

"I didn't have to 'get her' to do anything. I merely told her what you told me."

"Which was?"

"That you didn't love her, and that you had intended to break it off with her last weekend, but you got cold feet."

"You told her *that*?"

"Don't look so shocked. It's what you said, isn't it? In any case, she was hardly devastated, if that's what you're thinking. Sorry to disappoint you. She *is* very young, after all. Perhaps you overestimated the depth of her feelings. Without any prompting from me she said she wouldn't see you again."

Zach shook his head. "As simple as that."

"Yes, as simple as that. I thought you'd be relieved, since I did the dirty work for you. Besides, I never believed in two women competing for a man, and the best way to avoid that kind of nonsense is to meet face-to-face and talk it over."

"Of course," Zach said sarcastically, "sisterhood! And did you find her to be a 'sister'?"

For the first time Beth revealed a slight confusion. "No," she muttered, averting her eyes, "I found her to be ... strange. I have to tell you frankly, your taste in women surprises me."

"What's that supposed to mean?"

She looked at him with an expression of bemused superiority. "Honestly, Zach, was she the best you could do?"

He leapt to his feet and glared at her. Beth registered surprise at his unexpected ferocity, but she did not back away from him. For a moment they stared at each other, the air between them charged. Then between his teeth Zach murmured the single, high-voltage word: "*Bitch*."

"I understand that you're upset ..." Beth began calmly.

But Zach was already striding from the room. Beth followed and caught up with him at the kitchen door. "If you go to see her again, Zach, all bets are off between us."

Without pausing, Zach slammed the door behind him.

* * *

ZACH WAS NOT a man given to violence. He was too civilized. At this moment, however, he wished he were the kind of toothless lowlife who would pummel his wife, who could take out all his fury on her with his own hands. He hated her for what she'd done, hated her for intruding on his privacy, but more he hated her for the attitude she had assumed toward him. Like a parent with an erring child, Beth had taken it upon herself to extricate Zach from a jam he had gotten himself into.

On his way toward town Zach kept trying to imagine the interview between Beth and Luna. Had they really sat across a table at a coffee shop? What on earth could they have said to each other? Did they make small talk before they got down to business? Did they discuss the weather? Did they look for some common ground as women first? Try as he might, Zach could not conjure up any believable scene. He kept asking himself, what's wrong with this picture? The answer was that the image was absurd. Beth and Luna didn't inhabit the same universe.

Yet the interview had taken place. It was obvious from the queer look on Beth's features that she had met Luna.

When he reached Lark Street, Zach pulled his car into a space and mounted the stoop. He pressed her button and waited, but heard no scratchy voice on the intercom. He pressed it again. After a longer interval of silence, he pressed it a third time.

Zach looked at his watch. She was probably working at the shoe store today. He returned to his car and headed to the mall.

Amidst all the thoughts that careened through Zach's brain, there was an undercurrent of disappointment. He was hurt that Luna had willingly given him up. Had he really meant so little to her? Was Beth right that it was Luna's youth that made her so callow? Or had Beth's formidable presence intimidated her? Slight as she was, Luna did not seem a person easily frightened. Another possibility was that Luna had lied to Beth about her intention to give him up, but this seemed least likely of all. Zach could not imagine Luna telling a lie.

What was he saying? Everything about her was a lie, including her name! Why on earth did he continue to think that there was some absolute honesty about her?

The parking lot at Crossgates was crowded, but Zach quickly found a spot and hurried to Florsheim's. When he reached it, he saw Scott tending a customer. Luna was nowhere in sight. Impatiently Zach hung around outside the entrance until Scott was free. Then he hastened into the store.

"Hey, Big Guy," Scott said, recognizing him. He greeted Zach with a smile and his outstretched beefy hand.

"Is Luna here today?"

Scott seemed puzzled. "No. Didn't you know that she quit?"

"She *quit?*"

"Yeah. I thought you were her boyfriend or something."

"No. We're just ... friends. Why did she quit?"

Scott's face looked pained. "To tell you the truth, I was surprised. I told you what a good worker she was, how dependable and everything, but she came in this week and told me she was leaving the area and had to resign."

"Did she say where she was going?"

"No. I asked her that, but she said she wasn't sure. She didn't even have a forwarding address. When I asked her where I should send her last paycheck, you know what she told me? She said I should keep it for myself! Can you believe that? She offered me her last pay for the inconvenience she'd caused me by leaving. Well, even if I *could* have done something like that, I wouldn't have. I made her out a check right then and there for what we owed her."

Zach's mind raced. "Do you know any of her friends, anybody who might know where she went?"

Scott wrinkled his brow in thought. "Not really. I never saw her with anybody except for you." He paused. "I was really sorry she left. I had even thought about going into business with her. She had told me she was looking for a good investment because she had inherited some money."

Zach stared at him. "Inherited?"

"Yeah. That's why I was kind of surprised when you asked me about her father the last time. Remember? You asked if he ever came by the store. Well, that struck me funny, because she told me she had inherited the money three years ago when her father died."

* * *

ZACH STOPPED AT a phone in the mall and punched in Luna's number. It rang twice, and then, not to Zach's complete surprise, an indifferent mechanical voice informed him that the number he had reached was no longer in service. Zach stood for a moment in a kind of stupor, then hung up the phone and sat down on a bench.

For a long while he stared straight in front of him not knowing what to do. To himself he murmured, "I have to find her." But how? Blankly he watched the shoppers walk by, knots of people animated in their conversations, bustling along on their petty excursions. Zach was struck that they were all of them strangers, and as strangers they meant nothing to him. Yet among these anonymous faces, the image of Luna rose up in his mind, the dark eyes, the short hair, the solemn countenance, the deep voice with its odd questions and observations. *She* was known to him. Luna was *not* a stranger.

Abruptly Zach straightened in his seat. There *was* someone who might know, someone else for whom she was not a stranger.

XII

Fairy Tale

THE GIRL IN the ticket booth eyed Zach curiously. "Do you have an appointment, Mr.—"

"Tonner. Zach Tonner. No, but this is rather important. It's about ... Luna."

The name had an immediate effect. After conferring briefly on the phone, she said, "Mr. Rood said you can go right up. Do you know the way, Mr. Tonner?"

She directed him to a door marked "Private" in a small, vaguely Tudor building near the entrance. Once inside, the illusion of a quaint English village disappeared, and Zach found himself in a windowless hallway with pale green walls and a staircase covered with vinyl tiles. At the top of the stairs a receptionist pointed him to an open door down the hall.

Charles Rood's office was neither large nor ostentatious. Rood was not present, and while Zach waited, he scanned the various items on the wall. There were certificates from civic organizations, a colorful map of the Great Escape, photos of dignitaries who had visited the park. Zach was drawn to one photograph that pictured two gentlemen in business suits standing before a familiar storybook castle. They were shaking hands and smiling at the camera. The man on the right was a much younger Charles Rood. Zach drew closer to examine the other figure.

"It's Disney," said a voice behind him.

Zach turned around. Rood was hitching up his trousers as if he'd just returned from the lavatory. His white hair combed neatly in place, he was dressed in a short-sleeved shirt open at the neck. He strode to Zach's side and tapped the photo with his finger. "I'm quite proud of this. For a theme park owner to have met Disney is like a baseball player to have met Babe Ruth. We posed in front of Sleeping Beauty's castle at Disneyland a few years before he passed away."

Rood gazed at the photo. "People have criticized him, of course, for being more interested in profit than anything else. Well, the man was keen on making a dollar; that's for certain. He lived through the Depression like a lot of us did, and money held more than a passing interest to him. But people who see only the money miss the whole point. They also miss the point when they blather on about Disney ignoring the problems in the country and whitewashing history, as if it was his personal responsibility to correct every wrong in America. He quite rightly left that thankless task to somebody else. *His* job was making myths."

"Myths?"

"Yes. Myths are what artists deal in, and what most people forget about Disney is that he *was* an artist. He was the one who first put pen to paper and inked in that foolish-looking rodent. His canvas, God knows, got larger and larger until it became a whole little universe, but he knew what every true artist knows in his gut: your job, first and last, is to delight people. There are damn few individuals in history who have performed that task as well as he did. Disney will be around long after his detractors have slipped back into the woodwork."

A devilish twinkle appeared in Rood's eyes. "All that notwithstanding, I take some satisfaction from having beaten him by a year."

"Beaten him at what?"

"Creating the first theme park. You're standing in it. I built it a year before he built Disneyland. It was called Storytown back then. The theme was children's stories. I've always been a sucker for fairy tales. The park has expanded since then, but the core of it is still devoted to storybook fables, and at the very center of the park is a miniature castle. When Disney came to build Disneyland, what did he do? He centered his own fairy tale kingdom around Sleeping Beauty's castle there. I won't say that he copied me. All I'll say is that great minds often travel along parallel paths."

Rood laughed and stepped behind his desk. "But enough of modesty. Take a chair, Zach." When the two were seated, Rood looked at him expectantly. "So, what can I do for you?"

"I'm sorry to come without an appointment," Zach began. "I know you're busy, but I didn't know who else to turn to."

"You said this concerned Luna?"

"Yes." Zach took a deep breath. "Do you know where she is?"

"No. Should I?"

"I was hoping you would. She's disappeared."

"Disappeared?" Rood looked concerned.

"I don't mean disappeared in the police sense," Zach reassured him. "I'm certain she's all right. It's just that without warning she quit her job this past week and seems to have left Albany."

"Why would she do that?"

"I don't know for sure," Zach answered, a note of guilt coloring his voice, "but she had a conversation with my wife."

"Your wife?" Rood narrowed his eyes. "You were ... involved with Luna?"

"Yes."

"And your wife found out about it and confronted her?"

"Yes."

"Ouch!" Rood leaned back in his chair. "Well, I don't think I can help you. I haven't seen Luna since the two of you were here."

"You have no idea where she might go?"

"No."

"Do you know of anyone outside the area that she might visit?"

"No."

"Do you know of any friends she had who might know where she went?"

"No. Why is it so important that you find her?"

Frustrated, Zach made no reply except to shake his head disconsolately.

"Well, Zach, I'm a businessman, not a priest, so I'm not going to moralize to you. It sounds like Luna left to get away from a sticky situation. That's understandable. She told me once that she wanted to take a trip around the country someday to ride roller coasters. Maybe she decided this would be a good time to do it. It might be best if you just accept that she's gone and give her up."

"I can't."

Rood was silent for a moment. "Do you have children, Zach?"

"Why do you ask?"

"Children sometimes help you put matters in perspective, keep you from doing rash things."

"I don't have children," he muttered.

"That's a pity. Well, at least you have your work. You're an English teacher, right? That must be quite a demanding job."

"I'm not an English teacher."

"You're not? But I thought—"

"I'm not a teacher of any kind. I work for the State Education Department. I'm a bureaucrat, a damn paper pusher who hasn't set foot in a classroom for years. It's Luna who insists on calling me a teacher."

"Why?"

"I'm not sure. Maybe to wake me up."

"Wake you up?"

"Yes, like your Sleeping Beauty there, but in reverse. In this case it's the princess who hacks through the brambles." Zach looked the older man in the eye. "She woke up something inside me. I don't know exactly what it was, but it made me see myself, and I don't like what I see. Now I have to find her." There was a note of despair in his voice.

Rood laughed.

"What's so funny?" Zach demanded.

"Forgive me. I'm not laughing at you. You just reminded me of something. I had a Sleeping Beauty experience of my own once. Are you a religious man, Zach?"

"No."

"Good. I don't trust men who claim to be religious. So when I tell you this, you'll know that at least part of it is Grade A horseshit." Rood folded his hands on his desk and examined them. "I like to boast to people that when I first came to this area from western New York, I had only five thousand dollars to my name. It's one of those tedious rags-to-riches stories that wealthy men are fond of telling ad nauseam. And like other men who've made a fortune, I've also salved my conscience by giving a lot of money away over the years. Just look at the certificates on the wall." He made a sweeping gesture with his hand. "All of these organizations have benefited from my largess, and I've benefited from the tax write-offs. But then one night the Good Lord woke me up."

"The Good Lord?"

"That's the horseshit part. Have you ever heard of Hidden Valley, Zach?"

"It's a resort or something in the Adirondacks."

"At Lake Luzerne, yes. It's sort of a dude ranch, or at least it was. A lovely spot, with a lake, a lodge, cabins, swimming pool, Jacuzzi, the works. It fell on hard times, and I was approached as a possible buyer. I wanted no part of it. Then one day that summer I was walking around the park here, and I stopped at the monster trucks to chat with the attendant. An older couple was just lifting their granddaughter out of a wheelchair and putting her into one of the little rigs. While the ride was running, the wife of this couple came up to me. I don't think she knew I was the owner, but she must have figured I was some person of authority. Anyway, she told me how much the little girl enjoyed coming here every year, and how wonderful it was that we provided this place for unfortunate children.

"When I went home that night, instead of feeling gratified, I felt like a heel, a greedy son of a bitch who made money off kids in wheelchairs and got *praise* for it, for God's sake. Welcome to America, right? All that evening I couldn't get the image of the little girl out of my mind.

"Well, in the middle of the night that night, the Good Lord woke me up. That's how I usually tell the story, anyway. Who knows why I woke out of a sound sleep? Indigestion maybe, or the dog making a ruckus. In any case, lying there awake that night I conceived the idea of buying Hidden Valley and turning it into a camp for critically ill kids. The next day I put in my bid at the auction, and a few weeks later I was the proud owner of a failed dude ranch. People thought I was crazy, especially when they found out what I planned to do with it. That was five years and a couple of million dollars ago. Now the place has over a hundred and fifty children in residence."

"I never knew about it," Zach said.

"We've kept the fanfare to a minimum, except for a fund-raising bash we hold for well-heeled bigwigs once a year. The children's organizations and hospitals all know about it though. That's principally how we get our referrals."

Zach looked at him. "Why did you do it?"

"Don't you get it? We're talking about wake-up calls. Mine came in the form of a midnight fancy. Yours came in the form of a girl who loves roller coasters." Rood fell silent now. Leaning back in his seat again, he gazed at Zach. "I'm not sure if it will be of any help to you, but I think Luna's family comes from around here."

"How do you know?"

"She's familiar with the area. I could tell that from our conversations. She knew all the landmarks, all the local geography. You don't get that kind of intimate knowledge of the region living in Albany. She obviously grew up nearby."

"But where?"

"That I don't know. I never asked her. I'm surprised *you* didn't ask her."

"I did once, but her answer didn't tell me anything. She said she was born in the glen in springtime ... when the riverbank was knee-deep in wildflowers."

Rood snorted. "That's Luna, all right." He paused. "She said 'the' glen and not 'a' glen?"

"Yes. I remember that distinctly because I thought it was an odd way of putting it, as if I knew what glen she was talking about. Hell, I'm not sure I even know what a 'glen' is!"

"It's just a poetic word for valley." Rood reached for a map on the shelf behind him, then spread it out on the desk. "There's a small hamlet on the upper Hudson River called 'The Glen.' "

Zach stared at him. "What?!"

Rood stood up and drew a pair of spectacles from his shirt pocket. On the map he traced the swath of the Hudson River north from Albany until it narrowed to a thin blue line in the Adirondacks. Rood leaned over the map and examined the tiny print. "There it is, just north of Warrensburg." He pointed to the spot, then spun the map around.

Zach felt his pulse quicken as he read "The Glen" neatly printed at the intersection of Route 28 and the Hudson River, where the black line crossed the blue. "How far away is that?"

"No more than twenty miles."

"She may have gone home," Zach mused, still staring at the map.

"Possibly."

He committed the location to memory. When he straightened up again, Rood was watching him, his expression an odd mixture of wariness and envy. "I appreciate this," Zach said.

"I hope I'm not making a mistake. If you haven't noticed already, I have some paternal feelings about that girl, and I don't want to see her hurt." Rood looked thoughtfully at Zach, then glanced over at the photograph of himself and Disney standing in front of the impossible storybook castle. "But I am a sucker for fairy tales."

XIII

Mock Birth

ZACH SPENT THE night at a motel in Lake George. He knew, of course, that Beth would assume he was with Luna, but he didn't care. The next morning he got back on the interstate and headed north. It was a mere ten miles from Lake George to Warrensburg. From there he took U.S. Route 9 and then the smaller state highway, Route 28, northwest into the mountains.

The Adirondack Park is a five-million-acre preserve, larger than any national park, larger than the whole state of Massachusetts. A wilderness of mountains, forests, and lakes, it is crossed by few roads and dotted here and there with villages. Zach had visited some of the well-known resorts before, places like Saranac and Lake Placid, but the area he was entering this morning was more rural, its widely dispersed settlements thinly populated, and the only services an occasional general store with two fuel pumps outside.

The drive would have been gorgeous at any season of the year, but spring had a glory all its own. Everything was in bloom. As Zach drove deeper into the park, eventually he saw out his left window a lazy stream which, from the map, he knew must be the Hudson. The highway paralleled the water for several miles, and then, after a slight curve, Zach saw up ahead a steel bridge where the road crossed the river. He pulled his car over and stopped.

This far north, the Hudson was so shallow that one could walk across its pebbly bottom barefoot. Upon the bridge a boy with a fishing pole dangled his line into the water. There were no stores, no gas stations, no traffic lights. The only indication that Zach had reached the right spot was a rambling old farmhouse on the other side of the river. It had been converted into a commercial establishment, and a sign hanging over the porch read, "The Glen House, Bed and Breakfast."

Suddenly Zach realized the futility of his task. What was he looking for? How would he know when he found it? If Luna's family truly lived in this hamlet, how was he to locate them? Certainly not by the phony last name Luna had given him. The one clue Zach had was that their house was on the riverbank, but even this detail might be a fiction.

Nevertheless, he had driven all the way up here. The Glen was as sparsely populated as one could desire, so the number of residents must be limited. He resolved to drive along the river and at least look around. Who knows? If Luna had truly come here, he might be lucky enough to spot her car.

On the other side of the bridge the road split, Route 28 continuing north along the river and another route following the river south. Zach mentally flipped a coin, then made a right turn. He slowed as he passed the occasional house, examining the names on the mailboxes, peering down the driveways. There were no active farms any longer, but Zach saw people working in their yards this lovely Sunday morning. Occasionally they waved to him as he passed by, a rural custom he was not familiar with, but Zach waved back.

Seeing nothing promising after several miles, he returned to the bridge and faced an option he had hitherto resisted. He could *ask* someone. Though he had little enough to go on, not even a family name, he knew that country people are notorious busybodies. If the family lived here, someone in the area probably knew them.

He considered going into "The Glen House" to inquire, but

decided first to ask the boy who was still fishing off the bridge. He drove halfway across and rolled down his window. "Excuse me," he called, "do you live around here?"

The boy turned and waved. After carefully securing his pole to the guardrail, he strolled over to the car. A tall youth of twelve or thirteen, he had a friendly expression, not the bored, worldly-wise demeanor so common in city and suburban kids. "Lost?" he asked.

"No, I'm looking for a family that I think lives here."

"Who are they?"

"I don't know their name. I know the daughter though. I can describe her to you." Zach now launched into a description of Luna: her age, her height and weight, the color of her hair and her eyes. The more details Zach added, though, the more bewildered the young man appeared. Before Zach could finish, he was already shaking his head.

"No, I'm sorry," he said. "I don't know anybody like that. We just moved here last year from North Lake."

"Oh." Peevishly Zach wondered why the hell he hadn't volunteered this information earlier.

"You could ask Ruth," he suggested.

"Ruth?"

He pointed toward the route going south along the river. "She lives down there. I saw her in her garden when I went by. Ruth's been here a long time. She can probably help you."

Zach thanked him. Sighing disgustedly, he put his car in gear and made a U-turn, then turned left on the other side of the bridge. In a few minutes he saw a woman puttering in front of a small bungalow. Zach slowed and turned into the driveway.

The woman stood at his approach, a spade still in her hand. She wore a long skirt and an oversized straw hat. A collie that had been lying in the sun nearby leapt to its feet and barked a warning at the newcomer.

"Quiet, Walter!" the woman shouted. To Zach she added, "Don't worry. He won't bite unless you're selling aluminum siding." She appeared to be in her late sixties, had a thin, weathered face and intelligent gray eyes. Her features betrayed no wariness of the stranger. "Lost?" she asked.

"In a manner of speaking."

The collie thoroughly sniffed Zach, then returned to its former spot, circled a couple of times, and flopped back onto the grass.

"From New York?" she inquired.

"No, Albany."

"I ask because it's usually the New Yorkers who get lost up here. I can say that because I'm a former New Yorker myself—Manhattan."

The admission was hardly necessary, for Zach could hear in her voice the conspicuous tones of New York City speech. "Are you Ruth?"

"Yes. Who are you?"

"My name is Zach Tonner." Motioning vaguely behind him, he added, "The boy back there suggested you might be able to help me. You've lived here for some time?"

"Eighteen years. What can I do for you?"

"I'm trying to find a family, but part of the problem is that I don't know the name. You see, I know the daughter of this family, but her last name is different."

"What's her name?"

Zach hesitated. "Planitis."

Ruth thought about this for a moment, then shook her head. "No. I haven't heard of that one. I think I would have remembered it. Sometimes I learn the girls' married names after they leave, but that one doesn't ring a bell. What's her first name?"

"Well, her first name may not be of much help. I think it might just be a nickname, something she adopted—on her own, I mean."

"So, what is it?"

"It's ... Luna."

Ruth looked at Zach now for a long moment, recognition in her eyes and something else that he couldn't quite read. "That's not a nickname. That's her real name."

"You mean you know the family?" Zach asked excitedly.

She put down her spade and wiped her hands on her skirt. "Listen, Zach, do you want a beer?"

"Thanks, but I was kind of hoping you'd just point me in the right direction."

"I'll do better than that. I'll walk you there. It's just a little ways down the road, but let me get the beer first. Wait here. I'll only be a second." With that, she turned and strode toward the bungalow.

"Couldn't you just tell me where the house is?" Zach called after her. "I'm in a bit of a hurry."

"You needn't be," she said over her shoulder. "The house is empty."

* * *

"CHEERS." SHE TIPPED her bottle up, holding the straw hat with her other hand so it wouldn't fall off.

Zach took a small sip. "Luna's family doesn't live here anymore?"

Ruth shook her head, swallowed some more, then admired the bottle. "I know it's probably too early in the day, but there are few things in life better than Ballantine Ale swilled in the sunshine. You can't get this around here, you know. I have to drive all the way to Saratoga for it. That's the one thing I miss about New York. This was our vacation home at first," she said, gesturing toward the bungalow. "It became my permanent home after I got divorced. My husband was a stock analyst in the City. I named the dog after him," she added dryly. "So, you know Luna. How is she doing?"

"Fine. But what happened to her family?"

"Let's walk."

She led him across the yard to the road, the collie bounding ahead of them. "We were neighbors," Ruth told him. "Our properties adjoined each other, though there's a patch of woods in between. After eighteen years, I still can't get used to country lot sizes. Do you know how much land came along with my little house there?"

"No."

"Nearly fifteen acres, and that's with over a thousand feet of frontage on the Hudson River! I sometimes laugh to think what that riverfront real estate would cost in Manhattan. It's the same river, after all, and the same state."

"How long did her family live here?"

"I'm not sure, because they were here when I arrived, but I got the impression that the father had lived up here quite a while before Luna was born. When I moved in, Luna was seven years old. So she's married now, huh? Someone named—what was it—Planitis?"

"I don't think she married anyone. I think she just changed her name."

"Really? Luna Planitis." Ruth pronounced the name, as if to try it out on her tongue. "Well, it's got an interesting ring to it. I have to admit that it sounds a whole lot better than Luna Lewis."

"Lewis? That was her last name?"

"Yes. Can you imagine? I mean, Luna all by itself is a pretty name, but it just doesn't go with Lewis. I don't know what possesses some parents to saddle their children with monikers like that. I had a girlfriend whose last name was Otty, and her parents had the complete lack of foresight to name her Dorothy, so all through school the poor kid was called Dotty Otty. There was never a girl more anxious to get married than Dotty was. Two months after graduation she married a guy named Frumkin and considered it an improvement." Ruth laughed. "Good for Luna, though, to get rid of 'Lewis.' Hell, that wasn't even their real name."

"It wasn't?"

"No. It was shortened from Lubinski or Lupinski, something like that. Polish, in any case. Her father told me once."

Zach digested all this. "Then you knew her father."

"Albert Lewis? Oh, he was a real piece of work! Yes, I knew him. Mostly because I lived the closest, I became sort of a family friend, probably the only one they had. Here, this is where we turn."

They had reached a driveway. A crooked post still supported a mailbox, but rust had obliterated any name that might have been painted on it. Next to the mailbox stood a six-foot tall bracket made of pipe.

"Al had a television repair business," Ruth said, indicating the empty bracket. "The sign used to read, 'Lewis's TV and Radio.' Remember when there used to be television repairmen?"

"Was there much call for that up here?"

"Not after they invented transistors and printed circuits. You should have seen the collection of vacuum tubes he had in his shop. He must have had every possible size and shape, all of them in neat little bins and every one of them obsolete! Eventually he had to 'diversify.' He became a general fix-it man, fixed all kinds of electrical gadgets. Al was also an avid ham radio operator. He knew Morse code, and he taught it to Luna. She got so good at it that she could spell out my name almost as quickly in code as I could in English."

They came to a stop. The house at the end of the drive was a large, ramshackle, clapboard structure, once painted white, but now its paint peeling off, the weathered gray wood revealed beneath. To the left of the driveway stood a barn and a rail fence. Zach could see the yard behind the house too. Overgrown now, it sloped gracefully down toward the water, and at this season of the year the entire bank was—

"Knee-deep in wildflowers," Zach said aloud.

"What?"

"Nothing, just something Luna told me about this place." Zach turned toward the house. "So this is where her family lived."

"Yes, but all the time I knew them, the 'family' consisted of just Luna and her father."

"What happened to her mother?"

Ruth lifted her shoulders. "If Luna knew, she never told me, and neither did Albert. There were no pictures of her in evidence, something you might expect if she were dead, so it could be they were divorced. Al must have gotten married late in life, because he was already fifty-eight or fifty-nine when I moved here, which is kind of an advanced age to have a seven-year-old daughter. I admit to being curious about the mother, and though I never came right out and asked Al, I certainly made some broad hints and gave him several opportunities in case he wanted to volunteer the information, but he never took the bait. If Al didn't want to tell you something, he didn't tell you."

"What was he like—Luna's father?"

"Opinionated as hell, and conservative too. They always seem to go together, don't they? And no tact! He'd chew out his own customers if he thought they'd misused an appliance. He was also a world-class skinflint, hated spending a dollar on anything. But worst of all were his prejudices. He was from New York too, Brooklyn, I think. Blacks and Puerto Ricans had started to move into his neighborhood. That's why he came up here, so he wouldn't have to live next door to them. He would tell me these things without batting an eye, as if I agreed with him, as if *everyone* agreed with him. Since he was my neighbor, I kept my mouth shut to keep peace. I learned to just stay off certain subjects with him."

"What happened to him?"

"Come on." Ruth led Zach behind the house and through a field to the edge of the woods. A broad path, overgrown but still visible, led through the trees. "This is where Luna liked to ride."

"Nutty."

"That's right, Nutty. She loved that horse."

The collie sniffing along ahead, Zach and Ruth followed the trail to a steep rise that ended in a natural clearing at the top of a hill. Here they had an unobstructed view of the river valley below.

"Beautiful, isn't it?" Ruth observed. "Luna used to love to ride up here. She'd tie Nutty up to one of the trees. Then she'd sit for hours with her back against that oak there."

Zach saw a great, twisted trunk at the edge of the clearing. "What would she do up here?"

"Mostly she'd read. She loved to read stories, would devour books. Other times she'd just watch the hawks. It's a favorite spot for them because of the updrafts. Take a look." She pointed to the sky.

Zach saw the dark silhouettes of a pair of birds soaring over the river, their outstretched wings buoyed by the currents of warm air rising from the valley. They did not appear to be searching for prey. A mating ritual perhaps, or just some kind of avian diversion, one of the hawks appeared to be chasing the other, the pursuer making elaborate dives, the pursued always dodging just in time. This lofty gavotte came to a sudden end, however, when the pursuing hawk, anticipating the other's escape route, altered its flight at the last minute and intercepted. The two birds tumbled out of sight, and Zach was about to advance toward the edge of the promontory when he heard Ruth say, "Here it is!"

She had strolled to the far end of the clearing and was now looking at something in the underbrush. Zach joined her. Nearly obscured by the encroaching grass was a square stone marker set flat in the earth. Carved upon it was "Albert Lewis."

Zach gaped. "Luna's father is buried here?"

"His ashes anyway. Luna had him cremated."

"Why would she bury him here?"

"Why not? It's a nice spot. Would it be more appropriate in the azalea bed?"

"What did he die of?"

"Brain tumor. He lingered for a while. Luna knew it was coming."

Zach stared at the stone. "How did they ... get along, Luna and her father?"

"They got along all right. What do you mean?"

"Did he treat her well?"

"Yes, as far as I could see. What are you getting at?"

"I don't know. Just the two of them living alone. It's a little odd. You don't suppose he ever ..."

Ruth narrowed her eyes. "What? Molested her? Abused her? Is that what you're suggesting? That's the first thing people think of these days. Well, call me hopelessly naive, but I don't think so. Al Lewis may have been a cheapskate and a bigot and an all-around thorny bastard, but he would never have touched his daughter."

"I'm sorry," Zach said. "I'm just trying to understand some things."

"If you don't mind my asking—or even if you do—what is Luna to you?"

Zach was quiet for a moment, then answered simply, "We're lovers."

"Well, no one can fault you for beating about the bush. So why don't you just ask *her* all these questions?"

"She's gone off somewhere."

"Flew the coop on you? What was it? A misunderstanding?"

"Yes—and my fault. I was hoping her family could help me locate her."

"Well, I'm afraid dear old Albert can't help you." Ruth upended her beer now, draining the bottle, then started back toward the path, Zach following.

"What was she like, when she was growing up?"

"Why do you ask?"

"The Luna I know is such a strange person."

"Because she has a mind of her own and isn't afraid to speak it?" Ruth smiled. "Excuse me. My feminist side showing. I suppose Luna *was* an odd duck. There's no denying it, but it was an attractive kind of oddness, at least to me. I liked seeing a girl not act like a girl. She had none of that dreadful prissiness about her. She was a real tomboy, would go anywhere, do anything."

"Did she have friends?"

"Hardly any." Ruth chuckled. "She had one for a while, Ellie Prakken from down the road. Her parents were Al's customers. One time when I came over, the two girls were on Luna's front porch. They must have been nine or ten at the time. Anyway, Ellie was lying on the hammock making these God-awful noises like she was in pain. Her legs were spread open with a doll stuck under her dress, supposedly coming out of her. She was playing at giving birth. Her mother must have told her about it. And there's Luna watching this with the most horrified expression. I had all I could do to keep a straight face.

"Luna was always different though. When the other girls started wearing bras and make-up in high school, she wanted no part of it, kept to herself. The boys left her alone too. I never knew her to have a date. Of course, that might also have had something to do with her appearance. Her clothes always looked like she'd slept in them, which she very well may have done. She wore these oversized, shit-kicker boots. And her hair was always chopped short. Her father used to cut it himself—to save money, of course.

"Maybe it was spending so much time alone that made her different. I have no idea what it's like to be an only child. I come from a family of six, and we still call each other once a week, but Luna was alone most of the time. Her father would work in his shop, and she would spend her days by herself. She'd ride her horse for hours on end or go for walks. I'd see her sometimes along the river behind my house balancing on the stones, and I'd call her in for cookies. At first I thought she didn't enjoy coming over because she never smiled, but then I learned it was just her way. I came to really like her, odd as she was."

They had emerged from the woods now. Zach asked, "When was the last time you saw her?"

"A couple of months ago."

"She comes up to visit you?"

"No, I just saw her by chance. She comes to visit the house. She still owns it, so she looks in on it now and then. When Al died, he left Luna everything, which consisted mainly of this house and a little money he had socked away in the bank. She lived here alone for a while, but then moved and got a job down in Albany. I thought she'd sell the house, but she didn't." They came to a stop at the rear of the structure. "Do you want to go inside? I don't think Luna would mind."

"You have a key?"

"A key! Listen to him. You're in the country now, Zach. Besides, there's nothing to steal." Ordering her dog to stay put, Ruth mounted the small stoop and grasped the doorknob. The door resisted, but not from being locked, only from being stuck in its jamb. A determined push opened it.

They entered a spacious farm kitchen, with an ancient wooden table in the center. A sink, cupboards, appliances stood against the walls. Old metal canisters were lined up on the counter, and a set of ceramic bowls nested on a shelf. Except for the layer of dust covering everything, the kitchen looked as if it were still in use.

Ruth led him through a dining room and living room, both filled with old, well-worn furniture, then to a front room that Al had used as a shop. The bins of vacuum tubes were still there, and the shelves were littered with radios, phonographs, toasters, electric mixers, many of them in pieces. Copies of old electrical and mechanical magazines were strewn about the floor, and upon the workbench was a large television tube, its single great eye gone to sleep long ago.

Zach followed Ruth upstairs. There were several rooms off the main hallway. In one of them were a double bed and a rolltop desk filled with ham radio equipment. Above it hung a ham license. At the end of the hall Ruth pushed open a door. "This was hers."

It was a small chamber with wide, unpainted floorboards and one window, which faced the river. The furniture consisted of a single bed, a low dresser with a mirror attached, and an uncomfortable, straight-backed wooden chair. Zach had a sudden, vivid impression of the little girl who had once occupied it. He could see her sitting upon the chair and pulling on her great boots in the morning. He could see her looking out the window as she buttoned her shirt, planning the day's adventures. Zach ran his hand along the top of the bureau, glanced into the mirror and viewed the flowered wallpaper on the opposite wall. Almost to himself he said, "It's a ... wonderful little room."

"Do you *think* so? It always reminded me of a monk's cell. A little too Spartan for my taste, I'm afraid."

They descended the stairs and retraced their steps to the yard. Zach looked back at the house. "Why do you think she hasn't sold it?"

"Search me. It's much too big for one person. This is the sort of house you're supposed to raise a family in."

Zach was silent for a moment. "Does she have any other relatives?"

"She has an uncle, Al's brother Percy. He's the only one that I know of. I met him a few times when he came to visit."

"Do you think Luna might have contacted him?"

"Maybe. She used to be fond of him."

"Where does he live?"

"Ohio, near Toledo."

Zach turned to her. "Toledo?"

"That's what he told me. Why?"

"There's a roller coaster near Toledo." Zach paused. "How can I get hold of him?"

"I don't have an address, but he ought to be easy enough to reach. Find a tour book of Ohio and look under museums."

"He works in a museum?"

Ruth smiled sardonically and shook her head. "It's *his* museum, the only establishment of its kind, I gather—devoted exclusively to the New York World's Fair of 1939."

XIV

Super Wash

On the drive back home, Zach thought of the hilltop, the grave, the mysterious absent mother. He thought of the father and daughter living alone. Most of all he thought of the strange empty house and the young girl who had inhabited the bare little room on the second floor. He ached to clutch that girl to him.

Nearly back to Delmar he remembered Luna's uncle, this Percy person Ruth had mentioned. Zach made a detour to the bookstore and picked up a guide to Ohio. Back in his car he turned to the index, ran his finger down the listings, then flipped to a page and read:

> **New York World's Fair 1939 Museum.** One of the largest collections of original artifacts from the Depression era exposition, this unique attraction is housed in a stately Victorian residence located in the agricultural region of northern Ohio. In several rooms visitors may view photos, films, commercial souvenirs, and a wide variety of items used or exhibited at the fair. Open daily, 10-4, 5 mi. SE of Tiffin on U.S. 224. Admission: $6.

In the same book he looked up amusement parks. Thirty miles from Tiffin was Cedar Point, which boasted the largest number of roller coasters in the country. He closed the book.

Beth's car was missing from the driveway when Zach arrived home. On his bureau in the bedroom he found a brief note. "Zach," it read, "I'm staying at Jean's for a few days to give you a chance to get your stuff out of the house. I withdrew half the money from our checking account, and I'll be seeing a lawyer this week to draw up a separation agreement. Please let me know where you would like the papers sent." The note was signed simply, "B."

Zach put it down, stood silent for a moment, then picked it up and read it again. Practical Beth. Always efficient, she probably had a mental list of all the things to do in the event of a divorce, and now she could begin ticking them off. In an odd way she would enjoy this unpleasant but necessary legal ritual. She would appreciate its thoroughness, its finality. There would be no messy indecision any longer.

He carried the note into the kitchen, sat down and read it again. Then for several minutes he stared at nothing in particular.

It was the right moment for tears, but he didn't have any. Instead, Zach was remembering one of her many business trips. She'd gone to San Antonio for a week on some damn project or other, and when she returned, she gushed about what a wonderful time she'd had sightseeing, visiting the Alamo, having dinner on the Riverwalk. He should have shared her enthusiasm. That would have been the right thing to do. He should have listened attentively to her stories, asked questions, been happy for her success. A good husband would have done that. But Zach was hurt because she'd left him behind, and resentful because she'd enjoyed herself so much and so easily without him. Beth accused him of envy, and they both went to bed that night feeling angry, misunderstood, right.

So what was it? A bad marriage? Were they bad people? Was it his fault? Her fault? No fault? No fault divorce. That was the silliest notion of all, a California notion, that there should be a divorce and it was no one's fault. No, he'd take the blame. He'd earned it, for God's sake. Zach twisted off his wedding ring and looked at it. Why the hell don't they have a ceremony for this? Think of all the money spent and energy expended to celebrate the beginning of a marriage; yet there was much more wisdom to be gained at the end, after you've botched part of your life, wasted it beyond recovery. But when the end comes, it comes alone and in silence. He laid the ring on the table.

* * *

ZACH'S SECRETARY WAS surprised the next morning when he told her to hold all his phone calls and to keep all visitors away. Then he shut himself in his office. Resolutely, doggedly, he worked on the reorganization plan. He didn't break for lunch, and for one of the few times in his career he worked long past his normal quitting time. On Tuesday Zach closeted himself again, determined to finish. When he finally emerged from the office shortly after four o'clock that afternoon, he carried a thick folder in his hands.

"Zach, this is terrific!" Hugo rose from his desk, smiling broadly. "I'd planned to leave early. Eva's having company tonight, but when I got your call, I had to have a look before I left."

"Well, there it is," Zach said, tossing the folder onto his desk. "I think you can make all the reductions through the buyout and retirement."

"Excellent! Excellent! This is unofficial, but the governor told me they're going to back off now for a while, since we've been so cooperative. Sit down." He opened the folder, then noticed that Zach had remained standing. Hugo assumed a more sober attitude. "I'm afraid you were stuck with the dirty work here, Zach. I'm sorry. I gave you this job because you were the best qualified. I knew I could trust you to make the reductions judiciously and fairly."

"Thank you for your confidence, Hugo." His tone was unusually flat.

"I'll go over the nuts and bolts of this tomorrow, but I want to see how you sorted out the deputies." He skimmed the first page quickly, flipped to the second, then slowed down and began nodding his head. "Munser," he intoned thoughtfully. "Yes, good choice. Difficult choice, I'm sure. Win is a good man, a very good man, but he's been here a long time. Probably near retirement anyway, isn't he?"

"He's sixty-two."

"Good. Not that that has anything to do with it, of course, but it will be easier on him financially. Very good choice." Hugo continued skimming. Suddenly he stopped, looked up at Zach. "What does this mean?"

"Just what it says."

"You're recommending *yourself* for elimination?"

"Yes."

"But why?" When Zach did not reply, Hugo shook his head vigorously. "It's out of the question. You're much too valuable to me. You're going to have to choose someone else."

"I'm sorry, Hugo, but I can't."

"You can't? What do you mean?" He narrowed his eyes. "Have you had another offer?"

"No."

Hugo's voice grew softer. "Listen, Zach, I know this wasn't an easy thing for you to do. Cutting people is never easy, especially when they're your colleagues, but making a martyr of yourself is uncalled for. These cuts weren't your fault. You shouldn't take the blame."

"I'm not taking the blame, Hugo. Or even if I am, that's not the reason I'm leaving."

"Then what *is* the reason?"

A slight smile passed briefly over Zach's features. More to himself than to Hugo he said, "I don't have to do bad things anymore."

"What?! What are you talking about?" Hugo's face was an image of consternation. "What will you do if you leave?"

"I'm not sure. Maybe I'll go back to teaching—if they'll have me." He added, "I've included my resignation at the end."

Hugo read the short document at the bottom of the folder. "Three weeks? You're leaving in three weeks?"

"No, I'm leaving today. Those three weeks are accumulated time off. Beth and I never did get around to taking much vacation."

"Is there trouble at home, Zach?"

"Yes, but I'm taking care of it."

"If you've got marital problems, this is the worst possible time to leave your job. You *know* that." He paused. "I'm going to make a suggestion— as your friend, Zach. Don't leave yet. Postpone this decision for a while. Take those three weeks you have coming and go somewhere with Beth."

Zach snorted. "At the best of times Beth wouldn't take three weeks off. Even our honeymoon had to be limited to two."

"Then take the three weeks by yourself, damn it! What have you got to lose? If you feel the same way at the end of it, *then* you can leave."

Zach stood silent.

"Let me do you a favor," Hugo said, lifting the resignation letter and holding it sideways between his fingers. "We'll forget about this and pretend it never happened."

"Don't do it, Hugo."

The commissioner lowered the paper and shook his head. "Why are you trashing your whole career like this? You could have had a long future ahead of you here."

Zach nodded. "That's what I'm afraid of."

* * *

For some reason, it was a comical incident that Zach recalled as he drove back to Delmar. It had occurred many years ago when he first started at the Education Department, shortly after he left teaching. He was to attend a conference somewhere across town. With his improved circumstances, he'd already bought himself a new suit, a conservative gray much like the one he wore today, but he was still driving his old Ford. Zach was proud to be representing the Department for the first time, but not very proud of his car. At the very least he could get it cleaned. So, on the way to the conference he pulled into a car wash and splurged on the Super Wash, the most expensive cleaning and waxing job. Then he sat back while the automatic device pulled him and his vehicle into the tunnel.

Spouts of soap and high-pressure jets of water hit the hood of his car, and Zach watched with satisfaction as years of accumulated grime broke up and flowed off the metal surface. When the spray hit the windows, though, the water began to spurt freely through the top edge of his door where the weather seals had corroded. Horrified, Zach grabbed for his seat belt, fumbled trying to undo it, but it was already too late. The whole left side of his suit was spattered with rusty water stains, and the seat of his pants was wet to the skin. Cursing all the way, Zach drove home to change his clothes. When he finally arrived—late—at the conference, he was wearing a brown corduroy jacket and unmatched tan trousers, teaching mufti.

Zach smiled as he remembered it. He reached up now and unfastened the top button of his white shirt. With a deft side-to-side motion he loosened the knot of his tie, slipped it from his neck, and tossed it on the seat beside him. A few moments later he glanced at the shapeless bit of silk and recognized it: red with a pattern of little yellow diamonds.

XV

World of Tomorrow

By ten a.m. the next morning Zach was speeding west on Interstate 90. He rolled down his window to enjoy the mild air, but as he settled in for the long solitary hours on the highway, he could not help but feel some anxiety about what he was doing.

That Luna might be at his destination was only a possibility. Her uncle's proximity to the amusement park increased the likelihood perhaps, but likelihoods and possibilities are flimsy things to go on when trying to predict human behavior. Zach could have saved himself the trip, of course, by calling on the telephone, but if he had reached Luna, what could he have said to her? Please come back? And if she refused, would he have been prepared never see her again? The thought was intolerable. No, if Luna was there, he had to see her in person. He would take the chance.

Despite this anxiety, Zach was also aware of an undeniable elation, almost a giddiness. It was not just that he was free of the Education Department. He had before him the wild prospect of a life with Luna, something he was only now allowing himself to contemplate.

Zach crossed New York State, crossed the forty-mile panhandle of Pennsylvania, and entered Ohio. The tour book had described northern Ohio as an agricultural region, and it was certainly that. The flat, unvaried terrain seemed perfectly suited for the crop that grew here in greatest abundance: corn. Fields of corn stretched for a hundred miles in every direction. By two o'clock the next day Zach was on U.S. 224 heading toward Tiffin and looking for signs that he was approaching a populated area. What caused him to slow down, though, and then come to a complete stop was the roadside sculpture.

He recognized it immediately. He'd seen photos of the colossal original. For a brief moment in history the two geometric shapes formed one of the most recognizable images on earth. They had been a logo, perhaps the first logo of the modern world, instantly identifiable. Here, crudely recreated in miniature, on the edge of a dirt parking lot surrounded by Ohio cornfields, stood the Trylon and Perisphere.

Zach got out of his car and approached the sculpture. The Trylon was twelve feet tall, a three-sided needle, its blank faces tapering up to a point. The Perisphere was an enormous ball, less than half the height of the other form, but many times its girth. Near the base of the figures a stiff, narrow ribbon curved gracefully around them and, like an umbilical, connected one to the other. It was done in cement and painted white to match the original. Upon the broad face of the sphere was printed "New York World's Fair 1939 Museum."

There were no other vehicles in the parking area except a small, white Toyota—perhaps the proprietor's. As the guidebook had indicated, the museum building was an old Victorian dwelling. Though somewhat dilapidated, the three-story house appeared to have once been a handsome residence, the family seat of some prosperous farmer, perhaps, but now it squatted uneasily next to fields that were owned and tilled by another. Zach mounted the steps and opened the door.

"Come right in," a female voice invited him.

In the foyer was a small counter, behind which a matronly lady rose to greet him. She had a bubble of bluish white hair and large, bifocal glasses attached to a lavender cord around her neck.

"Are you open?" Zach asked.

"We sure are! Admission is six dollars. There are three rooms on the first floor, and one on the second. You can spend as much time as you like, but we do close at four."

Zach reached for his wallet.

"Where you from?" she asked.

"Albany, New York."

"You're a ways from home then. On vacation, are you?"

"Something like that." Zach handed her a ten-dollar bill, and she carefully counted out four singles into Zach's palm.

"Now, do you know about the World's Fair?"

"Not much, really."

She took a breath. "The New York World's Fair of 1939 was held in Flushing Meadows in Queens at the site of a former dump. The fair commemorated the hundred and fiftieth anniversary of the inauguration of George Washington as President in 1789. A sixty-five-foot-high statue of Washington stood near the theme center. The theme center was the Trylon and Perisphere. The Trylon was 610 feet tall, and the Perisphere had a diameter of 180 feet. The theme of the fair was 'Building the World of Tomorrow,' and many things that we take for granted today like television appeared for the first time at the fair. Now, as you go through the rooms, make sure you read the descriptive material. It's all self-explanatory. And when you go upstairs don't forget to watch the twelve-minute film. Just press the red button. If you have any questions, feel free to ask."

Zach thanked her and wandered into the first room, what had probably been the front parlor in the old house. A vast array of items was displayed, some hanging neatly on the walls, some lined up on shelves and tables, some protected by glass doors in unmatched cabinets. There were dishes, water tumblers, pitchers, ashtrays, even a complete set of flatware, and all had in common an image of the Trylon and Perisphere painted, etched, printed, or embossed upon them. Some artifacts had actually been cast in the form of the logo. A silver plated Perisphere held salt; a fattened Trylon held pepper.

Zach bent to read the "descriptive material." A typewritten index card informed him:

> This china cup and saucer was given away FREE with any purchase at the Japanese Tea Room at the Fair. Most people didn't save them because in those days anything that said "Made in Japan" on the bottom of it was considered CHEAP. How things change.

Another card read:

> A glass knife in it's original box. The knife is very sharp and can even cut steak, but blade has a tendency to chip, so not a *good idea to use.*

And another:

> The famous HEINZ PICKLE. One of the most popular souvenirs at the Fair. Millions of these little green plastic pickles were produced by the H. J. Heinz company to promote their products. Even wealthy ladies and gentlemen could be seen wearing pickle pins.

Zach straightened up and strolled into the next room, what

may have been the dining room of the old house. Indeed, it still had a wooden table and four chairs set up in the center, but these were part of the exhibit: a working-class kitchen set with the Trylon and Perisphere laminated on the table top and carved into the chair backs. A desk held postage stamps, guidebooks, maps, and stationery, all with the fair logo.

The second floor was hung with large advertising posters, and a television monitor had been mounted before a row of folding chairs. Zach pressed the red button as instructed, and a tape began to play, a grainy color film with voice-over narration. He watched for a minute or two, then stepped over to a table littered with newspapers and magazines dating from 1939. Zach skimmed a few of the articles. In the innocent, grandiloquent style of the time, the news stories shamelessly trumpeted the fair. Thanks to science, they assured the reader, this was the dawn of a new day. Zach recalled that before the summer of 1939 came to an end, the Second World War had begun.

Framed on the wall was a more recent newspaper article clipped from a local Ohio paper. It covered the opening of the museum and was accompanied by two black-and-white photographs, one showing the cement sculpture in the parking lot, and the other a lanky man standing in front of the building and holding a Trylon and Perisphere paperweight. The caption read, "Percy Lewis of Tiffin shows off one of the many hundreds of memorabilia he has collected from the 1939 World's Fair." Zach bent to examine the man's face. He appeared to be past fifty at the time of the photo.

Back downstairs again, Zach took a cursory look through the last remaining room, which adjoined the foyer. Here were jigsaw puzzles, toys, a cane that doubled as a stool, a bolt of cloth, a tiny blue vase that looked like Wedgwood but wasn't, a lamp, a radio, a wax candle in the shape of the fair logo, the wick rising out of the Trylon. Finally Zach stopped at a small display case hanging on the wall at eye level. The glass door was secured with a padlock, but through it he could see something glowing inside. He leaned toward it.

"That's the most valuable thing in the museum," said the white-haired woman, who was watching him. She fumbled around in the drawer and pulled out a bunch of keys. "Here, let me open it up for you so you can get a better look." She unfastened the padlock and swung the small door. What had been glowing inside was a light bulb, the size and shape of a standard incandescent lamp, except that the glass was clear. Inside, glowing an eerie purple, were the two geometric forms. "They made the filament in the shape of the Trylon and Perisphere," she explained. "It was used as a night light. Now, wasn't that ingenious?"

"Remarkable."

"What they didn't think of in those days!" She let Zach gaze a few moments longer; then she closed the door and carefully replaced the padlock. "A fellow came in one day and offered a thousand dollars for that bulb."

"Really?"

"Yes, one thousand dollars cash, and he wasn't the first to try to buy something. You'd be surprised how many dealers come in here expecting to purchase things." She returned to the counter, Zach following. "But this is a museum, the owner says, not an antique shop. Nothing is for sale, except the souvenirs, of course." She indicated the shelves behind her, stacked with coffee mugs, T-shirts, and baseball caps sporting the museum logo.

"Tell me something," Zach said. "How did the owner happen to begin this collection?"

The woman had obviously been asked the question before. "Percy Lewis was brought up in New York. In 1939 he had a season pass to the fair, so he used to go almost every day as a boy. That's when he started his collection. He has been collecting now for over fifty years."

"I see. And why did he locate the museum here in Ohio?"

"Percy married an Ohio gal, and he moved here." In a confidential tone she added, "The marriage didn't last, unfortunately."

Zach scanned the souvenirs behind the counter. "How much are the T-shirts?"

"Eleven ninety-five, except if you need XXL, but you don't look like you need XXL. Sizes start at medium."

"I'll take a medium."

She folded the shirt neatly and slipped it into a paper bag, then rang up his purchase.

Zach asked, "Is Mr. Lewis around today?"

"No, I'm sorry, he isn't."

"I was hoping to speak to him."

"Is there anything *I* can help you with?"

"No, I need to speak to him personally."

She narrowed her eyes. "You're not a dealer, are you?"

"No, nothing like that. Would it be possible for me to call him at home?"

"This *is* his home. Percy occupies the back of the house as his residence. It's the same phone number."

"Should I call him later this evening then?"

She appeared flustered. "He won't be home tonight. If I knew what you needed to see him about—"

"It's of a personal nature. A family matter," he added, "and kind of important."

She sighed. "Well, I don't suppose there's any point in trying to keep it a secret since it's been in the papers anyway."

"What's been in the papers?"

"Percy's in jail."

"*He's in jail?*"

She nodded. "Yes, the county jail in Tiffin."

"What did he do?"

"Oh, it was a silly thing. He built the sidewalk too small. Percy does contracting work for a living. This museum is more like a hobby for him. Anyway, the county contracted with him to lay a sidewalk along a stretch of road that didn't have one. Well, he dug it all out and framed it and poured the concrete, and only when it was done did the county come out with a tape measure and measure it. When they did, they found it was three inches smaller than they wanted. All county sidewalks are forty-eight inches wide, you see, and Percy had laid his forty-five."

"And they put him in jail for that?"

"Oh, no, it wasn't for that. Lord, no! What happened was, the county wanted him to dig the whole sidewalk up again and lay it the right size. Now Percy, he said he'd done the work proper and ought to get paid for it, since they'd never told him the size they wanted, and the sidewalk he'd made was plenty wide enough for any normal person to walk on. But the county said no, and they refused to pay him. Well, to make a long story short, Percy got so mad he drove his backhoe over to the county courthouse, and didn't he knock a nice big chunk right out of the corner of the building."

"My God!"

"Yes, so that's why they put him in jail. Percy does have a temper. Afterward, he offered to make repairs to the courthouse, which the judge is going to let him do, but not before he spends thirty days in the pokey."

"I can't wait thirty days to see him."

"You don't have to wait. He's not in solitary or anything. Visiting hours tonight are six to eight p.m."

"But I couldn't—"

"I thought you said this was important."

Zach hesitated. "Well, it is."

The woman looked at him. "What's the matter? Haven't you ever visited anyone in jail before?"

XVI

Bestowing Fire

Not only had Zach never visited someone in jail before; he had never set foot in a jail. Yet, at ten minutes past six that evening, he found himself sitting in the parking lot of the county correctional facility. It was a one-story, cinder block building surrounded first by a tall fence, then, like everything else in Ohio, by acres of corn.

Zach watched as a noisy old Pontiac with more rust than paint pulled up next to him. A stocky woman, who could have been eighteen or forty, stubbed out her cigarette, then unfastened a toddler from the back seat. Visiting her husband or her boyfriend, Zach surmised. Nearby a middle-aged couple got out of a pickup truck. The husband was a large, red-faced man in a checkered shirt, blue jeans, and muddy boots. His wife was small, her hair covered by a kerchief, her eyes hidden behind pointed sunglasses. They slammed their doors with a double thump. Visiting their son, he guessed. Zach left the safety of his own car and followed them into the jail. He had no idea what to expect. Would he be cross-examined? Would he be frisked?

In the lobby Zach was issued a request form that asked his name, his address, his social security number, his "felony convictions." When he handed the completed form to the woman at the desk, she checked it against another document. "You're not on this inmate's visitors list."

"No," Zach admitted. "I haven't been here before. I'm a friend of his niece."

"And the niece's name?"

"Luna. Luna ... Lewis."

The woman jotted it down. "Please have a seat."

Fifteen minutes later Zach was told he could proceed. After stepping through an open gate, he heard the solid clang of bars shut fast behind him—locking him in, never mind how briefly. The sound made his skin crawl. He was made to walk through a metal detector, then to remove his jacket, which was stored in a locker. These precautions out of the way, Zach was ushered into the visiting area, a large room divided into a number of booths equipped with telephones. The guard directed Zach to an empty one and told him he would have thirty minutes.

Zach sat down in front of a plate glass window and stared stupidly at the empty chair across from him. He felt oddly like he was in a movie, since his entire knowledge of the criminal justice system was gleaned from Hollywood. He also felt—and tried to ignore—the thumping in his chest.

Presently a tall man with longish, unkempt gray hair ambled in on the other side of the glass partition. He had a craggy face and beak-like nose, and he looked to be upwards of seventy years old, but Zach recognized Percy Lewis from the newspaper photograph. Percy's shirtsleeves were rolled up, and on his forearm was a faded tattoo of an eagle perched upon a rock. He glared at Zach for a moment through the glass, then mouthed something unheard. Zach hastily picked up the telephone. Percy sat down and did the same.

"What did you say?" Zach asked.

Out of the phone a gravelly voice demanded, "Who the hell are you?"

"My name is Zach Tonner."

"They told me your name, but your name doesn't mean anything to me."

"I'm a friend of your niece, Luna."

"Is that right?" Percy said suspiciously. "You a lawyer? I don't need a damn lawyer. Charge an arm and a leg, frigging lawyers!"

"I'm not a lawyer. I came to ask you about Luna."

"Ask me what?"

"I'm trying to find her. I'm from Albany, where she lived. I think she might have come out here to Ohio, and I was hoping you had heard from her."

Interested now, the old man tilted his head up and eyed Zach over his beaked nose. "What do you want with her? You don't look like a cop."

"I'm not a cop."

"You from a collection agency?"

"No, of course not. I told you, I'm a friend of hers."

"What kind of a friend? A boyfriend?"

Zach hesitated. "Yes, sort of."

A small, evil grin appeared on Percy's lips. "What happened? She ditch you?"

"Not exactly."

"It sure as hell sounds like she ditched you if she went off without telling you where she was going."

"Please," Zach said earnestly, "you're my only hope of finding her."

Percy leaned forward and looked intently at him through the glass. "Listen, Zachary, if that's your name, let me tell you how I view this situation. Evidently Luna doesn't desire to see you. On the other side, you desire to see her. Those two desires are mutually exclusive. Now, Luna's kin to me, whereas you're a complete stranger. So please enlighten me. Why in hell would I help you?"

Zach saw the inescapable logic. He also recognized the implacability in the old man's demeanor. He sighed. "No reason."

"I'm glad you see that, Zachary." The phone still held to his ear, Percy leaned back. "How'd you find out I was in here?"

"I asked for you at the museum."

"Doris told you?"

"Yes."

Percy grunted, looked annoyed. "The woman's got no imagination. Would it have killed her to make up something? Why couldn't she have said I was at a curators convention, for Christ's sake? Or out on a buying trip or some other damn thing. But no, she's got to tell the full-gospel truth! How the hell does it look to patrons when they hear the museum director's in jail?" The peevish mood passed as quickly as it appeared. He looked at Zach again. "So you came all the way out here from Albany."

"That's right."

"They used to make jokes about Albany when I lived in New York. They'd say people only went to Albany on business or by mistake. If Chicago is the city of big shoulders, Albany is the city of hall monitors. Is it as dull as they say?"

"It's pretty dull."

"What do you do up there?"

"Until Tuesday I worked for the state."

"Public employee, huh? Faceless drone? A boring job in a boring town. So what happened? You get shit-canned? 'Downsized' as they say nowadays?"

"No, I quit."

"Why? Boss breathing down your neck?"

"Something like that."

Percy looked smug. "That's why I went into business for myself. Couldn't stand bosses, frigging little tinhorn Caesars throwing their weight around. I'm my own boss now, do what the hell I please."

"So I see," Zach commented dryly, glancing at his immediate environs.

The jab was not lost on Percy, but his reaction was merely to cast a sardonic smile at Zach. He asked, "How well do you know my niece?"

"Not very well, really."

"Were you screwing her?"

A flash of anger shot through Zach. "That's none of your damn business."

"You must have been screwing her or you wouldn't be this interested in her. That's all right."

Something in Percy's tone made Zach feel as if the old man was giving his consent, and that only heightened Zach's rancor.

"Luna's a good kid," Percy continued. "I used to visit their place while she was growing up. Taught her how to play chess once, and then the little shit beat me." He paused. "Never had any kids myself. You got kids?"

"No, I don't."

"You married?"

Zach averted his eyes and did not answer.

"What's the matter? Can't remember?"

"My wife's asked for a divorce."

"Let me get this straight, Zachary: you quit your job, your girlfriend skipped town, and now your wife's ditching you? What's next? Your dog died? Hell, you're worse off than I am, and I'm in jail!" After a moment he said, "I was married once."

"Were you?" Zach made no effort to hide his total indifference to the subject.

Percy nodded. "Never do it again either. Let me tell you my candid opinion of married life: bad words and bad smells. That's how you can sum up the whole experience of wedlock. Bad words and bad smells."

"I didn't take you for a philosopher."

"Of course it might have had something to do with the woman I was married to. Her name was Charlotte. Charlotte the harlot I called her. She was a two-timer, must have screwed every son of a bitch in Seneca County. I met her in New York when she was visiting her aunt. We had what they call a whirlwind romance, and then like a damn fool I married her and followed her back here. After a while I didn't know whether to divorce her or shoot her. As it turned out, I didn't have to do either. Charlotte found religion and left me for a born-again Christian. The way I figured it, that pretty much settled the score between us. I couldn't wish her a worse fate than a lifetime of church suppers and Wednesday night prayer meetings and Praise-the-Lord summer camps. You ever been in the bible belt before, Zachary?"

Zach shook his head.

"The damn Christians are everywhere, smiling at you with their stainless steel teeth. You must have seen the frigging bumper stickers: 'Jesus—Don't Leave Earth Without Him.' 'God Said It, I Believe It, That Settles It.' Christ! It's enough to make you gag. Damn Christians wouldn't know an independent thought if it leapt up and bit them in the ass." He snorted. "Did you come through Mansfield?"

"No."

"In Mansfield they've got this attraction called the Hall of Living Scripture. I went to see it once, out of morbid curiosity. It's a Quonset hut, big as an airplane hangar, and inside they've got life-size dioramas representing famous scenes from the bible. Adam and Eve, for instance, reaching for the apple. They're manikins, and they're dressed in fig leaves, naturally, cause they're not going to show anyone bare-assed, not even a dummy. Eve looks like a grown-up Barbie Doll: blond hair, big tits, long legs. And Adam, he's a surfer: blue eyes, sandy hair, square-cut jaw. The two of them look like they stepped out of a goddamn Pepsi commercial."

Zach glanced at his watch.

"The whole thing is like that, Noah's flood, the parting of the Red Sea, the crucifixion, everything: a white bread, apple pie version of the scriptures. Anyway, at the end they've got the Last Judgment. On one side is a trap door with red light shining up through it, and standing over it is a devil who bears more than a passing resemblance to Bela Lugosi. He's got a pitchfork and this ghoulish smile, and I swear to God, he's the only one in the whole show who looks like he's having a good time."

"Listen, Percy," Zach interrupted, "I'm really not—"

"Wait a minute, wait a minute. You got to hear about heaven. On the other side is the fate of the righteous. Now I want you to ask yourself, Zachary, what your idea of heaven is. What does paradise actually look like? Well, I'll tell you: in the Hall of Living Scripture heaven is a goddamned suburb! There's a sidewalk that winds through a little neighborhood of individual homes, the kind you might see in a brand new housing development, complete with picture windows and—get this—chimneys, with smoke curling out the top! Apparently they need fireplaces for the occasional chilly night up there in the New Jerusalem." He laughed. "I have to admit that I did see some poetic justice in the notion that all these smiling Christians would be spending eternity in a subdivision."

Zach had been watching him impatiently. "Tell me something, Percy, if you hate it so much here, why the hell didn't you go back to New York?"

"Because, Zacharius, you can't go home again. You ought to know that." Percy flashed him a wicked smile. "The New York I knew is gone. You're too young to remember it. New York was the center of the world back in the thirties and the forties. People cared about it, were proud of it. And clean, not the shit-hole it is now with all the graffiti and trash. Things worked back then. Vending machines worked, trains worked, *people* worked. I stayed long enough to see the other fair, the world's fair in '64. Only went once. It couldn't hold a candle to '39. After that I realized everything I cared about was gone. I didn't even have any family left in New York. My parents were both dead, and my brother Albert had already moved upstate. So I decided it was time for me to go."

Zach thought of something. "Did you know Luna's mother?"

"Of course I knew her. Iphigenia." Percy pronounced the name *if-GAIN-ya.*

"Then she was ... Greek?"

"Yeah, she was a Greek and Albert was a Polack. Quite a combination, right? Only in America! And whenever I'd visit them, I'd tell Iphigenia all these Polack jokes. I'd do it partly to amuse her and partly to piss off Albert. He was sensitive about being Polish, you understand. But I used to say that as long as I was a Polack myself, I could tell any joke I wanted. Anyway, Iphigenia loved it.

She'd giggle so hard, her sides would ache."

"Do you remember what Iphigenia's maiden name was?"

"Andropolis, something like that. Her family were immigrants. Iphigenia only spoke a little English when Albert met her, and almost immediately after they tied the knot, Al took her up there to East Jesus to live. She was much younger than Albert. I think the only reason Iphigenia's father let them marry was that he wanted to get her out of the house. It was a big Greek family, and to him she was just one more mouth to feed."

"What was she like?"

"Iphigenia? A real pretty girl, much prettier than Albert deserved. Jet black hair and dark eyes. Stunning looking woman. And a good cook. She'd make all these dishes with grape leaves and wrinkled olives and salty cheese, dripping with oil."

"What happened to her?"

The old man frowned. "Died. She died having Luna. Internal hemorrhage. Poor kid bled to death."

"Did Luna know—I mean, how her mother died?"

"Of course she knew. Al told her."

Zach digested what he'd heard. More to himself than to Percy he said, "This might account for it."

"Account for what?"

"Don't you see? Her mother's death in childbirth, Luna left behind as a burden to her father. She must have felt responsible. That would explain why she is the way she is."

"'The way she is'?"

"You know, her unusual appearance, her odd behavior, the strange things she says."

Percy's features twisted into a nasty sneer. "The only thing worse than a goddamned psychiatrist is a goddamned amateur psychiatrist. You're trying to *account* for Luna? You're trying to explain why she is the way she is? Is that what I'm hearing? You, a piss-assed frigging bureaucrat from Albany, New York, *you* presume to explain Luna? Let me tell you something, Zachary, and this may come as a shock: you can't. You can't explain her. You can't add up A and

B and C and somehow come up with L. They don't add up to L. *Nothing* adds up to L. Luna is what she is, and there's no way you can 'account' for her."

Zach stared at him. "I ... I'm sorry. I don't *want* to account for her. I just want to—"

"You just want to *what*?" Percy spat the question at him.

"I just want to ... see her again."

The unexpected pathos in the simple statement caused Zach's upper lip to quiver. He averted his eyes and was silent for some time. When he glanced again at the figure on the other side of the glass, he expected scorn from the old man. Instead, he saw only a kind of sternness in his face, tinged by something else less clear.

Percy said, "I've never known Luna to have a boyfriend. What's so special about you?"

"God knows." Zach sat for a moment longer, then muttered into the receiver, "Listen, thanks for your time. I'm sorry to have bothered you."

He was about to hang up when he heard the gravelly voice say, "Wait a minute!"

Zach put the phone to his ear.

"What are you going to do?" Percy asked.

"I don't know," Zach answered honestly.

"You going home?"

"I don't know."

Percy watched him. "Where are you staying tonight?"

"A motel, I guess."

"Don't stay in a motel. Charge an arm and a leg, frigging motels. Stay at my place."

"Your place?"

"Yeah, behind the museum."

"No. Thank you, but no."

"Why not? It's empty right now, seeing as how I'm here as a guest of the taxpayers."

Zach shook his head. "That's nice of you, really, but I can't."

He stood and began to hang up again.

"Zachary!" shouted the other.

Zach looked at him, putting the phone back to his ear.

"You are a stubborn son-of-a-bitch. You don't even know when someone's trying to do you a favor." The old man stood up now too and glared at Zach through the glass partition. "Listen, the place is available. It's stocked with food and liquor, and the bed is clean. Doris takes care of that for me. The key is hung on a nail stuck behind the left post on the back porch. If you want to use it, it's yours. If you don't, the hell with you!"

Percy banged the phone in its cradle and without a backward glance stalked from the room.

XVII

Gadfly

Stay at his place! Not bloody likely, thought Zach as he drove away from the prison. First the old man refuses to help find Luna, then thinks he can suddenly become a nice guy by offering his flat to crash in. Nevertheless, even as Zach watched for a motel along the road, unconsciously he headed back in the direction of the museum.

There was no other traffic at this hour, and Zach slowed down as he approached the roadside sculpture for the second time that day. In the late afternoon sun the ersatz Trylon and Perisphere cast long, distinct shadows across the highway. Their expanded form appeared eerily like the famous originals. Again the museum parking lot was nearly deserted. The white Toyota was gone, but in its place was another car. Zach glanced at it as he drove by, turned away, then slammed on his brakes. From the middle of the empty highway Zach stared at the small black vehicle, pockmarked with rust.

Throwing his car in reverse, he backed up and pulled into the parking lot. After a quick look at the license plate on the other car, he dashed around to the back of the house and bounded up the stairs of a broad, unscreened porch. Only when he reached the door did he realize that someone else was on the porch. He came to an abrupt stop.

The slight, boyish figure had been seated in a wooden rocker, but now she leapt to her feet. "Zach!"

The two stared at each other.

"What are you doing here?" Luna demanded.

"What am *I* doing here?" he echoed. "What are *you* doing here? I've been looking for you."

"Why?"

"Because I wanted to see you."

"Why?"

"Because I ..." He hesitated, not knowing quite what to answer. "Why did you leave without telling me?"

"You told your wife that you didn't care about me."

"Yes, I told her that, but it was a lie."

"I don't like people who lie."

"You don't like people who lie!" More loudly he repeated, "*You don't like people who lie!* Everything you told me was a lie! Everything about you was a lie! The very fact that you're here proves it. Isn't this your uncle's house? It is, isn't it?"

Luna did not answer.

"It *is* your uncle's house. I know because I met him today, your Uncle Percy, Percy *Lewis*. And 'Lewis' is your last name too, not 'Planitis' like you told me. And your father wasn't 'Inachus, Lord of the River,' whoever the hell that was supposed to be. Your father was plain old Albert Lewis, a TV repairman from Upstate New York, and your mother was—"

Zach stopped suddenly. He had averted his gaze, delivering his harangue to the rocker, the porch floor, the row of trees that enclosed the small backyard, any inanimate thing, in fact, that might possibly sympathize with him. But now he looked at Luna again. She was dressed in a T-shirt and shorts, her feet bare. Quietly she asked, "What do you want, Zach?"

Seeing her solemn face, which he'd feared he would never see again, Zach felt the wrath drain from him. His features softened.

"What do I want? I want *you*, Luna. I don't care what you call yourself. I don't give a damn who your family is. I'm just happy to see you again. I'm sorry I lied about my feelings for you. I didn't have the courage to tell Beth the truth. Or to be more precise, I didn't have the courage to admit the truth to myself. I'm admitting it now. I love you. I need you."

Zach approached her. Hesitantly he put his arms around her, half-fearing that she might spurn him. Over her shoulder he said, "I've missed you, Luna. Did you really think I didn't care about you? Is that why you left Albany?"

"Yes." She added, "I was going to ride roller coasters."

"Did you ride them?"

She shook her head. "It wasn't fun anymore."

"Have you been to see Percy?"

Luna was silent for a moment, then said simply, "Yes."

The small word caused something to leap inside him. By acknowledging her connection to Percy, Luna was tacitly admitting everything Zach had found out about her. He pulled back so he could look at her again. "So your uncle knew that I'd find you here. Percy seems an unlikely Cupid." Zach paused. "He invited me to spend the night. I wouldn't think of accepting that invitation if you don't want me."

She stared at him with her grave, brown eyes. "Of course I want you."

* * *

IT WAS A spare room on the first floor, a chamber that seemed rarely used, guest quarters, perhaps, in a home that saw few guests. There was a double bed in the corner, a threadbare carpet on the floor, and thick, heavy curtains that framed a tall window. The last rays of the setting sun passed through the parted drapery and fell upon them as they made love. Zach bathed in Luna's odors, tried to rub them into his own skin. He inhaled her breath as if it were a drug. He spoke her name over and over again, its repetition stoking his passion.

Afterward they lay in each other's arms, Luna breathing softly on Zach's shoulder. The room had grown dark, lit only by moonlight. Out the window Zach could see fireflies, and he could hear the breezes rustling the trees in the backyard. He said, "Beth left me."

"Because of me?"

"No, because of me. And I left my job."

"You can be a teacher now."

"Well, I've proven I can be irresponsible. Whether I'll prove a good educator is another matter. The strangest thing is, without my marriage and my job, by rights I ought to feel terrible. Instead, I'm actually happy." He tilted his head so that his lips nearly touched her scalp. "I saw your house, the house you grew up in. I drove up to The Glen last week looking for you. It seems like a perfect place to raise a little girl."

"I should sell it."

"I hope you don't."

"Why not?"

"Because I want to go back there with you."

"What for?"

Zach watched the intermittent glimmer of the fireflies, pinpricks of light inscribing small, glowing arcs outside the window. "To live with you."

Luna sat up and stared at him. "You want to live with me?"

"Is it so outrageous an idea?" Zach sat up also. "Well, maybe it is outrageous. We hardly know each other, I suppose, and my prospects are anything but rosy. The moment I saw your house, though, it was the strangest thing. I imagined the two of us living there together. I imagined myself getting a teaching job in some rural school district. The pay would be pitiful, but I'd get the summers off. God, how I would love to have the summers off again!" He smiled at her. "Crazy idea, huh?"

Her brow wrinkled in thought, Luna remained silent.

"I can't blame you for being skeptical about me," Zach continued. "I'd be skeptical myself. I don't exactly come with sterling credentials. When you met me, I was someone looking to be unfaithful to his wife. Why the hell would you want to cast your lot with me? You'd be much better off with—"

"We could share expenses."

"What?"

"Fifty-fifty," she clarified. "The house is all paid for. There's no mortgage, only taxes, and I live very economically, so it shouldn't cost us very much."

Zach gazed at her. Luna's demeanor was businesslike, as if she were proposing a commercial endeavor instead of an affair of the heart, but that was just her manner. She was saying yes. She was agreeing to live with him.

"Does that sound fair?" she asked. "Sharing expenses, I mean."

He pulled her to him. "It sounds fair. It sounds very fair."

* * *

ZACH LAY AWAKE in the darkened room, Luna sleeping by his side. He was already imagining their life together in that idyllic house by the river. He saw them reclining on the broad, grassy bank, or puttering in the garden, or walking the country roads after a rain. But Zach was not naive. He knew that living with another human being involved more than just making love and playing house in a rustic paradise. Living together meant a host of banalities that don't find their way into romance novels. It meant brushing your teeth next to someone else and spitting into the same sink. It meant seeing stains on each other's underwear when you did the laundry. It meant mannerisms and quirks that would be noticed, catalogued. It meant foul moods that could not be disguised, petty remarks that could not be unsaid. In short, living together meant a thousand mundane intimacies. Instead of dreading them, Zach found he was looking forward to them, even craving them.

But there was another intimacy even deeper than these. Zach saw a tiny hand held in his. He saw the diminutive but perfect fingernails, the wrinkled palms that knew instinctively how to grasp. He saw the wispy hair, dark hair. It would have to be dark, because Zach's hair was dark, and so was Luna's, and that's how genetics worked.

* * *

WHEN ZACH OPENED his eyes the next morning, the full light of day shone into the room. He squinted, glanced over to the other side of the bed, then experienced a brief moment of panic when he found it vacant. Almost immediately, though, the aroma of brewing coffee drifted into the room. He looked for his clothes where he'd dropped them in a heap last night. Now they lay neatly folded upon a chair. After dressing, he made a quick trip out to his car, then joined Luna in the kitchen.

"Do you like omelets?" she asked over her shoulder.

She was standing at the stove, and Zach smiled as he watched her for a moment from behind. "I love omelets."

The kitchen table was set for two. Luna had obviously done the best she could with what she found among her uncle's supplies. Chipped white plates, unmatched mugs, and folded paper napkins were carefully laid upon the table, and Luna had picked wildflowers from the backyard for a centerpiece, the only cheery touch in an otherwise drab kitchen.

Luna poured coffee into the mugs and handed one to Zach. "You'll want an office," she advised him.

"An office?"

"In the house—to correct papers and things like that. There's a nice room upstairs in the front of the house. It's very private and quiet."

Zach took a sip of his coffee. "The whole place up there seems private and quiet."

"The house needs some fixing up," she added. "I'm quite

handy though."

Luna carried the frying pan from the stove and divided the omelet between them. "It has good water," she said as she sat down.

"That's comforting."

"Lots of houses up there have water problems, but mine has always been very good." She paused. "We can start back right after breakfast."

Zach looked at her. He realized that he had never seen her make conversation during a meal before, and though she was not smiling, he detected a kind of joy in her demeanor. He reached over and grasped her hand. "I feel like I'm getting to know you for the first time. There's so much I want to know about you."

"What do you want to know?"

"All kinds of things. Little things, big things." He grinned. "For starters, do you have any bad habits I should be aware of, since we're going to be sharing quarters? Do you squeeze the toothpaste from the wrong end of the tube? Do you leave toenail clippings on the nightstand? Do you forget food in the back of the refrigerator until it gets furry?"

Luna pondered this for a moment. Then quite seriously she confessed, "Sometimes I piss in the shower."

Zach laughed. "*Everyone* pisses in the shower! It's almost a national pastime. Don't worry about it. If that's your only fault, we're going to get along fine." Zach leaned back in his chair. "Which room do you want for yourself?"

"I'll take the one across the hall from yours."

"And what about the little room at the back of the house, the one that faces the river?"

She eyed him curiously. "What about it?"

"That was your room, wasn't it, when you were growing up?" Zach sipped his coffee. "Maybe another little girl will occupy that room someday, or maybe a little boy."

"I don't know what you mean."

"Don't you? I mean a child of our own."

Luna stared at him. "You want me to have a baby?"

"Not right now, of course. But I thought that eventually we—"

She stood up, confusion in her features. "You expected to have a child with me."

"I thought we might. Luna, what's the matter? I don't mean right away. I meant after the divorce is final and we're able to—"

"Is that why you wanted to find me?"

"I wanted to find you because I love you. If we have a child together, that will also be because we love each other."

Luna crossed the room. Her back to him, she gripped the sideboard with both hands as if to keep from flying off into oblivion. There was desperation in her voice. "I don't want to be a mother."

"But Luna, why not? You're a loving person. Why wouldn't you want to, someday?"

"The burrs, the nettles, the flies."

"Flies? What are you talking about?"

"The flies," she repeated. "Do you think the baby's sweet breath will blow them away?"

"What?!"

"It's bullshit!"

Stunned, Zach sat immobile for a moment. Then he rose and stepped up behind her. Slowly he raised his hands and touched her waist. She flinched a little, but he slipped his arms around her. "Luna, I'm sorry. I was wrong. I put the cart way before the horse. I'm still married, for God's sake. I had no business talking about this yet." In a lower voice added, "I think I know why you're worried. Percy told me about your mother, Luna."

"What did he tell you?"

"How she died. I'm sorry you had to grow up without her."

"There's nothing wrong with the way I grew up."

"No, there isn't. I think you grew up very well, but still it must have been lonely." He paused. "Listen, let's not drive home yet. It's a beautiful day out. Why spend it in the car? We could do something fun. Do you want to go to Cedar Point?"

"Cedar Point?"

"It's a big amusement park."

"I *know* what it is," she snapped.

"Well, it's only thirty miles from here. They claim to have the most roller coasters in the country. You've never been there, have you? But I bet you know all their names."

She turned around and inspected his face, disorder in her features. "The ... Blue Streak ... is the oldest. It's an out-and-back woody, designed by John Allen in 1964."

Zach smiled, returned to the table and picked up the paper bag he'd retrieved from the car. He slipped the T-shirt out and held it up so she could see the Trylon and Perisphere emblazoned on it. "I got you something to wear."

XVIII

Magnum

CEDAR POINT WAS situated on the southern shore of Lake Erie at the end of a long spit that jutted into Sandusky Bay. Among the scores of rides in the park, there were a dozen roller coasters, and in the course of the day Zach and Luna rode most of them. There were traditional wooden coasters, new steel ones, coasters that did loops and corkscrews, a coaster in which the trains were suspended below the tracks, and a coaster you rode standing up. If Luna was troubled by their morning's conversation, she showed no sign of it once they entered the park. To Zach's relief she began to regale him with facts, figures, and anecdotes about the coasters.

Late in the afternoon they queued up for a giant steel behemoth called the *Magnum XL200*. It was built right on the shore of Lake Erie, the great blue expanse providing a backdrop for the slender red parabolas of track. The *Magnum* was configured like an old-fashioned wooden coaster, though of gargantuan proportions, and it expended nearly all its accumulated energy on the first two precipitous drops. The initial hill was over two hundred feet high, twice as tall as the *Comet* in Lake George. The second hill, only slightly less tall, followed it like the subsequent hump of a colossal sea serpent, and the two towering arches stood starkly against the sky, higher than anything else in sight. When he first glimpsed it, Zach gasped audibly.

Though he wouldn't want to admit it, Zach was rather proud of himself. Not all men of forty-one would blithely go on high-speed thrill rides. As he craned to see the lofty crest of the *Magnum* twenty stories above him, however, he might willingly have forgone this particular thrill.

Luna had explained to Zach the many differences between a steel and a wooden coaster, and one of the most noticeable was the relative quietness. On a wooden coaster the iron wheels of the train roll on a flat iron strip nailed to the board tracks. This clash of metal on metal produces the characteristic noisy rattle so typical of traditional roller coasters. Steel coasters, on the other hand, employ high-impact plastic wheels that glide smoothly on tubular rails, thus producing a soft, whirring sound, almost a buzz, as they slide through the most complicated maneuvers. Even the chain is quieter. There is no ratcheting clatter as the cars mount the lift hill, just a series of low-pitched, solid thunks, like a high-tech cog railway.

The line for the *Magnum* was long, and as they shuffled slowly toward the station, Zach had ample opportunity to observe all these differences. Over and over again he watched the loaded train ascend the first huge hump and slip over the top, the shouts of the riders sounding like the faraway yelps of a thousand hounds in pursuit of a fox. Absorbed as he was in his own thoughts he was startled when he heard Luna ask, "Why do you want a child, Zach?"

He turned to her. There was no panic in her face this time, only curiosity tinged with something else. "Please don't think about that anymore, Luna. I'm really sorry I brought it up."

"But you *do* want a child."

He lifted his shoulders. "I've always wanted to be a father."

"Tell me why."

The simple question itself was not absurd. The absurdity lay in the notion that he could give her a simple answer—and give it *here*, in an amusement park, on a roller coaster line. But then, as he thought more about it, why not here as well as anywhere else? At least she asked him the question, something Beth had never bothered to do. Zach lowered his voice. "I can't pretend that it's important for me to pass on my genes, which are hardly extraordinary, as I'm sure you've noticed. And I'm not religious, and I'm not worried about the human race dying out. I'm not even concerned about having someone to take care of me in my dotage. It's none of those things."

"Then what is it?"

"I guess I want a child because ... I want to take part."

"Take part in what?"

"Life."

Luna watched him a moment longer, her brows knitted in thought, then turned away. After a few minutes, casually, perhaps unconsciously, she slipped her hand under his arm.

The loading platform looked like the terminal of a high-speed monorail transporting commuters to some city of the future. When they reached it, they climbed into the waiting train, and Zach was mildly alarmed to see how few restraints there were. Over the loudspeaker a mechanical voice iterated the now familiar series of warnings. Then the brake was released, and the cars began to move. Cheers accompanied the train as it slid out of the station. At the foot of the lift hill, the unending loop of chain latched onto the cars from below and began to raise them skyward.

No matter how many roller coasters Zach may have ridden, nothing could have prepared him for this ascent. It was the sheer height of the thing that was so terrifying. Two hundred feet up is not so tall when compared to a skyscraper, of course, but one does not commonly ride to the top of a skyscraper on the *outside* of the building—and in an open car.

As the train climbed the impossibly narrow scaffolding, the great blue expanse of Lake Erie filled Zach's field of vision. He caught sight of a sailboat miles away, its mast angled in the wind. The same breeze was stronger up here, and he felt the coaster sway. It would soon be over, he told himself. He knew from experience now. It was only the interminable lift hill that was so fearsome. The ride itself is never quite so bad. Unconsciously he dug his fingernails into the padded safety bar.

When they were a dozen feet from the pinnacle, Zach heard Luna say, almost to herself, "Sometimes it's better to jump out the window first, *then* decide whether you want to fall."

He looked at her.

The last of the cogs lifted free, and the sound of the chain ceased. For a brief instant an eerie quiet reigned, then was shattered by a volley of shrieks. Zach found himself facing the earth two hundred feet down.

His own scream joined in the chorus as the train dropped like lightning, the ground rising toward him even as he plummeted toward it. A living rush choked his lungs, death tickled his gut, and as he shot through the rails at breakneck speed, Zach felt the wicked thrill of escaping fatality one more time. The train's accumulated momentum sent it flying up the next great incline. There was no agonizing wait this time, no languorous chain to tarry for. The cars soared effortlessly up the hill and over the top, then earthward on the other side.

The train veered from the lakeshore at the far point in its career, then raced back in the direction of the station. Over a series of smaller hills, Zach's buttocks rose from the seat involuntarily. The cars tore through a tunnel, and Zach felt the shock of wetness on his face, a mist of tiny droplets sprayed from hidden water jets. When they emerged into the sunlight, the station loomed up ahead. Unseen brakes beneath the tracks grabbed hold of the cars, slowed them, then pulled them to a stop just short of the platform.

Zach heaved a great sigh of relief, then squeezed Luna's hand. "Do you want to ride again?"

She shook her head. "Let's go home."

* * *

ZACH SUGGESTED THEY have a drink before retiring. He turned

down the bed and propped up the pillows while Luna got something from Percy's store. She returned to the bedroom with two glasses and a bottle of single-malt Scotch. After they had undressed and climbed into bed, Zach clinked her glass with his, then took a sip. Immediately his mouth was filled with a rich, smoky flavor.

"Percy has good taste," Zach said, admiring the amber liquid. "He's quite a character. I would love to have had a crazy uncle like that when I was a kid. My relatives were all stuffy and boring."

"Tell me about them."

"Who, my relatives? Well, where shall I begin? My mother is a sixty-something genteel Connecticut lady. She should be gray, but for the last decade she's dyed her hair this appalling shade of brown that is dangerously close to orange. I call it 'forever amber.' She spends her days donating her time to worthy causes. She'll frown—audibly—over the phone when I tell her Beth and I have split up, and she'll try awfully hard to keep from implying that it was my fault. My sister Alice, on the other hand, will have no such reticence. She'll tell me in no uncertain terms that I'm to blame. Alice lives on the northeast coast of Massachusetts and has an irritating laugh that suggests lunacy rather than merriment. I think she got that cackle from living too close to Seabrook."

"What about your father?"

"My father, rest his soul, is dead. He was less genteel. He liked to drink, smoke, and cuss. He died young, fifty-seven. At least it seems young to me now." Zach refilled their glasses. "What about your family? Tell me about Albert."

"He had cancer. He died in the Glens Falls hospital. His last words to me were that I shouldn't let the damn doctors cheat me on the bill."

"So you were left all alone."

"Percy invited me to move out here, but I was old enough to take care of myself." Luna sipped her drink. "What else did Percy tell you about my mother?"

"He said she was quite beautiful, and a good cook, and liked to laugh. You obviously take after her. Well," Zach added with a chuckle, "two out of three anyway. Your father never talked to you about her?"

She shook her head. "I found a shoe once, a high heel. He must have missed it. He threw out everything else, but I found it at the back of the closet. It was shiny red, and the heel was very high. Why do women wear shoes like that? They're no good for anything. You can hardly even walk in them."

"Walking probably isn't the point. Pardon the expression, but in some circles those are known as fuck-me shoes."

She looked at him, puzzled.

Zach leaned back. "You know, we've never done this before, you and I, just sat together and swapped stories of our families. I mean, it's what all couples do after they meet, but we haven't done it—until now."

Luna put down her glass and slid into the bed. Zach drained his own and joined her. Luna's smells were abundant, for she had stood long in the sun. Zach drank them in and felt his passion for her rise again. He pulled her thin body close, felt her ribs, the hollow of her belly. With his mouth he brushed the down of her upper lip. He kissed her nostrils, her eyelids, her hairline. When he reached for the packet of the condoms on the nightstand, Luna seized his wrist.

"Don't put it on, Zach."

"What do you mean?"

"Come into me."

"Luna, I can't. You know what might happen."

"Come into me," she repeated.

"You don't mean that. Please forget what I said earlier. This is the wrong time."

"No, Zach," she said evenly, "this is the time."

He stared at her. His mind affected by the Scotch, he could not keep rein on his imagination, which was already miles away, years away. He saw the phantom child again, the dark-haired infant who looked like Luna and—impossibly—like himself as well, the child who would assure him of his own humanity, the child who would link him to Luna for eternity. Zach stared into her eyes, which were staring up at his. In this strange young woman's slight hips was the promise of immortality, the hope for meaning in a random universe. Her breath beckoned him. Her blood beckoned him.

"Come into me," she said again.

And he did.

XIX

Minerva

THERE WAS A CHANGE—subtle, indistinct. What was it? A minor shift in her demeanor? A slight alteration in her expression? A different light in her eyes? He could look at her now without the unaccountable embarrassment he had felt so often before. And occasionally when he smiled at her—just occasionally—she smiled back.

They had left Ohio the next morning, Luna driving ahead, Zach following behind, their two vehicles attached as if by an invisible, mile-long cord. The small convoy stopped frequently, sometimes for food, sometimes for gas, sometimes just for society during the long hours on the interstate. At the halfway point they had spent the night in a motel, and there made love again. Now as Zach drove along, watching the small black car far ahead of him, he thought about the implications of what he was doing.

He may have had an excuse that night at Percy's. There was the Scotch, after all, and Luna had urged him, but there was no excuse last night. Without a word spoken between them, they had just done it. What did that mean? That Zach ignored the consequences of his actions? Beth observed once that he never did anything without thinking, and it was true—then. Had *he* changed too? He searched himself for doubts, regrets, but couldn't find any. The only thing that alarmed him was a giddy excitement he could not keep down.

They crossed the broad horizontal axis of New York State in a little over six hours, and at Albany turned north without a pause. The drive up to The Glen took another hour and a half, and they accomplished this last leg of the trip without a break. When they exited the highway and turned onto Route 28, Zach rolled down his window so he could smell the fresh air of the Adirondacks again. He followed Luna to the little steel bridge, past Ruth's bungalow, then into the driveway marked by a crooked mail box and a bracket made of pipe.

Before going inside they stood for a moment next to each other gazing up at the old structure. It was so different from his house in Delmar, larger, shabbier—sagging and furrowed like an old face. Yet in some odd way it already felt more like home than anyplace he had ever lived. Zach put his arm around Luna's shoulders.

"It hasn't been painted in years," she said.

"Then we'll paint it."

"We could have a garden this summer. It's too late for peas, but we could plant tomatoes."

"Let's plant them."

"And peppers. We could plant peppers."

"Let's definitely plant peppers."

She flipped on a light switch inside the door, knowing where it was without looking. She opened the window over the sink, propped it up with a stick that lay on the sill for that purpose. She clomped down to the basement to turn on the hot water heater. And Zach watched in fascination, touched for some reason by the not-very-remarkable fact that she knew her way around. Before unpacking they made a quick trip to Warrensburg to buy food. At the supermarket Zach pushed the cart while Luna pulled items from the shelves, and there was something magical in the homely domesticity of the scene. That night, upstairs in what was probably her parents' bedroom, they made love again, and once more the packet of condoms remained unopened.

* * *

THERE WAS MUCH to do in the days and weeks that followed. Zach called Beth to tell her his new address. In an awkward but civil conversation, they arranged a convenient time to get the rest of his things from Delmar. They spoke about how to proceed with the separation and divorce, how to divide the property they held jointly. There was no discord or conflict in these matters. Both leaned over backward to be fair. Neither wanted to appear grasping or mean spirited—and therefore common. Just before she hung up, as if it were an afterthought, Beth asked, "Are you staying with Luna?" Zach replied, "No, I'm living with her."

Luna lost no time in getting a job. She was hired at Oscar's Smoke House, a pork store in Warrensburg, where she worked at the counter slicing ham and packaging meat. Dismayed that she would want to do such menial labor, Zach suggested to her that she go back to school to get a college degree. He assured her that she was smart enough and young enough for a professional career if she wanted one, and he offered to support her while she pursued an education. Luna weighed his suggestion for some time and said she would consider it, but in her customary practical manner, she asked how he could support her when he had no job himself. Zach bowed to her logic. He had already contacted all the schools within driving distance and sent resumes to those that had openings in the fall, but he had little hope of landing a teaching position at such short notice.

During these early weeks Zach and Luna fixed up the house they would be living in. They spent one whole day cleaning the kitchen. After they'd sponged down the cabinets, Zach helped Luna stack her china in them, the dishes with the sentimental images of country life. They hung her roller coaster posters in the living room, his prints of French cathedrals in the hall. And daily they took walks together. Luna enjoyed hiking up to her favorite hilltop. At first Zach thought it was to visit her father's grave, for she regularly swept the leaves from his stone, but otherwise she ignored it and merely sat under the oak and watched the hawks.

They planted the garden too, and one afternoon while they were hoeing the first crop of weeds, they heard a voice call out, "Welcome Wagon!"

From the path that connected their two properties Ruth emerged carrying a six-pack of beer and a large cellophane bag. She kissed Luna on the cheek and handed them to her. "It's supposed to be bread and salt," she observed, "but I thought you'd prefer Ballantine and pretzels."

"Zach's moved in with me," Luna announced.

"I knew that," Ruth assured her. "Not much goes on along this little road that I'm not aware of, but I thought I'd leave you two alone for a while before I came over with the official greeting." She gave Zach a rather formal handshake, tilting her head back and eying him over her nose as if to size him up in his new role. "So the city boy's going to take a stab at country life."

"Not city, Ruth, suburbs—since the cradle."

"Even worse. Listen, you two, I've got a million things to do right now, but come over for dinner tonight. I'm making lasagna." Before turning on her heel and heading back toward the path, she gave Luna a hug and said in her ear, "It's good to have you back, Hon."

When Zach's things arrived from Delmar, he spent several days fixing up his study. He built bookshelves and organized his volumes, happy to have them around again. He bought a floor lamp, set it up next to an easy chair. Then, as if to try the room on for size, he sat for an hour reading. Zach also bought a TV set. Luna's father may have been a television repairman, but not a single one of the many old TVs in his shop worked. After they set it up in the living room and began watching it, Zach realized that Luna seldom saw television, for she knew next to nothing about the current fare. And though she was happy enough to sit by his side, she seemed oblivious to the humor in the sitcoms; nor could she understand why Zach would want to watch nature shows when he had the woods right outside his door.

Some nights they drove to the multiplex in Saratoga. Zach was an avid moviegoer, and on the ride home afterward he enjoyed analyzing what they'd seen. Unused to such discourse, Luna was clearly puzzled by his comments on cinematic technique, but she was quite capable of talking about the story and had surprisingly strong opinions. She seemed to have no sense of moral relativism. While Zach might argue that a corrupt world justified ethical compromise, Luna would entirely disagree, prompting Zach to reevaluate his own beliefs.

And many evenings they did nothing but sip wine at the kitchen table and talk. They caught each other up on what they'd done before they met, a chronicle of facts and anecdotes, important and trivial. During these late night conversations as Luna narrated the story of her life, Zach had the distinct impression that, by the very act of recounting it to him, she was accepting her own history for the very first time.

* * *

IN EARLY AUGUST Zach got a call from Minerva Central School to come in for an interview. There was an opening for a high school English teacher in September. They were forced to reopen their search, he was told, when their first-choice applicant backed out. Feeling some loss of esteem at being a second-string candidate, Zach nevertheless agreed to come.

On the appointed day he put on a business suit for the first time in months, and he felt butterflies in his stomach for the first time in years. The school was twenty miles away, a hop, skip, and a jump by rural standards. The building turned out to be as drab as one could desire, and even smaller than Zach had imagined. As he parked his car in the nearly vacant lot, he considered the irony in the school's name. Minerva was the local community, but it was, of course, also the Roman goddess of wisdom. The humble brick and cement block edifice didn't look much like a temple of wisdom. Zach wondered if he should forget the whole idea.

The main entrance was open, and presently Zach found himself in a deserted foyer. He stopped and sniffed. He would have been hard-pressed to identify the specific source of the odor, but there was no doubt about it: the place smelled like a school, and the scent quickened something in him. He looked down the darkened hallway, pierced at regular intervals by daylight shining through the classroom doors. He looked at the endless rows of lockers. The halls were empty now and quiet, but he could see them filled with students rushing from one class to another, opening their combination locks, banging the metal doors, laughing, calling to each other at the top of their lungs.

Against the wall there was a trophy case filled with framed photographs of sports teams: goofy kid faces, baggy uniforms, an arm cradling a tennis racket, a foot resting on a soccer ball. There were trophies, miniature golden athletes perched upon gaudy marble pedestals. Zach felt an odd tingle, the same kind of thrill he'd felt on the first day of his first teaching job nearly twenty years ago. Suddenly the drabness of the school faded. He glanced at his watch and strode toward the principal's office.

Five administrators and senior faculty members interrogated Zach over the next two hours. They asked why he wanted to return to teaching after such a long absence. They expressed dismay at the severe cut in salary he would sustain. Having anticipated this line of inquiry, Zach affirmed that his work for the Education Department had been rewarding, but he'd been restless in Albany, so far removed from the classroom. He described the electricity in the air when new ideas took hold of a young person's imagination. He told them about introducing *Macbeth* to a class of tenth graders, seeing them repelled at first by the unfamiliar language, then slowly enthralled by the story, caught up in the horror.

There was passion in Zach's voice; nor was he insincere. Yet it was also true that this was what Zach did best. During his years in the highly political state bureaucracy, he had honed his skills at answering difficult questions, turning a handicap into an advantage, getting people to come around. Never did his verbal dexterity stand him in better stead. The principal, the vice-principal, the senior teachers who sat around the broad table listened intently to his answers, nodded as he spoke. Two days later Zach received a not-entirely-unexpected phone call from Minerva Central School. They were pleased to inform him that he was being offered the position. That night Zach and Luna shared a bottle of the best champagne that could be found in Warrensburg.

During the remainder of August, when he was not working with Luna in the garden, or strolling the country roads with her, Zach drafted lesson plans, formulated assignments, read textbooks. He even studied grammar, relearned the parts of speech. Luna was pleased that Zach was going to teach again, but she was also distracted. In those last weeks of summer, as the days began to shorten imperceptibly, she had skipped her menstrual cycle for the second month in succession.

XX

Ancient Notes

Luna had no regular physician, and she accepted Zach's offer to make an appointment with his general practitioner in Albany. They could have bought an over-the-counter pregnancy test at any pharmacy, of course, but Zach urged her to see a doctor. By her own admission, Luna had not seen one in years.

They drove down to Albany together, and when she emerged from the examining room, Zach could tell nothing from her somber expression. It was only after they were outside again and walking toward the car that Luna said simply, "March."

Zach stopped and peered into her eyes. "March?"

"The baby's due in March."

Slowly, involuntarily, a great, crooked smile crinkled his face. Paradoxically he was also very close to tears. He clutched her to him. Over her shoulder he asked, "How do you feel?"

"All right."

He pulled back and searched her face again. He saw something else in her solemn features. "No, Luna, how do you *really* feel?"

"Scared."

"It's going to be all right. It *is*, Luna." He hugged her again. "March will be here in no time. Next week is September." He smiled.

"Do you think it's a girl?"

"I don't know. He said we can find out later on if we want to. He gave me the name of an obstetrician in Glens Falls."

"We should celebrate, go somewhere for a drink."

"I can't drink."

Zach pulled back again, looked confused. Almost immediately, he smacked his temple with the palm of his hand. "I'm sorry. I forgot. We'll toast with something else, fruit juice or something. Would you like to go somewhere for lunch?"

She was silent for a moment. "Could we go to Lake George?"

"Lake George? Why?"

"I'd like to ride the *Comet* again."

Zach was horrified. "You can't!"

"Don't be silly. It won't hurt anything this early."

He was dubious, but he could see how much it meant to her. On the way to the car he chuckled.

"What's funny?" Luna asked.

"Who's going to tell the little one?"

"Tell the little one what?"

"That the first thing we did when we found out she was in there was to take her on a roller coaster."

* * *

IT WAS ONE of the last golden days of August, still warm but with a hint of briskness in the air. At the Great Escape they rode the *Comet* three times in rapid succession. Then Zach prevailed upon Luna to eat something. She'd had no lunch, and she needed to keep up her strength. She was eating for two now, he reminded her, repeating the old cliché, though he knew well enough that Luna *always* ate like she was eating for two.

They got a pizza at an outdoor patio across from a diminutive train station. Swan boats passed along the channel by their table. Zach ate very little, leaving most of it for Luna. As he sat in the sunshine watching her, he could hardly believe that this odd young woman with tomato sauce on her chin was going to be the mother of his child. He had met her barely three months before, and in many ways she was still a stranger to him.

"How are you doing?" he asked.

"Fine."

"Not getting too tired?"

"Of course not."

In a quieter, more serious tone Zach asked, "Do you have any doubts about this? Having the baby, I mean."

A floppy slice of pizza was balanced precariously on her fingers. Now she lowered it to the paper plate. "Do you have doubts?"

"No, no," Zach assured her. "But I'm not the only one concerned here. I need to know how *you* feel."

She looked puzzled.

"We could wait," he explained. "We could wait a year or two until my divorce is final. We'd be able to get married then, if you wanted to. That might be a better time to have a child."

"But I'm already pregnant."

"Yes, I know, but you're only two months along. If you don't feel ready, it's not too late to change your mind."

"What do you mean?"

"Well, we could get an abortion."

Luna's eyes opened wide. "An abortion?!"

"I'm not suggesting it. I'm just telling you that if you think this is too soon, you have the choice."

Flatly she echoed, "I have the choice."

"Yes." Zach searched her features. "I hope I didn't offend you. I guess I never asked you how you felt about abortion. It's one of the many things we've never even talked about. If you're fundamentally opposed to it, I mean on moral grounds, I can certainly respect that. I think there are good arguments on both sides."

She gazed at him, her expression more bafflement than anger. Slowly, steadily she said, "You've always wanted to be a father, Zach. Today we found out that we're expecting our child in March. We came here to celebrate. Please tell me why you would say now that

I have the 'choice' to destroy it?"

Zach felt like he'd been punched in the gut. He lowered his eyes, feeling such disgust with himself that he wanted to flee from her sight. After several minutes, barely audible, he whispered, "Please forgive me, Luna. You can't know how sorry I am to have said such a thing. I'm ashamed of myself. I have no excuse except my own stupidity. All I can say is that I was wrong. I do want the child with you, more than I've ever wanted anything. My God, Luna, it's the one thing on earth I'm sure of."

He felt her hand brushing the hair from his forehead. When he looked up into her dark eyes again, he saw someone else. She was no longer just his lover. Foreign though she might still appear to him, she was a blood ally now, and they were confederates in a venture that involved mortality and eternity.

"Come on, Zach," she said, "let's go ride the *Comet* one more time."

* * *

THE NEXT DAY Luna called the obstetrician, a Dr. Gundy, and made an appointment for later on in the week. She also drove to the library in Warrensburg and returned with an armload of books on pregnancy, childbirth, prenatal and postnatal care. Several of them open on the kitchen table, she poured over the volumes with Zach that afternoon, comparing the information, examining the charts and diagrams, studying the line drawings of a baby's development in the womb. Considering Luna's former aversion to motherhood, Zach was amazed at her diligence now and the assiduous care she took to learn what was best for her child.

On Thursday they drove together to Glens Falls for her appointment. Dr. Gundy was a well-favored man in his mid-thirties. Dressed in clean blue jeans and a red plaid shirt, open at the neck, he introduced himself as "Tom." Obviously a father himself, he had framed snapshots of children on his desk and children's artwork hung on his examining room wall. Though Zach was initially put off by his casual manner, he was impressed by Gundy's competence, and he eventually concluded that Luna was in good hands.

With all the excitement, Zach had barely thought about his new job. The first day of school came the following Tuesday, and with it a drenching rain. Having spent the entire summer with Luna, Zach was reluctant to leave her that morning. He gave her the phone number of Minerva Central and kissed her at the door before making a dash for his car. In the faculty lounge amidst complaints about the weather, Zach's fellow teachers welcomed him to the school, and at 8:30 Zach stood alone before his first class, thirty pairs of eyes sizing up the new teacher. Despite his self-assured eloquence at the interview, Zach was nervous. His voice quavered and he stumbled badly over the students' names. He tried to remember the advice a professor had once given him: Speak slowly. Allow silence after a question. Always say something good about a response, even if it's wrong. And for God's sake don't pace.

After teaching four classes that day, Zach was more exhausted than he'd felt in all his years at the Education Department. The irony was that he also felt good. Animatedly he told Luna stories over dinner. There was the fat, freckled kid in second period who announced that Edgar Rice Burroughs was the greatest writer who ever lived. There was the misunderstanding in third period when he'd asked, "What are a man's basic needs?" and a curly-haired girl at the back of the room responded, "He's got to be tall." There were his colleagues: Mr. Van Cleve, the elderly science teacher whose ancient teaching notes looked like they'd been typed in 1962; Mr. Goss, the gym teacher, who drove an old red Cadillac with a license plate that read "CATCH UP"; Miss Montano, the French teacher with the bleached blond hair and Long Island accent.

Zach apologized to Luna for going on at such length. He asked her about her own day, and she reported mildly that she'd thrown up that morning. It came upon her unexpectedly when she was getting ready for work, and she couldn't reach the bathroom in time. She'd cleaned up the mess, though, she said. For no reason he could fathom, Zach took her in his arms.

Over that fall while Zach taught at Minerva, Luna divided her time between her job at the pork store and several projects at home. She put the garden to bed and preserved the last of the vegetables. She sorted through her father's things, a job she had postponed after he died. She boxed up his radio equipment and cleaned out his old shop. To Zach's alarm one day, he came home to find a pile of dusty picture tubes and bulky television cabinets that Luna had carried out for the trash by herself. Luna also began fixing up the little second-story room that would be the nursery.

All during the fall Zach watched Luna's body change. Her breasts swelled, and her belly grew, imperceptibly at first, but then inexorably. Zach found something hopelessly endearing about this transformation. He needed to touch Luna often, to lay his hand on her when they sat together. As she began to outgrow her clothes, he offered to drive her to Saratoga so they could buy maternity wear, but Luna would not hear of it. Instead, she started wearing hand-me-downs of her father's that made her look rather like a character out of Dickens.

In November Dr. Gundy determined that Luna was indeed carrying a girl, and he also confirmed that the child was healthy and that everything was proceeding normally. Gundy predicted that the baby would arrive around the thirtieth of March, "give or take a month," he joked, since first births are notoriously unpredictable.

On Thanksgiving Zach had much to be thankful for. He and Luna cooked a large turkey in the old gas oven, and asked Ruth over to share it with them. That night when they went to bed, Zach fell asleep against Luna's back, his arms around her, his hands protectively on her belly where he could feel his daughter every time she moved.

XXI

Lost in the Wood

"GREAT VIEW," BOB said, looking around as he shook hands with Zach in the driveway. He'd stopped by to visit on his way back from a school inspection in Plattsburgh. "Cold though," he added, shivering in the January chill.

"Come on in."

Zach ushered him to the living room and watched as his friend took in the dilapidated furniture, the bare wood floor, the roller coaster pictures on the wall. "Nice place," Bob commented. "Looks ... comfortable."

"Don't overdo it. You want a beer?"

When Zach returned from the kitchen, Bob was examining a stack of student compositions on the coffee table. "You have to correct all these?"

Zach nodded, handed him a bottle.

"Boy am I glad I don't have to do this anymore. I used to hate it when I'd have a bunch of papers like that. They would just sit there and glower at me for weeks until I finished them." Bob lifted the top sheet and read: " 'Henry the Eighth was King of England from 1491 to 1547. He is known for holding fantastic banquets where he'd stuff himself.' You teaching history now, Zach?"

"It's a book report."

"I think the kid saw the movie. Remember Charles Lawton throwing the chicken leg over his shoulder?" Bob dropped the paper back on the pile. "Tell me the truth, though, Zach. Don't you ever miss the good old days at the Ed. Department—the politics, the jealousy, the backbiting? They're implementing your changes now, you know. The whole damn place is in an uproar. You're like the guy who starts a fight in a bar and then leaves. Hugo is hopping around the building from one unit to another all day long. Now that he doesn't have you to salve people's egos anymore, he has to do all the schmoozing himself. Lots of units are moving. *Mine* is moving."

"Is it?"

"Next week. Everything: desks, filing cabinets, rubber tree plants, Dilbert cartoons. How much do you think it's going to cost?"

"No idea."

"The move for my unit alone is gonna set them back twenty-two grand."

"Where are you moving to?"

"Three doors down the hall." Bob took a long draft of his beer. "So how is it to be teaching again?"

"The first semester I wanted to quit. It's a little better now. The kids seem to like me, and the faculty, if you can believe it, actually treat me with deference."

"Well, you're the emissary from the tabernacle. Maybe you'll get to be principal someday."

"All I want to do is teach."

At that moment Bob looked up as Luna entered the room. She wore baggy corduroy trousers and an oversized flannel shirt, its sleeves rolled up and collar frayed. Her clothes were spattered with light green paint, as were her forearms and her face. She was seven-months pregnant now, and if the roominess of her outfit had been able to hide her condition, her awkward pigeon gait would have given it away. Zach could detect the mild shock on his friend's features, even though covered by a smile. Bob stood up, and Zach introduced them.

"It's nice to meet you," Luna said, extending her hand. "I'm sorry I didn't come down sooner. I was painting the nursery." She glanced at her belly. "I'm pregnant."

Bob also glanced downward as if noticing her situation for the first time. "Well ... congratulations!"

"Zach said you worked together."

"We did. Well, Zach worked," Bob clarified. "I read the newspaper and did crossword puzzles. I didn't want to risk doing something that might waste the taxpayers' money."

If Luna recognized that Bob had made a joke, she showed no sign of it. She sat down and talked with him for a while, trying in her own way to be a good hostess. As Zach looked on, he could surmise what Bob was thinking. Why would Zach abandon a good wife and a prestigious job for this pitiful ragamuffin?

"Can you stay for dinner?" Luna asked.

"Oh, I don't want to put you to any trouble."

"Please stay," she urged, and left the two friends to talk while she repaired to the kitchen.

"Nice girl," Bob said after an awkward silence.

"Don't lie. You think I'm crazy, don't you?"

"Of course not."

"Then you think *she's* crazy."

With less conviction Bob protested, "She's not ... is she?"

Zach snorted. "To tell you the God's honest truth, I don't know. And you want to hear the strangest part? I don't even care."

"When is the baby due?" Bob asked.

"March."

"Are you going to assist?"

"Well, I'm going to be there. I don't know how much assistance I'll be. Luna wants natural childbirth. She read that drugs can harm the baby, so she told the doctor she didn't want any."

"That's what Judy said the first time too, but once she started labor, she changed her mind real fast. Do you go to classes?"

"Every Wednesday night."

"Yeah, we did too, at the YMCA. Thirty pregnant women on rubber mats and their husbands crouching over them with stop-watches." He paused, sipped his beer. "Does Beth know?"

Zach looked at him. "What business is it of Beth's?"

Bob merely shrugged his shoulders and looked uncomfortable.

"You don't approve of any of this, do you?" Zach concluded.

"It doesn't matter what I approve or disapprove of."

"But still, you don't approve."

Bob frowned pensively. "I miss seeing you guys, you and Beth, I mean. That part is true. We had a lot of fun together over the years. Listen, Zach, I'm not a brain like you are, but there's one thing I've learned."

"Tell me."

"You can never know from the outside what's between two people. Beth was a smart, cultured lady, and I liked her, but I didn't live with her like you did. I don't know what your marriage was like. I *can't* know. It might have been warmed-over hell, so I'm not going to be the one who tells you that you should have stayed with her. This girl Luna is different. Yeah, she looks a little funny, talks a little funny. Maybe she does seem a little crazy to me, but none of that matters. The only important thing is what she means to you."

Zach looked toward the door. Quietly he said, "She means everything."

* * *

THE SECOND WEEKEND in March turned out to be a surprise preview of spring. Though there was still a thick snow cover in the woods, the temperature rose into the fifties on Saturday, and then into the low sixties on Sunday. The soft air together with a brilliant blue sky coaxed Luna outdoors, and she prevailed upon Zach to take a walk with her. They chatted for a while as they strolled the dirt road arm-in-arm, then fell silent, enjoying the warm sun and mild breezes. After several minutes and apropos of nothing, Luna said, "I went to Cape Cod once."

"And you told me you'd never been anywhere!"

"I was twelve years old."

"Albert took you?"

"He thought I should see the ocean. On the way back home we went to an amusement park near New Bedford, Lincoln Park. I'd never been to an amusement park before. It was the middle of summer, and it was filled with people. There were colorful buildings and dozens of rides: a carousel, a whip, little jet planes, a fun house, a giant sliding board. And there was food I'd never seen before: candy apples, fried dough, funnel cakes, corn dogs, cotton candy."

"A culinary paradise," Zach observed.

"There was a roller coaster," she continued. "It was an old wooden coaster, only sixty feet tall, but it seemed huge to me. It was gleaming white. I couldn't keep my eyes off it. I remember looking up into the maze of wood and thinking how easy it would be to get lost in it."

"Did Albert let you ride?"

"He didn't want to. He was afraid of roller coasters, but he let me."

"And you rode it all by yourself?"

She nodded. "The coaster had been baking in the sun. It smelled of warm wood and grease. The train rocked from side to side as it went up the lift hill, and the chain made a noise that would wake the dead. At the top of the hill I could see far away, even outside the park. There were trees and houses and people in their backyards. It was as if I were invisible, spying on them."

"You had a lot of time to look around when you were at the top. Weren't you scared, even a little?"

"I wet my pants."

Zach laughed.

"I couldn't believe the bugger could go that fast. It was only a rickety train on old wooden tracks, but it raced down the hills. I thought I was going to fly out on the turns. It terrified me, but on the way home I couldn't get it out of my mind. I kept thinking of that maze of white wood, the smell, the sound. When I found out that there were coasters all over the country, I wanted to travel around someday and ride every one of them." She paused. "When I met you, I thought we could do it together."

There was a note of despair in her voice. "Luna, we can still do it," Zach assured her. "Once the baby's old enough. We'll take her with us. I get the summers off. We'll do it."

Luna seemed to be breathing a little heavier now.

"Are you tired?" Zach asked. "Do you want to go back?"

They turned around, Zach taking her other arm. "I have an idea," he said. "This summer why don't *we* make a trip to the Cape? It's not that far away. We'll bundle up the baby and do a weekend, maybe even a week. It would do us good to get away for a while. And we can make a side trip to Lincoln Park so you can ride that roller coaster again. How does that sound?"

"It's closed," she said mildly. "The park went out of business a long time ago."

"Oh."

"I drove out there once, after it closed," she added. "They'd torn down everything but the coaster. The white paint was peeling off, and weeds were growing up through it."

"It must have been sad to see it like that, with no one riding it anymore."

"Oh, they were still riding it."

Zach looked at her. "What do you mean? Who was riding it?"

Idly she caressed her belly. "Ghosts."

XXII

Crowning

CHILLY AIR RETURNED to the Adirondacks Monday morning, and there were even predictions of snow for the afternoon. Zach reluctantly pulled on his boots and donned his heavy overcoat, then said good-bye to Luna.

"How are you feeling?" he asked.

"Fine."

"Well, listen, you've got the day off today, so take it easy. Put your feet up and watch TV or something. No cleaning out the attic, okay?"

"Okay."

They kissed at the door.

In Zach's first class he drew a sketch of the Globe Theater on the board. The students giggled when he told them that boys their own age played the female roles in Shakespeare's plays. They groaned when he assigned the first act of *Julius Caesar*. In Zach's second class he explained that the two parts of a compound sentence can be separated either by a comma and conjunction or by a semicolon. He warned them not to employ the semicolon, though, unless they were absolutely sure about its use. His third class was reading *Huckleberry Finn*, and Zach asked them what Huck thought of slavery. A young man sitting near the window asserted that Huck disapproved of it, and Zach was just forming a response when the door opened. A gray-haired, bespectacled lady, the school secretary, stuck her head inside.

"Excuse me, Mr. Tonner. Can I see you a moment?"

Zach put his chalk down and slipped out into the hallway. "What is it?"

"I'm sorry to interrupt your class, but there was a phone call for you from a Ruth Frankel."

"That's my neighbor. What did she want?"

"She was calling from the Glens Falls Hospital. She said she's there with Luna."

"Luna? What happened to her? Is she all right?"

"Oh, yes. She's fine," the secretary assured him, smiling. "It's just that she's gone into labor."

"*Into labor?!* She wasn't due for another two weeks!"

"Mrs. Frankel said not to worry. The doctor is on his way."

"I'm going to have to get down there. I'm supposed to *be* there." Zach looked at his classroom, confusion on his features.

"Go ahead," she said, patting his arm. "We'll get someone to mind your class. Go ahead, Mr. Tonner."

* * *

TWO WEEKS AHEAD of time! Zach shook his head as he sped down the road. What if he were late? What if Luna had the baby before he even got there? Zach pressed down on the accelerator.

The drive to Glens Falls ordinarily took a little over an hour, but Zach made the trip in forty minutes. Luckily the snow held off until just before he pulled into the hospital parking lot. Zach hurried through the main entrance and took the elevator to maternity, a special ward on the second floor called "the Snuggery." He bounded into the waiting room and found Ruth calmly reading a magazine.

She looked up. "Nice of you to drop by."

"Has she had the baby yet?"

"Listen to him! I wish it happened that easily."

"Where is she?"

Ruth got up now and very deliberately put her hands on his shoulders. "Calm down, my boy. Everything's under control."

"Why didn't she call me?"

"I don't think she knew it was for real. Luckily, I stopped in at your place this morning."

At that moment Dr. Gundy and a nurse entered the room. "How are you, Zach?" Gundy greeted him. "This is Jenny. She'll be assisting today."

"Hello," Zach said absently.

"How was traffic on the Northway?"

"I ... uh ... it was okay."

"Not snowing yet?"

"No. Yes. I mean, a little." Zach looked intently at Gundy. "How *is* she?"

"Luna? Oh, she's fine. Just a little ahead of schedule; that's all. She's apparently been in labor for about five hours."

"Five hours?"

"Yes. Did she mention any pains to you this morning?"

"No."

"Well, it looks like you've got a very impatient baby. I was just coming out one last time to see if you'd arrived. Are you ready to suit up?"

"Yes."

"Good! If you'll just go along with Jenny." Gundy turned to Ruth. "Were you coming in too, Mrs. Frankel?"

Ruth shook her head. "Being present at my own was quite enough, thank you. I'll be waiting right here." With that she resumed her seat and picked up the magazine.

The delivery room was done in homey wallpaper and comfortable furniture, more like a suburban bedroom than an operating theater. There were several people present, all in surgical garb as Zach was, and in the center of the room was an adjustable bed.

Upon it lay someone who looked at once familiar and unfamiliar.

Her face pale, bathed in sweat, her dark brown eyes focussed on the ceiling, Luna seemed dwarfed by the great protuberance at her midsection. Her belly was partly obscured by a hospital blanket carelessly thrown over it. Her knees were bent, her legs spread apart. Seeing her splayed like that, Zach felt a wave of compassion for her, that she should be so exposed in front of strangers.

Gundy beckoned Zach over to the bed. "Luna," he said, "look who finally showed up."

Luna turned her head and gazed at Zach, a distant recognition in her eyes.

"You can touch her," Gundy prompted. "She's not contagious."

Luna's hand was damp and cold. "How are you doing?" Zach asked softly.

She appeared distracted. Gripped suddenly by pain, her face grimaced, and she squeezed Zach's hand hard.

Gundy said something to the nurse, and both bent over and peered between Luna's legs. "That's good; that's very good," he said to Luna. "I was telling Zach outside that you have a very impatient little girl there." With his heel, Gundy pushed a low stool into position, then sat down. "Come over here and take a look, Zach."

Zach moved to the foot of the bed. Over the doctor's shoulder he could now see the hairy, bloody grotto that was the focus of their attention. He suddenly felt nauseous.

"There's the head. Can you see it?" Gundy pointed. "Just the tippity top, see?"

Inside the ring of hair was something else, hairy also and matted with blood.

"I hope you like brunettes, Zach, because it looks like—"

He was interrupted by a cry so forlorn, so desolate, it might have come from a soul in hell. Zach's eyes darted to Luna's face. Her features were contorted, her mouth agape.

"You're doing fine, Luna," Gundy soothed. "We'll have your little girl out before you know it. We can see the top of her head already. Zach can see it, can't you, Zach?"

Zach looked again, nodded.

"Let her know that you can see it," Gundy urged. "Tell her."

"I can ... see it."

"Now let's bear down, Luna," Gundy said. "Try to push, gently but firmly."

Zach watched the muscles of her upper body tense, saw her dig her elbows into the cushions. Then she howled again.

"That's all right," Gundy reassured her. "That's good. Let the pain out. Just let it go. Now keep breathing. Go ahead and push again."

Contracting her muscles once more, she wailed piteously.

Zach leaned over to Gundy. "Can't you give her something for the pain?"

"I know this is hard to watch sometimes," Gundy said softly, "but it *is* normal. Unless it gets really bad, I'd like to honor her wishes and avoid analgesics." To Luna he said, "You're doing very well. We're making good progress here."

But Zach could see no progress. The baby's head had not moved. "Bear down a little more," Gundy coaxed. "Push just a bit more this time, gently but firmly." A nurse wiped the perspiration from Luna's forehead, and the excruciating process continued. Gundy urged her more insistently. "We just need you to push a little harder, Luna. Your little girl needs some help from you. Now try to concentrate. Breathe steadily and give us a nice, good push."

Gasping for air, Luna tensed again. Then she screamed, a long, ear-splitting screech that rent Zach's heart.

"It's crowning," Gundy said with some relief.

The top of the baby's head seemed to be crowned by the circle of Luna's own tortured skin.

"Excellent! Let's do that again," Gundy urged. "Firmly, very firmly, push!"

Luna let out another horrid shriek.

It was ludicrous, Zach thought, that anything so large could issue from so small, so delicate a portal. Seeing her bloody ring of hair, the fiery locus of that unspeakable pain, Zach lost his desire for children. He lost his desire to be a father. All he wanted now was for Luna to be freed from her torment. Then he heard her scream, *"I hate you!"*

Zach straightened up. Luna was staring at him, her face twisted with rage. *"I hate you!"* she cried, spittle on her lips.

Zach tried to speak. "I ... I—"

She roared, stretching the words almost beyond recognition, *"I ... hate ... you!"*

Gundy stood up and spoke quietly to Zach. "Don't take this to heart. You have to understand, she doesn't know what she's saying. She'll forget all about it afterward."

Luna thrashed, locked her eyes on Zach again. Through clenched teeth she hissed, *"You did this to me, you fucking prick!"*

Appalled, Zach staggered backward.

"It will be all right," Gundy soothed. "Trust me. I've seen it before. It's just the pain."

Over the doctor's shoulder Zach could see Luna's head whipping from side to side, a nurse trying to steady her from behind. Another nurse held onto her hand. "Just the pain?" Zach repeated. He turned on Gundy. "*Just the pain?* If it's the pain, damn it, give her something for it! Can't you see she's in agony?"

As if to underscore what Zach had said, Luna screeched again, shattering the air in the room. Gundy bit his lip. Without turning around he said, "Fifty milligrams of Demerol, Jenny."

"Yes, Doctor."

Gundy returned to his stool. When Luna caught sight of Zach approaching her, she shouted, *"Get away from me! Don't come near me! Don't touch me!"*

"Luna, you don't mean that," Zach said. He reached out his hand.

"*NOOOOO!*" she yowled, flailing so violently that the nurses could barely restrain her.

Gundy said, "Zach, it would be better if you waited outside. She's very agitated."

"But I can't leave her!"

"The most important thing right now is Luna's safety and the safety of the child. We need to deliver that baby, and I don't think Luna can do it while you're here."

Zach gazed at her, writhing upon the bed. "All right."

As Zach left the room he heard Gundy say, "Fifty more milligrams, Jenny."

* * *

Slowly Zach removed the gown, mechanically draped it over a chair. He returned to the waiting room where Ruth was still reading a magazine.

"Is it over?" Ruth asked, arching an eye.

"Not yet."

"You look like you've seen a ghost. What's the matter? Blood get to you?"

"No ... no. Luna was a little upset, so they thought it might be better if I waited out here."

"Just as well. They didn't do this sort of thing when I had mine. They stashed the father away where he couldn't do any harm. Better that way, if you ask me. I don't know why anyone would willingly want to see such a bloody mess to begin with. I sure didn't want Walter to see me in that state. It was bad enough he had to see me when I woke up in the morning."

Zach tried to smile but couldn't. He sat down next to her.

"Something wrong?" Ruth asked.

"She ... got angry at me in there."

Ruth waved her hand dismissively. "Don't hold it against her. During my labor, I got so pissed at the doctor that I called him a horse's ass. He actually *was* a horse's ass, but I wouldn't have said that to his face if I didn't feel like I had a watermelon stuck in my pelvis."

Zach looked at the floor.

"Here," Ruth said, handing him a magazine. "Take your mind off it. Read about who's sleeping with whom in Hollywood."

Zach glanced at the stylishly dressed people on the cover, not really recognizing them. He opened the magazine and began leafing through, reading nothing, seeing nothing. Twenty minutes later it lay on his lap open to an automobile ad. He was staring blankly at it when he heard someone enter the waiting room. It was the head nurse, a fortyish woman Zach had met on an earlier visit to maternity. He stood up, the magazine dropping to the floor.

"Zach," she said evenly, "there's been a complication in the delivery—a serious complication."

"What happened?"

"Luna experienced some difficulty in breathing, accompanied by an accelerated pulse rate. While the doctor was trying to determine the cause, she went into cardiac arrest."

"What?!"

"The resuscitation team is with her now. They're trying to revive her."

"Is she going to be all right?"

The nurse hesitated. "We don't know yet. They're doing everything they can." She paused. "I'm going to stay in close contact with them, and I'll tell you as soon as I know something."

She left the waiting room. Zach turned to Ruth who was standing by his side.

"It's a good hospital," Ruth assured him. "They'll know what to do."

Zach went to the door, peered out helplessly toward the nursing station, his mind a chaos. He turned and started pacing, needing to move. Ten minutes passed, then ten minutes more. Intermittently Zach returned to the door and looked out. Meanwhile a deep silence settled onto the hospital ward. The normal institutional sounds, carts clattering down the hall, sneakers padding around the corridors, distant voices, all ceased. Finally, almost noiselessly, another figure appeared in the waiting room. Zach spun around.

Beads of perspiration dotted Gundy's forehead. He was still wearing his blood-spattered gown, his mask still dangled from his neck. Clearly shaken, he stood for a moment looking at Zach. "I'm sorry," he said. "We lost her."

Zach felt Ruth grasp hold of his arm.

"We were able to save the baby, but not Luna."

"What do you mean?"

"She died during the delivery, Zach. I'm very sorry."

Zach stared at him. "She wasn't sick. She didn't come here because she was sick." Unconsciously Zach's hand strayed to his eyes, and he backed away. Ruth helped him to a chair.

Gundy sat by his side. "We tried everything we could to save her. The procedure is always to save the mother first. That's usually the best way to protect the baby as well. But there was nothing we could do."

"I can't believe it."

Gundy gazed down at the carpet and shook his head. "I can't believe it myself. I've never lost a patient before. You don't expect to lose patients in maternity. It's one of the reasons I went into obstetrics. I've got three nurses back there crying their eyes out, and I feel like joining them."

Zach turned to him. "Did she ... bleed to death?"

Gundy looked puzzled. "No. What gave you that idea? She wasn't hemorrhaging. She had complete cardiopulmonary failure."

"But why? It couldn't have been a heart attack, not at her age."

"We won't know for a while, but the symptoms indicate an embolism."

"An embolism?"

"A blockage, probably a blood clot. If it gets lodged in the pulmonary artery, it can be fatal. An embolism is rare in someone as young as Luna, but it does happen, and for reasons we don't fully understand, pregnancy increases the risk."

"You mean this happened because she was pregnant?"

"No, it's just that the risk factor goes up. All pregnant women have a higher incidence of embolism, but the danger is still very slight, only about one in fifty thousand."

"One in fifty thousand," Zach repeated. He got up from the

chair and walked to the other side of the room. "I had breakfast with her this morning," he said softly. "We sat in the kitchen together eating cereal. She put too much sugar on hers, like she always does ... did." Zach closed his eyes. "Oh my God. The last thing she said was that she hated me."

Gundy was at his side. "Don't think of that, Zach. She didn't mean it."

"I should never have put her through this."

"You couldn't have known. She was at the ideal age to have a baby."

"You don't understand. She never wanted to have a child. She only did this for me."

Gundy put his hand on Zach's shoulder. "If she decided to have a baby because she loved you, that was the best reason in the world. I saw her many times over the last six months, and I can tell you without hesitation that she wanted the child very much."

"She did," Ruth agreed, squeezing Zach's arm. "She might have been worried, but she really did want the baby."

"And now she doesn't have it." Zach breathed deeply. "*I* have it. I have the child I always wanted, but I don't have Luna."

XXIII

Nor'easter

WHAT HAPPENED AFTERWARD remained a blur in Zach's memory. There was paperwork to do, absurd paperwork before he was permitted to leave the hospital. The baby would stay overnight for observation, but he was led up to the nursery to see her before he left. An attendant with a melancholy smile lifted the child out of the crib and placed her in Zach's arms. Seven pounds, four ounces, Zach was told. The infant had a small, red, wrinkled face, and a full head of dark hair. Zach gazed down at the child, not knowing what he was supposed to feel, not feeling much of anything. After a few moments he wordlessly handed her back.

Before Zach left the hospital, Gundy stopped in to see him one more time, and again the doctor expressed his sorrow. He told Zach not to hesitate to call him if he needed anything. Ruth offered to drive Zach back to The Glen, but Zach refused, telling her he preferred to be alone for a while. She promised to visit him that evening.

The snow was falling steadily now. Zach negotiated the familiar roads, barely able to keep his mind on what he was doing, or even to remember where he was going and why. He stared blankly in front of him, thinking of her. Beginning, middle, and end were now known. Her time had amounted to a piddling twenty-five years, a brief interval at the end of the twentieth century. She should have spent most of her life in the new millennium, and instead she didn't even live to see it. The news she'd heard on the radio this morning, important, trivial, had been processed by her brain. The news tomorrow morning, whether a flood in the mid-west, a war in Asia, or the extinguishment of the sun, would not be processed. It would fall in that infinite void of time that would come after her. Who in the wide universe was going to remember that slight, odd-looking, insignificant person who liked roller coasters?

When Zach pulled into his driveway, he stopped for a moment and gazed at Luna's car. Snow was accumulating on its roof. He walked over and looked in at the driver's side. There were cracks in the vinyl upholstery, and the floor mat had holes worn through. Where had Luna gotten this piece of junk, he wondered. There were so many things Zach had never asked her, never thought to inquire about. He always figured there would be time later on, and now, without warning, he'd run out of time.

* * *

RUTH SEEMED TO know instinctively what to do. When she arrived that evening, she took a look at the nursery to see that it was ready to accommodate an infant. She satisfied herself that the crib was sturdy, the bedding sufficient, the heating adequate. She looked in the cupboards and closets to see what baby supplies were already there. She told Zach she would go with him to the hospital tomorrow, and on the way they would buy some more necessities. Ruth made Zach a late dinner, which she insisted he eat, and afterward Zach pulled out a bottle of whiskey and poured for both of them. He drank his first glass down immediately, and promptly refilled it.

"You've got a perfect right to drink tonight," Ruth said after a moment, "and frankly I don't mind joining you, but we've got to talk about some things beforehand."

"All right."

"They'll ask you tomorrow about the disposition of the body. Did she ever say how she'd like to be buried or where?"

"No."

"You'll have to decide, and what kind of a funeral you'd like."

"I know. I will."

"And people will have to be notified, like Percy. Do you have his phone number?"

"Yes."

"And her boss. Who else can you think of?"

Zach pondered the question. "Charley Rood, the owner of the Great Escape. He knew her."

"All right. And who else?"

He thought for a moment, then shook his head. "There is no one else."

"What about friends and family?" Ruth pressed.

"She had no other friends or family."

"No, Zach, I mean *your* friends and family."

He looked at her. "Mine?"

"People who care about you will want to know."

"Of course," he said, closing his eyes. "I'm sorry. I'm not thinking very clearly."

"I'll help you make the calls if you'd like."

"No, I'll do it. Tomorrow." Zach drank down another glass of whiskey.

"I don't suppose she had a will."

"No, of course not."

"Well, I'm not a lawyer, but I think that means everything will go to her daughter, or at least in trust to her daughter, and as the father, you'll have to make all the decisions. That's lucky in a way. Otherwise you might have lost this house to her crazy uncle."

"It doesn't matter," Zach muttered. "I don't plan to stay anyway."

"Where will you go?"

"Back to Albany probably."

Ruth looked at him, sipped her drink. After a few minutes silence she said, "So you're going to fly the coop, huh? Pack it up and pack it in."

"Something like that."

"It's none of my business, but why?"

"I only moved here because of Luna. Without her, there's no reason to stay anymore."

"What about your job?"

"I'll finish out the term. I don't know who I was trying to kid anyway, pretending to be a teacher again. I've been a bureaucrat too long. Who knows? Maybe I can get my old job back." He smiled grimly as he refilled his glass.

"And what about the baby?"

"What *about* her?"

"Are you taking her back to Albany too?"

"Of course. I can't leave her here."

"Something tells me you'd like to if you could."

"What's that supposed to mean?" he asked angrily.

"Sorry. Putting my nose where it doesn't belong." She paused. "Do you know what you're going to name her?"

"We hadn't decided yet. We'd talked about 'May' because we met in May."

"May! That's a nice, old-fashioned name."

Zach fell silent and gazed into his glass.

"Well, I ought to go so you can get some sleep." She rose and put on her coat.

Without looking up, Zach said, "I have to be practical, Ruth. I can't stay here. I'm going to be a single parent, for God's sake. I'm going to need day care. Where the hell would I find day care up here?"

Ruth shrugged her shoulders. "I don't know."

"And babysitters. I'm going to need them on a regular basis. How easy would it be to get babysitters here?"

"Not easy, I suppose."

"And when the time comes, I'm going to want to send her to a decent school. The schools up here aren't worth a damn. I ought to know."

Ruth eyed him for a moment, then finished buttoning her coat. "You're probably right," she said. "The schools up here can't be very good. After all, Luna went to one of them."

* * *

THE WHISKEY HELPED Zach fall asleep, but when the alcohol wore off in the early hours of the morning, he woke with a start. For one impossible moment he thought he was waking from a bad dream. He glanced over to the other side of the bed, hoping to see the slight figure lying peacefully next to him, her body heaving rhythmically as she breathed. But in the silent moonlight Zach could see that the bed was empty save for himself. He rolled over and sniffed Luna's pillow, trying to catch some scent of her there. He buried his face in the linen and inhaled deeply, but the more he pursued the fragrance, the more elusive it became.

It was hours before dawn, but he rose, dressed mechanically, then went down to the kitchen and made a large pot of coffee. He sat alone at the table, in his mind that last view of Luna, trussed up so hideously on the hospital bed, her face contorted with rage, cursing him. He was still sitting at the kitchen table when the sun came up and Ruth arrived.

In Warrensburg that day they arranged for a simple funeral to be held on Friday. Zach decided to have Luna cremated as she had her father. On the way to Glens Falls they stopped at the supermarket where Ruth filled the cart with diapers, infant formula, plastic baby bottles, and many other items that she assured Zach he would need.

There were more forms to be completed when they reached the hospital. After the bills had been paid and the rest of the business concluded, Zach was taken up to maternity again. The baby was wrapped in a hospital blanket, and as Zach held her in his arms, a nurse sat down with him and outlined the basics of infant care. It was obvious that she had given this talk many times before, but never to a lone man, never in this situation. From time to time she eyed Zach dubiously as she spoke. When they finally left the hospital, Zach asked Ruth if she would hold the child on the way home. "No, my boy," she answered. "She's yours. You might as well get used to it. I'll drive."

On the way back to The Glen, May fidgeted a while and whimpered, then promptly fell off to sleep, lulled by the vibrations and incessant hum of the engine. When they had asked him what name should be filled in on the birth certificate, Zach had said, "May Tonner." Now as he gazed down at her, he wondered what features she might share with the Tonners. Would she have Zach's mouth, perhaps, or his sister's chin, or the brow of a great-grandfather Zach never knew. And what would she inherit from her mother? Would Zach be startled by her smile some day? With a shock of recognition would he see the joy that once shone on Luna's face the first time they rode the *Comet*? When May was serious, would Zach recollect Luna's habitual grave demeanor? And some day when May was cross, would he note in her childish features that fury he had seen in Luna when she screamed at him the last hour of her life?

At home once more, Zach carried the child up to the nursery, and Ruth watched as he lowered her onto the mattress and arranged the linen around her. Then they returned to the kitchen, and Zach began making phone calls.

The school secretary at Minerva Central had already heard the tragic news, and she conveyed to Zach the condolences of the principal and the entire faculty, whose prayers, she said, were with him now. Percy was not at the museum when Zach called, but Doris expressed her sympathy and jotted down the time and place of the funeral. Before he hung up, Zach said, "Tell Percy he can stay with me while he's here."

Next Zach called Bob, and Bob's happy surprise at hearing his friend's voice quickly turned to a stunned disbelief as Zach explained what had happened. He stammered, "This is terrible, Zach, just … terrible," and asked if there was anything he could do. Zach thanked him and merely requested that he pass on the news to the Education Department and to other mutual friends. Zach knew that he would also tell Beth.

Zach called Luna's boss at Oscar's. He called the Great Escape and left a message for Charley Rood. Finally Zach phoned his own family. These two calls were far the most difficult for him. Several months before, when Zach had informed his mother and his sister that Luna was pregnant, they had expressed subdued felicitations. Now, having never even met Luna, they were obliged to express sorrow at her death, and, more than that, travel hundreds of miles for her funeral.

After Zach completed the calls, Ruth gave him a crash course in baby care, elaborating on the nurse's instructions. She showed him how to prepare the formula, how to test the temperature. She demonstrated how to pick the child up, how to hold her while feeding her, how to burp her afterward, how to change her diaper. She advised Zach to hold May often, and for extended periods of time. She suggested he get used to carrying her around the house while he did other things no matter how awkward that was. At the end of it, she asked Zach if he had any questions.

"I know I should," he said, "but I can't think of any."

"You will. Call me when you do. They don't come with an owner's manual, and even if they did, you, being a guy, wouldn't read it. You'll need help. Ask for it."

After Ruth left that evening, Zach poured himself another whiskey, and with this in hand went up to the nursery. He stood for a long while at the side of the crib gazing down at the sleeping infant, but when he raised the glass to his lips, he stopped suddenly. No, better not. What if she got sick during the night, or had trouble breathing? He would need his wits about him. He sighed and lowered the glass, then with his free hand reached into the crib and adjusted the covers.

* * *

THE SNOW THAT had begun falling on Monday continued into Tuesday. Then on Wednesday the radio warned that another storm would arrive within twenty-four hours. A "classic nor'easter" they called it. Shortly after midnight the wind shifted and the snow began to fall in earnest. By noon Thursday most of New York and New England were blanketed, and airports all over the northeast were closed down.

Zach's sister Alice called first. Her flight from Boston was cancelled, she said, and there was no way she could get there in time for the funeral. She apologized in the most authentic tones she could muster, and Zach said he understood. Zach's mother called next. Her flight from Hartford was also grounded. Her apology was more sincere, but there was still an element of relief in it. Zach had not really been looking forward to seeing them, but when he hung up, he realized that he was angry and hurt that neither member of his family would pay her respects to the mother of his child.

The only other person who had to travel a long distance for the funeral was Luna's uncle, and Percy had not called. Zach phoned the museum, and once again it was Doris who answered.

"Doris, this is Zach Tonner. Is Percy there?"

"No, I'm sorry, Mr. Tonner, he isn't."

"Do you know if he's on his way here?"

She hesitated. "No, I don't think so."

"You did tell him about the funeral, didn't you?" Zach asked, getting annoyed.

"Oh, yes. I told him the same day you phoned, and I gave him all the information."

"Well, he never called me back. Does he intend to come?"

Her voice was uneasy. "I'm sorry, Mr. Tonner. I don't know what to say. Percy … doesn't like funerals."

"He doesn't like funerals!" Zach repeated. "Well, that's just fine!"

"I'm really sorry, Mr. Tonner. That's just the way Percy is."

Zach hung up. For several minutes he fumed, glaring at the telephone. It was one thing for Zach's family not to show up, but

Percy was her own uncle, her only blood relative. Why couldn't the bastard get off his ass and come here? He doesn't like funerals! Well, the hell with him!

By early Friday morning the snow had finally stopped. The plows had been out all night, and the roads, though slippery, were passable. Zach wrapped May in a warm blanket, and Ruth drove them along the winding route to Warrensburg. The funeral director, a thin, sober-faced man named Mr. Wedekind, helped them off with their overcoats and commented about the improved weather that would make driving easier that day. Then he led them into the chapel.

At one end there stood a dozen or more wreaths of flowers whose heavy fragrance filled the airless room. On their wrought iron stands they formed a semi-circle around a closed wooden casket. Chairs had been arranged in four or five rows facing it. Zach walked up the aisle to the casket and stood for a moment staring at it, not knowing exactly what to do. He looked down at the kneeling rail. Whom could he pray to, and for what?

He walked behind the casket and examined the cards stuck in the various flower arrangements. There was one from his sister, one from his mother, one from Ruth, one from Bob and Judy, several from former colleagues, but none, he noted, from Beth. The largest wreath by far, an enormous horseshoe-shaped spray, was given by Charley Rood. The card read, "To Luna. We will miss you aboard the *Comet*. From your friends at the Great Escape."

Despite the weather, many people attended the modest funeral. Luna's coworkers from Oscar's came, as did most of the faculty and many of Zach's students from Minerva Central. Several members of the Education Department came, driving up from Albany with Bob, and when Charley Rood arrived, he had in tow more than a dozen employees from the Great Escape.

Considering Luna's indeterminate religious convictions, and Zach's own lack of them, he had requested a nonsectarian service—no false assurances of a better life, no empty promise of heaven. The minister, bowing to his wishes, allowed those present to conceive of the Infinite in any way they saw fit, and he encouraged them to remember Luna for her life, not her death.

Zach held May in his arms as people greeted him afterward. When it was Charley Rood's turn, he tickled her chin with his great index finger. "Looks like my granddaughter," he said as he grinned at the infant. "That's nonsense, of course," he amended. "They all look alike." He stared into Zach's eyes. Quietly he said, "I won't try to console you for your loss. Luna was a treasure, irreplaceable. But I will say that I don't think she was truly happy until she met you. Take some comfort from that, Zach."

When everyone else had gone, Zach and Ruth stood in the foyer with Wedekind, who told them he thought it was a very nice service. He also told Zach to stop by in a few days for the ashes. Zach hesitated, not ready leave yet.

"Do you suppose I could spend a minute or two longer?" he asked, motioning vaguely toward the chapel.

"Of course, Mr. Tonner."

He let Zach back into the room. Once more Zach walked up the aisle, May in his arms, and he came to a stop in front of the casket.

Wedekind stood for a moment behind him, then inquired, "Would you like to see her, Mr. Tonner?"

Zach was about to say no, that he wanted to remember Luna the way she was. Instead, he found himself nodding mutely.

Slipping past him, Wedekind deftly lifted the half lid. Zach took a step closer to the casket and gazed inside.

Luna was dressed in a white frock, one of the very few dresses she owned. Zach had found it in her closet, though he had never seen her wear it. He looked at her face, her pallid features, solemn as they had been in life, but so still now.

"I'll leave you for a while," Wedekind said softly.

Zach heard his footsteps as he left, heard the door close behind him, but he continued to stare at the pale figure lying in front of him. Zach glanced at the infant in his arms, his daughter, her daughter. May's eyes were open, but in their baby fashion, they did not focus on anything specific. Carefully Zach lifted May so that she could see into the coffin.

"You don't know what you're looking at," Zach said quietly, "and you won't remember it anyway, but you should see your mother at least once. This is the last day of your life that you'll be in the same room with her. When you're older, I'll tell you about her, and I'll tell you about this day. You'll wish you could remember it." He lowered her back into the crook of his arm.

Slowly Zach knelt at the rail, his knees settling onto the pliant cushion. He wished he could pray, that there might be some comfort for him in prayer, but there was none. Zach stared at Luna's delicate features, so close to his own face now. He reached over the rail and touched her hair. "I never knew you," he whispered. "I lived with you. I loved you. But I never knew you."

XXIV

Wildflowers

WHEN ZACH RETURNED to Minerva Central the following Monday, his fellow faculty members welcomed him back, and his students were unusually well behaved. Zach read from his notes in class, tried to keep his mind on what he was doing, got through the day. Ruth had offered to look after May while Zach taught, and after school he picked her up at Ruth's house and thanked his neighbor.

Over the following weeks Zach learned what all new parents learn, to eat quickly and to sleep lightly. When May demanded attention in the middle of the night, Zach would get up and often stay up until dawn. He found it best to sleep only when May slept, so any hour of the day or night might find him correcting papers or preparing lesson plans. During these midnight watches, he also read. Something drew him to the *Iliad* and the *Odyssey* again, and the Greek tragedies.

The worst times for Zach were those hours when May slept and he could not sleep. Then Luna would haunt his thoughts. He would play over in his mind their first meeting by the river, their first dinner together, their first lovemaking, their first ride on the roller coaster, then that horrid last view of her in her hospital bed.

Zach would sit in his study, a book open but unread in front of him, and he would stare out into the darkness and see the fine, grave features of the young woman who wasn't there.

March became April, and April became May. The snow disappeared from all but the tallest peaks of the Adirondacks, and the banks of the Hudson River erupted in wildflowers once again. Zach was surprised at how quickly his daughter grew and took on an individual personality. She had brown eyes like both her parents, and she could charm Zach merely by flashing them at him, or turning them shyly away when she smiled. What astonished Zach, though, and even frightened him, was how quickly and how fiercely he had come to love her.

As the spring drew on, Zach began to prepare for his move back to Albany. The principal at Minerva was disappointed when Zach told him of his intention to leave at the end of the term. He considered Zach a gifted teacher, and he encouraged Zach to give it more thought, which Zach promised he would do, though in fact his mind was made up. Bob was keeping him apprised of job openings and real estate listings.

On a Saturday afternoon in early June, Zach hauled the old power mower out of the barn and coaxed it to life. He did the front yard first, then debated whether to mow the riverbank behind the house. As he leaned on the mower watching the wildflowers wave this way and that, he heard a vehicle pull into the driveway. An old Dodge pickup came to a stop, and a lanky, grizzled man with wild gray hair got out. Zach cut the engine of the mower.

"You do good work, Zachary," the old man observed, surveying the lawn.

"Hello, Percy. I hardly recognize you when you're not behind bars."

"Nice to see you too." Percy glanced up at the house. "The old place looks the same. How do you like living here?"

"I'm moving."

"Where to?"

"What do you want, Percy?"

"I came to visit. You invited me."

"I invited you three months ago for the funeral, and I haven't heard from you since."

Percy shrugged his shoulders. "Been busy."

"Too busy to come to your own niece's funeral?"

"She wouldn't have known I was there."

"Why the hell didn't you call me at least, or write?"

"What for?"

"To say you were sorry. To say *something*—anything! You were her uncle, damn it."

"I see. Social niceties even in the face of the Grim Reaper." He smiled wryly. "Aren't you going to invite me in?"

Zach was tempted to say no, to tell Percy to go back to Ohio, or to hell. Instead he merely grunted and strode toward the house. At the door Zach stepped aside and let the old man precede him.

Percy looked around the living room, nodding to himself as he recognized things. Then he flopped on the sofa and picked up a book that had been lying there. "*The Scarlet Letter.* You reading this, Zachary?"

"I'm teaching it."

"I read it in school. I remember the girl. What was her name?"

"Pearl."

"That's right. Obnoxious little snot. I couldn't stand her. Why the hell are you teaching this?"

"Because I like it," Zach snapped. "And also because the school owns enough copies of it. Poor districts can't buy new books every year. Any more questions?"

Percy tossed the book back on the sofa, then shifted around in his seat trying to find a comfortable spot. "Albert was one cheap-assed son of a bitch. Where the hell did he find this lumpy furniture? This is the same damn couch was here when I came ten years ago. The tightwad probably bought it second-hand. You must have money, Zachary. Why didn't you buy Luna some new furniture?"

"She didn't want any."

"Well, she may have said that, but let me tell you something about women: they all like new furniture. They can't help it; it's in the genes. Now if you ask me, what you should have done—"

"Listen, Percy," Zach interrupted, "will you cut the crap and tell me why you're here."

Percy sat up straight now, his brow furrowed, his eyes trained sternly on Zach. "I've come to collect my inheritance."

"Inheritance? What inheritance? All she had was this house and a little money in the bank."

"*Did* she now?" Percy's voice rose along with his eyebrows.

"Yes, but as far as I'm concerned, you can have the house, and if you want the money too, you can—"

A booming laugh cut him off. "I don't know what my niece saw in you, Zachary, but it sure as hell wasn't your sense of humor. Can't you tell when you're being joshed? Thanks for the offer. Mighty generous of you, but I'm not interested. Got a house of my own, thank you, and I don't want your money."

"Then what *do* you want?"

Percy's voice was quieter now. "Two things. I came to see Luna's grave, and I came to see her little girl. Is that all right with you?"

Zach was oddly touched. "Of course it's all right. May's at my neighbor's. I can take you over there."

"I appreciate it. And the grave?"

"Come on."

They passed through the backyard to the woods, then took the winding path up to the top of the hill. Zach led Percy to the far side of the clearing where two stone markers were set next to each other in the earth. One had "Albert Lewis" carved upon it. Percy looked at the other and started. "Luna Planitis! What does *that* mean?"

"That was her name."

"The hell it was! Her name was Lewis, same as mine."

"She changed it."

"When?"

"I'm not sure. I never asked. There were a lot of things I never asked."

"Where'd she get a name like that?"

"She made it up."

Percy stared at him, consternation in his features. After a moment his face softened, and he looked at the grave again. "Well, why shouldn't she change it if she wanted to? She sure as hell didn't owe the Lewises anything." He crouched down for a moment or two in silence, then touched the stone with his fingertips. Quietly he said, "See you, Kid."

They climbed back down the hill and then took the well-worn path to Ruth's house. As soon as Zach knocked, the dog began to bark.

"Quiet, Walter!" Ruth shouted over her shoulder as she pushed open the door. When she saw Percy, first she looked surprised, then bemused.

"Hello, Ruth," Percy greeted her. "Long time no see."

"Hello, Percy. What is it they say about a bad penny?"

"They don't say it anymore, Ruth. You're showing your age. How are you?"

"Very well, thank you. And you?"

"Couldn't be better."

Zach interjected, "Percy came to see May."

Ruth led them into her kitchen where a crib had been set up.

"Has she been behaving herself?" Zach asked as he carefully lifted her.

"You've got an angel on your hands," Ruth replied. "If she doesn't start acting like a normal baby soon, you're going to miss all the joys of parenthood."

"You don't see her at night." Zach dandled her for a moment, pressed his nose to her forehead and sniffed her, then turned to Percy. "Would you like to hold her?"

Percy began to demur, but Zach was already passing May into his arms. "She'll cry," Percy warned, awkwardly cradling her. Indeed, his craggy face and wild hair must have been a terrifying apparition. For a while May stared up at the scowling visage, her expression wavering between apprehension and curiosity. Then, turning away shyly, she broke into a disarming smile. Percy could do nothing but grin foolishly at the tiny creature in his arms.

* * *

Back in Zach's living room, Percy accepted the offer of a drink. "Glenlivet!" he exclaimed as he watched Zach pour. "You drink nothing but the best."

"I got it for you when I thought you were coming." Zach handed him a glass, then touched it with his own. "To Luna," he said.

"To Luna." Percy sipped. "Good juice!" he pronounced it, then settled back in his seat.

Zach watched him for a moment. "Percy, what did you mean up there on the hill?"

"What are you referring to?"

"When you said Luna didn't owe the Lewises anything."

Percy eyed him, took another sip of Scotch. "She wasn't related to the Lewises."

"Wasn't related?!"

"That man up there that you buried her next to wasn't her father. Old Albert couldn't have any kids. He and Iphigenia tried for years. Al even sent her to a doctor to see if she was okay. When she checked out, he went himself and found out *he* was the culprit."

"Then how did Iphigenia get pregnant?"

"Use your imagination."

"Someone else was her father? Who?"

"There's the sixty-four-dollar question."

"You mean you don't know?"

"No one knew, except Iphigenia, and she wasn't telling. She used to go down to New York by herself to see her family. It was probably somebody she met down there. Like I told you, she was a nice-looking woman, and Albert was no prize."

"What did Al do when he found out?"

"Happily, I wasn't present that day. All I know is that Al decided to raise the child as his own. He never forgave Iphigenia though. After she died he got rid of everything that might remind him of her—clothes, jewelry, pictures, everything."

"Everything but one shoe," Zach murmured. "And what about Luna? Did she know?"

Percy nodded. "As soon as Luna was old enough to understand, Albert told her he wasn't her real father. Some moral lesson he wanted to convey, I guess, so she wouldn't grow up to be a tramp like her mama. If it was me, I never would have told her. Let sleeping dogs lie, I say."

"My God. She hasn't got a mother, and then she finds out she hasn't got a father either. It explains everything." He shook his head, gazed at the floor, then looked up at the old man again. "It explains everything, but it explains nothing. Percy, tell me the truth: was there something wrong with her?"

"What are you asking me? If she was insane?"

"No, of course not."

"No, of course not," Percy echoed. "I forgot. No one is insane anymore. Nowadays people only suffer from depression or paranoia or some other damn thing that you can treat with Prozac. When you see what passes for sanity in this world, it's no great shakes to be sane anyway." He cast Zach a wicked smile and took another sip of his drink. "She changed after Albert told her about her mother, drew more into herself, but the truth of the matter is that she was always different, even from when she was small. Does that mean there was something wrong with her? I don't know. But I can tell you this: Crazy or not, that girl had one thing that a lot of 'sane' people don't have."

"What?"

"Heart. She had heart. She was able to love things. She loved her horse. She loved the hill up there. She loved those damn roller coasters, loved them with a passion. How many frigging people love *anything* with a passion?" He paused. "And, fool that she was, she loved you, evidently."

"She did—God knows why. She would have stayed with me

for the rest of her life, and I could have stayed with her for the rest of mine." Bitterly he added, "I wasn't satisfied with that. I wanted something more. I wanted a child too, and she died trying to give me what I wanted."

Percy shook his head. "She died trying to be normal."

"Normal? Who wanted that? I didn't. I loved her the way she was. I didn't care if she never smiled. I didn't mind the odd things she'd say, the way she looked. There was something wonderful about her. She wasn't like anyone else. Who wanted her to be normal?"

Percy drained his glass. "*She* did."

* * *

IN THE MORNING Percy said he had to get back home. He didn't want to leave Doris running the museum by herself too long. The woman had no proper business sense, he said. In the driveway Percy extended an invitation to Zach and May to visit him in Ohio. Before he got in his pickup, he also extended his hand.

Zach watched him drive off, watched until the dust had settled and there was no reason to watch anymore. Then, almost mechanically, he walked back toward the house. He looked at the lawn. It was another good day to mow, he thought. He could finish the job he started yesterday. It would probably only take an hour or so. It would be a good use of the time.

He sighed, mounted the stoop, and passed through the front door. He stood for a moment in the living room. His copy of *The Scarlet Letter* still lay where Percy had tossed it on the sofa. Zach looked at the roller coaster pictures on the wall. Maybe it was time to take them down. What were they supposed to be, anyway? Some kind of memorial to Luna? Why be so morbid? They didn't belong in a grown man's living room anyway. Zach considered removing them that very moment, while he was thinking of it. Instead he climbed the stairs to look in at the nursery.

May had gotten him up twice last night but now was sleeping peacefully. Zach looked around at the small room. How cramped it seemed, how ill lighted. May would be better off in Albany. He could give her a bigger, brighter place to grow up in, a room where she could do her homework, listen to music, invite her friends. Zach leaned over the crib and adjusted her covers unnecessarily.

He descended the stairs. In the kitchen he picked up the coffee cups he and Percy had used that morning and put them in the sink. He considered washing them. No, he thought, there was no hurry. He glanced at the dishes in the drainer, then lifted a plate and was about to replace it in the cupboard. He stopped for a moment and looked at it. Painted on the surface was the picturesque image of a rusty-red schoolhouse, trees and hills in the background, snow falling.

He raised the dish to put it on the stack. Once more he hesitated, staring at the painted scene. "You hated me," Zach muttered. "You said you hated me. Well, I hate you. I hate you for being so simple, so absurd." His hands trembled; his voice grew louder. "I hate you for filling your head with nonsense. I hate you for living such a pointless, useless life." He lifted the plate high in the air. "And most of all I hate you for liking these *stupid fucking dishes!*"

He smashed it to the floor. The pieces skittered over the pine boards even as Zach threw himself down upon them. He let out a loud, unintelligible roar as the tears filled his eyes. "I hate you for dying, for leaving me." His body twisted as he pressed his face roughly on the sharp fragments. "I'd go. Don't you know that? I'd go myself. They could throw the dirt on me if it would bring you back. Or I'd join you there," he sobbed. "But there is no there, and there is no back." Harsh, guttural sounds emerged from his throat. "I see you in her eyes. Every day, I see you in her eyes."

Bellowing and groaning, he writhed upon the floor and would willingly have lost himself in the maelstrom, but out of his anguish he felt a hand touch his shoulder.

"It's me," Ruth said softly. "I was at the door, and—"

Zach clutched her arm. "What am I going to do, Ruth?" he

cried. "I loved her. I love her *now*. I love her so much."

"I know you do."

"I thought she was crazy. My God, it was the rest of us who were crazy. She had character, convictions. She had an integrity I could only dream of. She was complete, a single, genuine human being out of a million, million counterfeits. And now she's gone. What am I going to do, Ruth? What the *hell* am I going to do?"

From the pocket of her skirt Ruth drew a handkerchief and daubed his cheek. "You're bleeding."

"My God, Ruth, how am I going to live without her?"

"You're bleeding," she repeated. "Finally."

* * *

RUTH CLEANED THE cut under Zach's eye and later sat with him in the old farm kitchen. Zach nestled May upon his lap as he related to Ruth the story Percy had told him.

"She made up a myth about herself," Zach concluded. "She made up a name, and she made up a history. Since no one was willing to claim her, she was free to claim whoever she wanted. She told me she was born of a river god, and I accused her of lying. That says more about me than it does about her."

"You wanted to find out who the real Luna was. There's nothing wrong with that."

He shook his head. "The closer I got to the 'real' Luna, the more Luna herself faded, until she finally disappeared."

"Don't blame yourself, Zach. It wasn't your fault."

"As a matter of fact, it was." He was quiet for several minutes. "I've been rereading mythology lately. The Greek gods were supposed to live forever, yet the Greeks made fun of them. That's fascinating, isn't it? Since the gods couldn't die, they were trivial. It was the human being who was important—mortal, fragile, and unknowable."

Ruth looked at him.

As May began to fidget in his lap, Zach rocked her gently

with his knees. "Sometimes in the morning I still expect to see her lying next to me."

"It'll be easier for you back in Albany, fewer things to remind you."

"Maybe it's best not to flee the ghosts."

"Are you thinking of staying?"

Zach touched May's palm and thrilled for the umpteenth time to feel her tiny hand close around his finger. "Do you think she'd like growing up here?"

"I don't know. Luna did."

"I wonder if she'll like roller coasters."

"Probably, unless she thinks you want her to. She'll be as contrary as possible if she's a normal teenager."

"I wonder if she'll be a normal teenager."

Ruth glanced at her watch. "I should get back," she said, standing now. "I haven't fed Walter yet. He's liable to eat the sofa."

Zach looked up at her. "Thanks, Ruth. Thanks for everything."

"Don't mention it. Shall I take May with me so you can finish mowing?"

"No, I'm done."

"Done? What about the backyard? It's a foot high back there."

Zach smiled to himself as he gazed down at his daughter. "It's not a foot high. It's knee-deep."

photo: Mary Trev Thomas

Richard Matturro, a native of Rye, New York, holds a doctorate in English with a specialization in Shakespeare and Greek Mythology. After sixteen years at the Albany *Times Union*, he now teaches in the English Department at UAlbany and lives on a farm in the foothills of the Berkshires. *Luna* is his second novel.